A TALE OF TWO COLORS

GRAY & BLUE

VOLUME II

VICKSBURG, MISSISSIPPI

ETCHING BY HARPER'S WEEKLY, FEBRUARY 9, 1861

A TALE OF TWO COLORS

GRAY & BLUE

VOLUME II

ANTHONY
WOOD

TIREE
PRESS

an imprint of
THE OGHMA PRESS

OGHMA

CREATIVE MEDIA

Bentonville, Arkansas • Los Angeles, California
www.oghmacreative.com

Library of Congress Cataloging-in-Publication Data

Names: Wood, Anthony, author.
Title: Gray & Blue/Anthony Wood | A Tale of Two Colors #2
Description: First Edition. | Bentonville: Tyree, 2022.
Identifiers: LCCN: 2022935253 | ISBN: 978-1-63373-731-0 (hardcover) |
ISBN: 978-1-63373-731-0 (trade paperback) | ISBN: 978-1-63373-731-0 (eBook)
Subjects: | BISAC: FICTION/Historical/Civil War Era |
FICTION/War and Military | FICTION/Action/Adventure |
LC record available at: https://lccn.loc.gov/2022935253

Lee Press hardcover edition May, 2022

Cover & Interior Design by Casey W. Cowan
Cover art by Thure de Thulstrup (1848-1930)
Siege of Vicksburg: Assault on Fort Hill 1863, Oil on canvas
Editing by Gordon Bonnet & Amy Cowan

This book is a work of historical fiction. Apart from the well-known actual people, events, and locales that figure in the narrative, all names, characters, places, and incidents are the product of the author's imagination or are used fictitiously. Any resemblance to current events or locales, or to living persons, is entirely coincidental.

Published by Tiree Press, an imprint of The Oghma Press, a subsidiary of The Oghma Book Group. Find out more at www.oghmacreative.com

To Mamaw Wood, who told me stories about my ancestors when I was a child.
She's planting flowers in Heaven somewhere now.

ACKNOWLEDGEMENTS

WRITING THE ONGOING story of a historical fiction novel series is often like waking up every morning not knowing what the world will throw at you. I like that, especially when the chaos of creative thought and feeling is brought to order through the flow of the pen, or in my case, pecking on a laptop keyboard. In *White and Black,* I honored a number of people who made writing my historical fiction series, A Tale of Two Colors, possible. Here I want acknowledge four others who had a deep impact on my writing. They were my teachers.

My fifth grade teacher at Washington Elementary, Mrs. Bryant, had a knack for making history come alive in her storytelling and historical accuracy. After reading a number of my research assignment efforts, taken mostly from World Book Encyclopedia in those days, she asked me to enter the Daughters of the American Revolution essay contest. I don't remember the topic about which I wrote, but I won first place. She told me, "Keep writing."

Mrs. Ferguson, my seventh grade geography teacher at Morgantown Junior High, saw past my ability to disrupt her class to see an adventurous young man who had a passion for going anywhere and everywhere and knew the geography to back it up. She said, "Wherever you may travel, write about your experiences."

My tenth grade English teacher, Patricia Stansbury, encouraged my writing throughout my high school years. She inspired me to enter a college level short story contest as a senior. Though she typed the story for me, she refused to edit it, saying, "You will win only on the merits of your writing." I won second place against a number of college students. Miss Stansbury told me I would be an author one day.

I cannot forget my eleventh grade English and Literature teacher, Mrs. Carolyn Carter, who taught me to understand stories and a better use of grammar, and coached me as I served on the staff of our high school literary magazine, the *Compendium.* One day in class she was discussing diagramming sentences. I was laughing and "cutting up" when Mrs. Carter said, "All right Mister Wood, since you feel you don't have to pay attention, come diagram the sentence on the board. My heart dropped when I saw the three-line, thirty word sentence waiting for me. My buddies laughed, the girls snickered, but in a matter of moments, I had the sentence diagrammed. Her jaw dropped but then she smiled and said, "Mister Wood, I want to see you after class. It was then she opened the door to a wider world of writing possibilities.

For my teachers, it never was about winning a contest or getting a story published in the *Compendium.* They stretched me to become the best writer possible. They saw in me what I could not see in myself. It was the foundation I needed to be the author I am today. To you four and all my teachers, I am forever indebted.

DRAMATIS PERSONAE

ANNIE FANNY: Lummy's sassy and frisky snuff-dipping friend who cared for his shoulder injury he suffered during a ferry crossing the Mississippi River from Vicksburg to Desoto, LA in search of Susannah. She's a mess.

BENJAMIN FRANKLIN "BENNY FRANK" TULLOS: third child of Archibald and Mary Tullos, and Lummy's older brother who moved with his family to Winn Parish from Choctaw County, MS in the mid-1850s. He is foreman on James T. Gilmore's farm. Lummy and his family in Choctaw Co., MS have not seen nor heard from Ben and family since the moved.

COLUMBUS "LUMMY" NATHAN TULLOS: Archibald and Mary Tullos's sixth child born in Holmes County, MS in 1834. As the main character in this series, Lummy leaves his home in Choctaw Co., MS in search of his love, a young slave woman named Susannah, which begins his adventurous journey in search of her and a life of peace.

DAN CREEKWATER: Choctaw Indian who befriends Lummy not long after he leaves home. Dan refused to leave when his people were herded west on what became the Trail of Tears. He nicknames Lummy "Crazy Deer Dancer."

DORCAS TULLOS: Ben's wife and Lummy's friend and confidant.

J.A. KILLINGSWORTH: a recruit who befriends Lummy at a Confederate Army enlistment rally in Winfield. They leave together to go to war.

MR. AND MRS. DAVIS: owners of a mercantile in Winfield, LA who provide Lummy with friendship and his first job in Winn Parish.

MR. JAMES T. GILMORE: Winn Parish landowner and gambler who wins Susannah in a card game in Choctaw Co. and takes her to his farm. Generous to a fault, he wins slaves gambling only to set them free to live and make their way on his farm.

MR. WILEY: old Mexican War veteran and the first person Lummy meets when he arrives in Winfield, LA. Mr. Wiley takes Lummy under his wing and helps him get his first job at Davis's mercantile. Mr. Wiley dies and Lummy performs his funeral service.

OLD BART: former slave, now secretly a freedman, who works with Ben and Lummy farming for Mr. Gilmore. Old Bart becomes like a grandfather to Lummy.

RAINY MILLS: a gun dealer who saves Lummy from hungry coyotes on the road to Winn Parish, LA. Rainy pays Lummy to deliver a shotgun to his older brother Ben whom he has not seen or heard from in several years.

SUSANNAH: a young slave woman and Lummy's first love who was taken from Choctaw County, MS to Winn Parish, LA when James T. Gilmore won her in a card game. Lummy leaves his home to find her and does so in Winn Parish. Lummy eventually marries her Christmas Day, 1861.

THOMAS "POOLE" POOLE: Lummy's childhood best friend who lives in Choctaw Co., MS.

SCAENA

CHOCTAW COUNTY, MISSISSIPPI: founded and created in 1833 from lands ceded by the Choctaw Indians and named for them. Lummy's parents, Archibald and Mary Tullos, bought land and settled there as pioneers in 1835. They helped start one of the county's first Baptist Churches, New Zion, in 1842. Lummy grew up in Choctaw County.

DESOTO, LOUISIANA: a small but important town at the eastern end of the Vicksburg, Shreveport, & Texas Railroad, which only extended from the Mississippi River to Monroe, LA in 1860. The village serves as a ferry site and railroad depot for travel, goods, and mail just across the river from Vicksburg. Lummy meets Annie Fanny in Desoto.

GREENWOOD, MISSISSIPPI: a major cotton center where Lummy worked for a spiritually minded man named Jake long enough to buy a ticket on the steamer Dime to travel to Vicksburg. Not far downriver on the Yazoo, Lummy has an encounter with a large alligator.

VICKSBURG, MISSISSIPPI: important river port and railroad town that links east and west of the growing United States. Lummy boards a ferry there one night in search of Susannah and suffers a shoulder injury crossing the Mississippi River to Desoto, LA.

WINN PARISH, LOUISIANA: established in 1852 from lands once belonging to surrounding parishes. Erroneously nicknamed the "Free State of Winn," young attorney David Pierson was elected to vote "no" to secession at the convention called in Baton Rouge in January, 1861. He, along with few others, refused to change their "no" votes at the end of the session when asked so as to make the decision unanimous. No documentation substantiates the claim the Winn Parish was declared a "free state." Though raising eight companies for the Confederate Army, nearly half of the parish's young men hid rather than go fight for "rich men's slaves." Others joined the Union Army. Several Winn Parish slave owners freed their slaves before war began. James T. Gilmore owns and farms land not far from Winfield, the county seat.

A TALE OF TWO COLORS

GRAY & BLUE

VOLUME II

CHAPTER 1

DESOTO AND ANNIE FANNY

MARCH 6, 1862

The bluffs of Vicksburg rise like thunderclouds on a hot summer's day.

THE TRAIN BOXCAR sways back and forth as the steam engine spews heavy black smoke. My soul bounces between my head and my heart. Should I enlist? Should I stay home? I still have a little time before we reach Desoto and the steamboat south to New Orleans.

Here I go again. Lummy Tullos. On my way to who knows where and what I don't know. My new friend, J.A., surrenders to the motion, and his head bobs over to rest on my shoulder. He snores softly, but his eyes are open. Who can sleep at a time like this? Who can sleep with their eyes open?

I gently elbow him. "If I don't get back home, it'll be my own fault, J.A."

He lifts his head, snorting like a hawg. "That ain't gonna happen, Lummy boy. You've got me to get you home."

I tell myself I had no choice when President Davis ordered a Conscription Act. But I did. I could have hidden in the swamps or hills like some men. I'm just not the hiding kind except what I feel deep in my heart right now.

It's been three years since I went through DeSoto the first time. Seems like just yesterday I left Choctaw County in search of Susannah. I found her and married her. Now I leave her. Watching tears stream down her cheeks as I boarded the train headed east was the hardest thing I've ever done. I want to desert this army before I even enlist. There's no salve made that can soothe my aching heart.

As we barrel down the railroad tracks, the bluffs of Vicksburg rise in the distance. Though it was night the last time I passed through, I took a good look back at them as I walked the train tracks west toward Winnfield. Those bluffs looked like mountains to a Mississippi boy. They rise up like thunder-clouds on a hot summer's day.

The train chugs, jerks, and spits hot steam. We slow to a stop.

Sarge yells, "We'll board a steamer south to New Orleans tomorrow, boys!"

I don't know what I'm headed for, so I'll just go whichever way life's river flows. It's worked so far. I hope it'll keep me alive.

One of the boys yells over the roar of the engine, "We heard Lincoln painted a target on Vicksburg not long ago. Guess we'll be a part of that bullseye soon enough."

Silence is the only sound. Reality has set in, and all the hurrahs have disappeared. We don't want to hear it, but rumor is there'll be serious fighting around here soon. What we do hear as the train stops is the hustle and bustle of a large army readying itself for battle. I'm just ready to get out of this cattle car.

DeSoto, Louisiana, sits on a sandbar jutting into the river like the finger of an invader pointing to his prize. It doesn't take a genius to figure out this hairpin bend in the river is God's way of saying to the Yanks, "You ain't get-tin' by here that easy with your fancy pants gunboats."

J.A. nudges me with his shoulder. "You sound like a Reb newspaperman. Better watch that talkin' out loud, boy. And I'm pretty sure God ain't had nothin' to do with it." I agree.

DeSoto is all important to the future of the Confederacy. Eastbound sup-ply trains bring fresh troops, food stuffs, and military supplies from the west here. Soldiers unload trains and load ferries to take them across Ole Man River to be sent to the armies in the east. It was on one of those ferries I got knocked senseless by a demon tree that rose up out of the dark waters when I crossed back in '59. My shoulder still aches.

"Wait a minute!" I plum forgot about her in all the commotion. "Dang it all to Hell."

J.A. elbows me. "What you squawkin' about?" I shake my head.

It was here I got chased by that tobacco-spittin', possum-eatin', hairy-legged, cannonball-shaped woman who wanted me to bed her with no thought given to wed her. The boys will give me hell if they find out. I'll keep my eyes peeled like fresh-cut taters and hope I don't cross paths with that woman. "I need to stop cussin' before the Lord gives me what I deserve. It's probably too late. My whoopin's comin'."

J.A. yells, "What'd you say?"

I shake my head. "Something big is goin' on, look up there."

DeSoto looks like black ants escaping a burning stump. Men rush around in all directions—some barking orders, some following them, some ducking and dodging them.

The door to the boxcar slides open. Fresh air rushes in like cool water pouring over my head.

A stocky Cajun wearing three stripes on a gray jacket stomps up. "Sergeant Kelly from Winn Parish? Get these pretty little chickens out of the henhouse and line 'em up."

Sergeant Kelly snaps a crisp salute. "Yassuh, Staff Sergeant Boyette." Nobody moves.

"*Now,* damn you." We fall over each other like beans spilling out of a can trying to get out. We form the crookedest line a man ever saw. But we're all smiles—brave men come to rescue the just and holy Confederacy from the evil blue oppressor threatening our homes, families, and sweethearts.

Sergeant Boyette runs to me with his nose less than an inch from mine. "What the hell are you smilin' at, boy? Is the man next to you ticklin' your ass? Yeah, betcha you'd like that wouldn't you? Speak up, tadpole." He has to stand on his toes to look me in the eye.

"Nawsuh, no tadpole here, suh! Ain't no grab-ass goin' on neither, suh. Just volunteers from Winn Parish lookin' to whoop some blue-belly Yankee ass. That's why we're smilin', Staff Sergeant Boyette. We're the Winn Rebels, suh."

A timid cheer rises up from our company.

"That's what I want to hear, tadpole, 'cause before this army's done with you, you're gonna lose your tail and make a damn good bullfrog. You'll be eatin' them damn Yanks like flies."

Somebody yells, "Winn Rebels give 'em hell!" We all slap each other on the back, happy with our new friend, the sergeant.

"Attention in the ranks, tadpoles. Nobody said to start no damn sissy party. Shut the hell up and start runnin' toward the river. I want you to see the greatest city on the Missip where you might be stationed if you're worthy. Run like hell, get back here quick, and tell me what's flappin' in the wind by the bank so I know you went to the edge of the river. If you don't have the right answer, I'll run you 'til your tongues drag the ground."

He stomps his foot. "The last five back will dig latrine ditches before supper. Makes for a good appetite." We just stand there like schoolboys lined up for a footrace hoping to get a first place blue ribbon.

Sarge pulls his Army Colt, which I believe he'll use to signal the start. He aims it at us. "Run, dammit, or I'll shoot every last one of you shit-stompers in the ass!" We bolt like scalded dogs hoping he won't shoot us in the back. He laughs as we kick up dust.

I grin at J.A. "See you later, boy." I bolt out front like a cat with his tail on fire. My long legs leave him behind. It's every man for himself. Friends are friends, but digging shit ditches is another thing. I won't be in the last five.

We get to the river, and it looks so peaceful, and I'd like to stay. A blue and white flag snaps in the breeze at the Hall's Ferry dock, and I take off back. Three men sprint ahead of me. They're just too dang fast.

I remember Mr. Wiley's words. "Do nothin' to make yourself stand out. That'll just get you a medal and a coffin. Do your job, and if you do good, they'll let you know." Good advice.

I get back third out of four front runners, breathing hard. The rest of the pack trickles in behind us. J.A. is in the middle of the group. The last five, a bit overweight, straggle in with sad looks on their faces. They know punishment is coming.

I'm congratulating myself when Sergeant Boyette yells out, "Last five, front and center. What'd you see, you slow-as-hell land turtles?"

The five boys look at each other. "A blue and white ferry flag?"

"Why are you askin' me? Is that what you saw or not? You silky sack o' tater-bellies."

They straighten up. "Yassuh, Sergeant Boyette, that's what we saw." The youngest of the five lets out a giggle at being called a tater belly. He can be no more than seventeen.

"Do I amuse you, son? Straighten your lard ass up, or I'll kick you so hard you'll have a new set of eyeballs." Sergeant Boyette draws back his fist, and the tater belly cringes. Boyette stops, then smiles, cutting his eyes my way.

"First five, front and center to get your prize for winnin' the race." My chest swells. "This is how this man's army works, ploughboys. You men who ran quick as scared chickens escapin' a Sunday dinner will help the tater-bellies."

It's like my jaw just hit the ground and stuck in the mud. I don't dare look Sergeant Boyette in the eye. Our Sarge Kelly covers his mouth trying not to laugh. Sergeant Boyette ain't playing. J.A. winks and grins at my misfortune.

"You special boys best help these wormy peckerwoods lose them tater bellies their mommas gave 'em so they can run a mile without breakin' a sweat. You got it?"

I yell, "Yassuh, Sergeant, suh." Mr. Wiley said I'll say those words so often I'd do it in my sleep.

Sergeant Boyette walks slowly up to me, hands on his hips, his unlit cigar tickling my chin. I close my eyes waiting for a bloody nose.

"Sergeant Kelly, you learn him that, or is he just lucky?"

Before Sergeant Kelly answers, I jump in. "Never had much luck, suh. An old Mex War soldier gave me some advice, suh. He told me to do good and get back home. That's all, suh."

Sergeant Boyette rolls his cigar around in his mouth, smiling. I don't know if he's going to slap me or hug me. "Next time, tadpole, you wait for my permission to speak, you hear?"

"Yassuh."

"Y'all hear that? Do good and get back home. Do that, and you'll make it home to your sweethearts. What's your name, Winn Rebel?"

"Columbus Nathan Tullos, suh."

Sergeant Boyette huffs a cough. "Cully Nathey wha-a-at?"

"Columbus Nathan Tullos, suh. Folks just call me Lummy, suh."

"All right then, Lummy Tullos, you take these nine well-bred Looseaner gents to that tool shed over yonder by the commissary. Tell them I sent you and to give you ten diggin' spades. Can you do that, Lummy Tullos?"

"Yassuh, right now, suh." The other nine look scared to death but happy I'm getting all of the Sergeant's attention. I bark, "Let's go."

Sergeant Kelly winks out of the corner of his eye. "Lummy, dig 'em over yonder. I don't want to smell a shit ditch whilst I'm eatin' my finely-prepared army meal." I throw a wave his way and take off with the tater bellies in tow.

Sergeant Boyette turns to our Sarge. "Fine bunch of men Winn Parish has sent President Davis. You done good."

We hustle over to the tool shack. It's strange to be ordering men around. It's not my nature and certainly ain't my plan. I just ain't the orderin' other people around kind. It can drag up my anger because sometimes I don't know who to please.

The fastest runner whispers, "Why'n the hell we gots to dig shit ditches? We're suppose't to be leavin' out of here tomorrow, right?"

This complaint comes from a man who earlier talked big about bravery on the battlefield and getting medals but who knows little about the daily life of a buck private. I don't know either, except what Mr. Wiley told me. He told good stories. I hope to live to tell some of my own one day.

I can't say I'm afraid of what's coming. Pa pretty much beat the fear out of me and my brothers. But I am apprehensive about leaving Susannah, not being right with Ben, and I'll admit, about going into battle. I hope it'll keep me sharp and alive when the fighting comes. Any fear is more about not getting the chance to live the peaceful life I've always wanted. I throw a shovel over my shoulder and hum "Oh Susanna."

When we get to the latrine area, a couple of the boys double over and puke. One gags and ties a cloth to cover his mouth and nose.

"O-o-owee, what in the hell have these boys been eatin'? Damn, that stank's so thick you gotta wipe it off your teeth."

I point my shovel at him. "Shut up, fool, and dig so we can get the shit stank out of our snouts before we go eat. It'll be darker'n a coon's moon out here soon."

He stands up straight like he'd seen me do a few minutes ago with Segeant Boyette. "Yassuh, General Columbus Nathan Tullos, suh." We laugh and keep digging.

I can't eat after finishing our work, so I save my dwindling stash of home food and stuff the army rations in my pack. I stare into the stars. I miss Susannah something terrible already.

THE QUIET OF the morning sun greeting a peaceful cool morning breeze is blasted away by the unfamiliar sound of a bugle.

J.A. rolls over rubbing the sleep out of his eyes. "Ole Gabriel blowin' his horn already?"

Sarge kicks a few late sleepers. "Winn Rebels, I thought we'd be here a few days, but it ain't so. Get your gear, choke down your breakfast, and get your sorry asses down to the river. The boat's early, and we will be too. Lummy, get 'em goin'."

I don't have to. Men scurry like mice in a corn crib chased by a barn cat. We stand ready at the river by seven o'clock sharp. Sarge splits us into three single file lines to board a steamer.

J.A. peeks down the line. "Hey, what's goin' on down there?"

Nicely-dressed ladies hand packages to each man. The closer we get, the sweeter the perfume. I daydream about Susannah as the line moves slowly.

Then I see her. "Oh hell," I cry out softly. It's Annie Fanny in all her big backside glory, flirting with every man who passes. Dang, I'm in her line.

I start to duck out to another line. Sarge barks, "What's wrong with this line, Lummy?"

I can't tell him the truth. "Just gonna step behind them barrels for a minute, Sarge, before we get stuck on that boat."

Sarge grabs my head and turns it toward the river. "See that boy? Your tiny little pot of piss ain't gonna make a bit of difference to Big Muddy. Do it after you get on the boat. Damn, boy, we got a war to get to. No time for your lolly-gaggin'."

My only hope is to pull my hat down. It doesn't work.

"Well, hellfire blazes blowin' my skirt up and over my head if it ain't my good friend, Lummy Tullos." She rears back and bellylaughs. "How long has it been, my sweet darlin'? What? Three years since I had your pants off the night I patched you up? My Lord, don't you look better'n honey on a fresh-baked biscuit."

I hang my head but to no avail. The boys cheer, one yelling, "Dang, Lummy, if you can take her on, I hate to see what you'll do to the blue-bellies."

J.A. scratches the back of his neck. "Da-a-amn, son. She's ugly enough to scare a buzzard off a gut wagon."

"Shut the hell up, or I'll slap your ass sideways."

He laughs, and I can't help but laugh too. I look up at Annie, who realizes she can cause me a lifetime of misery or tell the truth.

"Now hold on boys. Time to fess up. I tried to get this fine young man's britches off, but he'd have no part of it. He stayed right as rain to a girl he was followin' to Winn Parish. I hope he found her, 'cause if he didn't, he's mine for the claimin'."

J.A. yells out in my defense. "She's right. Lummy got hitched in Winnfield. I wasn't there, but he's got a ring on his finger to prove it."

I hold up the band. "Say something now." They all laugh. I sigh and give Annie Fanny a thank you nod.

But just to make an awkward moment go away, I peck Annie Fanny on the lips. "Good thing I'm hitched, boys. This here's as fine a specimen of woman ever formed by the Good Lord himself." Annie blushes. I wipe the snuff juice off my lips without her seeing.

Annie pops me on my backside. "You're still a good man, Lummy Tullos. Take care of yourself. Come on back, and I'll roast us a corn-fed possum with sweet taters."

I wink. "Yes'um, sure will."

The steamer casts off and starts for the channel. The captain blows the whistle, and black smoke bellows into the wind.

Sarge comes by. "Damn, son, if you ain't the sight. You get caught up in the middle of things without even tryin'."

"Yassuh and steadily doin' my best to stay out of it all. It just ain't workin' out so good."

Sarge pops me on the shoulder. "You're gonna do fine, son."

As we turn south for New Orleans, I look back at the Confederate flag on top of the Warren County Courthouse snapping in the river breeze. For some reason, it just doesn't look right.

CHAPTER 2

DOWNRIVER TO
NEW ORLEANS

MARCH 7, 1862

"You gotta keep movin' like that muddy river."

IT'S EARLY MARCH, and the air is a bit breezy this morning. Our steamer, the Trent, paddles along navigating sandbars and logs with the ease of deer slipping through the forest. I pull my coat around my neck and watch eddies and whirlpools swirl in the mile wide current.

The sky feels so big and our boat so small in the middle of this river. I look out over the great expanse of the flowing stream. Security, peace, and even tranquility washes over my soul like short river ripples lapping on a nearly exposed sandbar. "The One watchin' over me commands all of this. What have I to fear?"

J.A. elbows me. "Nothin', Lummy. You just gotta keep movin' along like this big ole river."

This steamboat ride is much better than the train. Tightly packed in a stuffy boxcar with no way to rest or relieve myself is a stark contrast to this smooth ride out in the open with plenty of fresh air. Soaking up the mid-morning sun watching the riverbank gives me time to meditate.

One of the boys pokes a log. It explodes high into the air and lands in the boat. Sarge yells, "Don't let it get away! Gar fish is good eatin'." The ugly fish is at least five feet long and weighs over fifty pounds.

J.A. laughs. "Alligator gar rise up from the deep to get sun on their backs."

Sarge orders one of the fellas to grab the fish and take it to the cook.

J.A. yells, "You ain't eat good 'til you had fresh fried gar balls."

A city boy cries out, "Gar balls? I didn't know fish had...."

Sarge licks his lips. "No, fool, you get the meat off the bones, roll it up in cornmeal and spices, and fry 'em up. Put 'em with fried taters, and you got yourself a fine meal."

I ask J.A., "A fish jumpin' into a boat. You ever seen anythin' like that?"

He scratches his ear. "Nope, ain't never even heard of anythin' like that."

The river runs smooth and dark, almost silky, like the sweet coffee milk we drank as children. The water is thick with silt, like it has something to hide underneath like when I crossed it back in '59. My shoulder ain't been right since.

Occasionally a stump rolls up from the bottom, like a great beast rising only to sink down again. Ole Man River hides his true feelings about us riding his back like ticks on a dog. At any time he can hurl death from the depths. The dragons stay deep today. So do my feelings.

Sarge leans against the rail. "Peaceful, ain't it?"

I whisper, "Oh Susanna, Oh don't you cry for me, For I come from Mississippi with my banjo on my knee."

J.A. stands up from where he's been napping in the sun. "You've been hummin' that ever since we left Winnfeld. What's it called?"

"'Oh Susanna,' my favorite tune. Susannah is my wife's name. It keeps me thinkin' about her."

"Yeah, I miss mine, too. Wish I had a song for her. Maybe I'll come up with one."

"Maybe so."

Everyone thought this war would be over before it got started good. Some still think we'll go home without firing a shot. Sarge reports that two river forts surrendered in Tennessee. That just means the Yanks'll be heading our way soon.

I watch the rolling waters. As peaceful as the flow appears, it's a smooth ride that can kill a man. The man who thinks he'll have a smooth ride in this war could get himself killed. I'll need a dragon to roar up in my soul if I'm going to survive what's coming. The evil I fight within will rise to face men who try to kill me. I tried to leave my anger in Choctaw County. Doubt creeps into my soul. Can I do this?

None of us really know what we've signed up for and surely don't know how badly we'll want this war over. No escaping it now. There's no circling back like a swamp rabbit throwing off the hounds. This war has its mark on us now, and the color is gray. Death has our scent, chasing us until the right moment. I look down at the swirling waters. Will I make it back home?

"It's like this big river flowin' to the sea. Nothin' can stop it. And, like this war, we're runnin' straight at it like crazy men." I quiet my out-loud talk. Like this river, the war will have bends, shallows, eddies, and backflows, but eventually the water all runs the same direction—to the vast ocean where it doesn't matter if you wear blue or gray. Death doesn't care what color you wear.

I envision the scene. We march through the countryside and line up in some unknown field. Death advances in a long line with muskets aimed at my heart. However death finds me, the color of his jacket will be blue.

A quiet hush like a preacher calling us to prayer falls over us at the front of the sternwheeler. We all feel it at the same time. We stare out into the wide, empty river expanse. I pray for the boys next to me, for my brothers, Ma, and Mr. Gilmore. And Susannah.

The trip downriver is uneventful. We send up a cheer and fire a three-cannon salute at midday as we pass the fort at Grand Gulf. Stopping at the small town for wood gives us a few minutes to go behind a bush or walk along the riverbank. The whistle blows, and we're off again.

Except for being so crowded, I enjoy the lazy float down the stream in the warm sunshine. There's not much to do. Most of us sleep on the decks at night and cover up to stay out of the heavy morning dew. We catch a few fish, but the boat moves too fast to let the lines settle on the bottom for a catfish.

Our progress is slow, dodging river debris and navigating sandbars that rise out of nowhere to threaten the steamer. I learned to spot them floating down Big Sand Creek with Dale back in '59. The steamer accidentally runs up on a bar, but fortunately the boat's tail end is swept around by the current. The captain reverses the engines, and it pulls free. It's a nervous kind of fun, twirling like a toy top, but there's plenty of room in this river.

We pass several boats patrolling and transporting troops south. Except for a long stop at Natchez to pick up a few distinguished passengers and officers, there isn't much to write Susannah about.

Sarge speaks above the hum of the sternwheeler. "Get a good look, boys. This is close as you'll get. Natchez-Under-the-Hill is the best place in the world to lose your money and catch a disease." I don't want either.

"Been here, boys, and got a reminder that won't ever go away. Stay on the boat, or I'll have your asses whooped. It's for your own good." I watch the roustabouts tugging ropes, unloading and loading at the landing. They look rougher than cobs in an outhouse.

J.A. asks, "You ever been here?"

"No, but Pa said he and Uncle Silas once brought moonshine here to sell. The road to Natchez was dangerous. Ruffians preyed on honest people trying to make a livin'. Uncle Silas told his father, who I call Grandpa Temple, he could handle any saw-toothed, pumpkin-headed outlaw tryin' to rob a man who whooped the British with Andy Jackson at New Orleans."

Pa and Silas, first cousins cut from the same cloth, ran together like two hound dawgs. Pa spent more time with Grandpa Temple than his own father, Willoughby, who treated his sons worse than his slaves. Pa didn't like how his father treated his slaves. It made an impression. Pa never owned a slave. But he did learn Grandpa Willoughby's heavy-handed meanness.

"There wouldn't have been any trouble in Natchez had Uncle Silas not insisted on seeing a steamer and having a beer down by the river. Pa wanted to make the sale and go home, knowin' Uncle Silas's temper showed up every time he drank too much.

"After they finished dickerin' for the best price at the trading post atop the bluff, they settled down at a little table outside a fancy saloon facin' the river at Natchez-Under-the-Hill. Uncle Silas was quiet, but much of a man. He never started trouble but never was afraid to end it. He and Pa had just finished their first beer when a flatboat docked. A man in black pants and a red shirt wearing a big black hat with a long red feather jumped on the dock waving his arms.

"He yelled, 'I'm Mike Fink, king of the Mississippi River. Anybody wantin' to travel her has to kiss my boot or whip my ass!' He looked around for a taker. Uncle Silas started to get up, but Pa pulled him down before Fink saw him. He was too late.

"Fink called Uncle Silas a yellow striped skunk-belly and said his mother wouldn't know him when he was done whoopin' him. Uncle Silas bristled but kept his seat. Fink wouldn't let it go. Fink taunted him again. Uncle Silas stood up. Pa didn't try to stop him this time.

"They lit into each other like two wildcats with their tails tied together. Uncle Silas was stronger, but Mike Fink moved like lightning. They slugged and kicked, tussled and tumbled, bit and scratched, and fell in the river twice. Uncle Silas got him in a head lock, and Fink tried to bite his nose. Finally, it ended, and they both lay exhausted. Fink threw his hand over to Uncle Silas, offering to call it a draw and to buy Silas a beer. Since Fink made the challenge and didn't win, he gave Uncle Silas his black hat with the red feather. Uncle Silas wore that hat until the day he died. I'm glad I got to know that man."

J.A. grins. "Damn good story. It ought to be in a book. You think we're tough as them?"

"Oh, hell no. But the story should be in a book."

Catching the smells of a river town makes it strange knowing Pa and Uncle Silas once looked down on this very spot. If I had the time, I'm sure there's an old timer still around who could tell the story of that fight years ago.

Uncle Silas and Mike Fink—two men who lived very different lives. One, a woodcutter, trapper, and farmer who made his way in the wilds of the Mississippi Territory. The other, a roustabout, braggart, and brawler who worked flatboats up the Mississippi. Tough men I wouldn't want to tangle with. I'll have to be like them when the fighting starts.

We shove off from Natchez stopping only at Baton Rouge for supplies, mail, wood, and to pick up three officers at Port Hudson. We finally tie off just above New Orleans.

Sarge walks through the crowd of soon-to-be soldiers. "You boys get your beauty sleep tonight. We're marchin' out of here in the mawnin'."

I cover my back with my coat to get the last few hours of rest. I think about Uncle Silas's fight. "Can I be that tough?"

J.A. whispers from underneath a tarp. "Hell no, Lummy, you ain't never gonna be that tough. Shut up, and go to sleep."

He's right. We'll move out in the morning to where I don't know. Doesn't matter, I'm rolling like that muddy water straight to an ocean of war.

CHAPTER 3

ENLISTMENT

MARCH 16, 1862

You can really only give your true heart to one purpose. Mine has dark curls.

THE MORNING SUN sends a bright shimmer across the dancing whitecaps on the river. To the south, New Orleans stretches as far as the eye can see.

Sarge draws a deep breath. "Biggest city most of us will ever see." He stretches for a better look. "See them gunboats bein' built down there? The funny lookin' ones are rams."

Our rag-tag bunch lines up to march. Sarge barks, "Attention! We're headed to Camp Walker. We'll be there a few days, then hop a train north to training camp."

This is happening way too fast. I like to know where I'm going and what I'll be doing when I get there. Putting my life in the hands of men who don't know any more about what's ahead than I do makes me nervous. The man who holds my life in his hand also holds Susannah's. I don't like it.

We camp for the night. There's little shelter, and men complain about mosquitoes. I cover my head with my coat and draw my hands inside the sleeves. Complaining never helped a soul feel better about anything. Still, it makes me wonder why God created those bloodsucking devils.

After breakfast, Sarge shouts, "Let's go! Leave nothin' behind. We won't come back here."

J.A. yawns and stretches. "It's Sunday, ain't it? They must want the priest to bless us."

Some boys are against going to a papist service. Heck, I'm happy to get a blessing of protection from anyone who claims to follow God.

We stop at Camp Todd. Sarge lines the Winn Rebels up nicely with six other companies. We look like a grand army, except there's hardly a musket between us. If we're attacked, I guess we can throw rocks at the Yanks. I did once at a bully and was pretty accurate.

We line up in front of tables where men have papers in neat stacks. When my turn comes, a doctor examines me and declares me perfectly fit to be a soldier. He calls out my description to a corporal, "Hazel eyes, black hair, and dark complexion." The corporal raises his head when the doctor spits out, "And six feet six inches tall."

"Damn, boy, what's your momma been feeding you?"

J.A. yells, "Peas and cornbread grow'd Lummy taller'n a sawtooth oak." Everyone laughs. I grin, but I am shocked. I've never measured my height, but it's official now. I sign a three-year enlistment paper and line up with the other men in front of a raised platform.

A Sergeant dressed in a new gray uniform shouts, "Attention!" We straighten up. "At ease men. Stand straight and tall, plant your feet shoulder width, and when I tell you, raise your right hand." Some men have to be shown which hand is right.

He walks down the line. "You men'll know right from left very soon when you get to Camp Moore. Trust me. Learn it now and save the pain of gettin' your foot stomped every time you miss a step." We look to see who's coming.

"Atte-e-ention." The Sergeant salutes a colonel making his way up the platform steps followed by a couple of other officers.

J.A. whispers, "Lummy, we're fixin' to become soldiers in the army of the great Confederate States of America." We straighten up, and though we don't have a stitch of a uniform amongst us, we look determined.

The colonel raises his hand to quiet the crowd. "This is an important day in your lives and for the life of these great Confederate States of America. You will rendezvous at Camp Walker and then be taken by train to Camp Moore where you will be made into fighting infantrymen. I know you will do your best to serve your country and do your families proud.

"Let me introduce to you the man we are proud to have lead you in repeating the oath of allegiance to the Confederacy—Lieutenant David H. Todd. He's none other than the brother of Mary Todd Lincoln, wife of the illustrious President Lincoln of the invading United States of America." We cheer but quiet down as the lieutenant walks toward the platform.

Todd mounts the stage energetically and cocks his jaw. "You men serve a cause as great as that of our forefathers who threw off the red-coated oppressor from across the ocean. With the help of God and you good men, we shall throw off the blue coated oppressor and become free forevermore."

We cheer, and Todd throws up his right arm. "Before we take this oath together, men, you know that the tyrannical commander-in-chief of that other nation is none other than my sister's husband. I claim no kinship to him or his ideals. And with regard to that trespasser from Illinois, he's the greatest scoundrel yet unhung."

We cheer again.

"Now men, in all seriousness and sanctity of heart, stand straight and proud, raise your right hands, and repeat after me. Say your name loud and clear so all of Washington City can hear it."

Seven companies in one voice repeat the oath. I clear my throat and half yell, "I, Columbus Nathan Tullos, do solemnly swear to support...."

So there it is. We're soldiers in the newly formed 27th Regiment Louisiana Volunteer Infantry. I like the sound of it.

After the oath, the colonel announces, "You will be fully trained and equipped to meet the enemy on any ground of his choosing and defeat him soundly. You'll be paid eleven dollars a month, fed, clothed, and housed by the Army."

J.A. elbows me. "Three years. Looks like we'll be together for a spell, huh, Lummy boy?"

"Should be more'n enough time to get this war over with, you think?"

I wander away from the crowd. What did I just sign up for? A lot can happen in three years. It's a long time for a newly married man. "Keep me safe, Lord." I take out a pencil and paper.

Camp Todd, New Orleans, Louisiana
March 16, 1862

Dearest Susannah, brightness of the sweetness in my life. I miss you dearly. We got to New Orleans safe and sound. We're in good hands with Sarge and the generals. We hope to get home in less than a year with the way the Reb army is whoopin the Yanks. We got sworn in today by none other than Abe Lincoln's brother-n-law himself. He told us Abe ought to be hung by now. What do you think of that? Soon we'll head north to train at Camp Moore. Don't worry, and don't think I won't be comin home. The Lord watches over us all. Give my best to all back home.

Your loving husband,
Lummy Tullos

CHAPTER 4

TRAIN RIDE TO CAMP MOORE

MARCH 28, 1862

Generals are always happy to point the way to death.

A TRAIN WHISTLES long and loud as we leave the station near Camp Walker. Staff officers and local dignitaries stand tall and proud waving little flags as the rail cars start north. I wonder how many of them will face a bullet.

It's a seventy-five mile ride to Camp Moore on the New Orleans, Jackson, and Great Northern Railroad. It's a fine way to travel except they put too many of us on each car. They load us on livestock cars like cattle going to market.

Sarge yells, "It's an eight-hour trip standing up, unless you all agree to sit down."

I like the sound of the engine and the clickety-clack of the wheels on the iron tracks. A man can go anywhere in this world he chooses if he just hops a train or steamer. I look across the peaceful countryside. I don't know where I'm headed, but it means being farther from Susannah. I feel my pocket for the crossed cannons Mr. Wiley gave me and the alligator tooth the Captain gave me on the Yazoo River when I almost got eaten by one. I expect to meet more good people like them on this path.

We pass swamps filled with cypress trees like in McCurtain Creek swamp back home.

A man complains. "What an ugly worthless chunk of land."

I can't let that go by. "Beauty can be found anywhere on God's good earth.

Cypress swamp or rocky hillside, Big Muddy or Big Sand Creek, ploughed field or oak forest, beauty is there if you look."

J.A. laughs. "Amen, preacher."

"Don't call me that."

Once we leave the lowlands, the sweet smell of pine forests fills the air. Seeing farmers working their mules reminds me of why I give myself to this cause. A young boy runs a water bucket to his daddy. He wipes sweat from his brow and takes a long drink. He hugs the boy and rustles his hair. That's why I'm here.

J.A. licks his lips. "Cool water sure would be good right about now."

I drift back to those days working the farm with Pa and my brothers. I wish I had one more day in the field with my daddy again. I wander deep within myself to hear Pa gee-hawing the mules in the springtime. He's smiling, happy to be working. He strains to keep the two mules headed in a straight line.

I can hear him now. "Lummy, walk straight like I plow this field. Watch yourself, and don't do nothin' foolish." Pa had his moments. I just wish he hadn't whipped us with plow lines to teach us. I'll never feel good about that. I vow to never do that to my child. Lord, help me.

I remember reaching up to hug him once, but he kept moving. "No time for that, boy, keep plowin'."

An overwhelming pungent smell shocks me back to the clickety-clack of the train and the closeness of the men.

A city boy with a red ribbon for a tie pinches his nosed closed. "Oooooowee, who shit in their breeches?"

J.A. laughs. "It's a hawg farm, you dern fool. Nobody shit their britches unless it was you."

Holding his nose and breathing through his mouth, he doubles over to puke. With tears forming in his burning eyes, the city boy cries, "How do y'all live with that foul smell?"

I grin. "Smells like cash dollars to some folks. Keep breathin' in and out your mouth like that and you'll be wipin' that smell off your teeth." He shuts his mouth quickly.

"Let me change your thinkin'. You know that good smoked ham your momma cooks for breakfast, bacon fryin' in the skillet, ham hocks in the black eyed peas, red eye gravy, and...."

"I get it. I just never knew somethin' that good could come from somethin' so stanky."

A man in the back yells, "Don't forget about them good ole fried chitlins."

Another yells, "Yeah, I like 'em boiled up tender and peppered hot."

J.A. laughs. "Hand slung, stump whooped, and creek washed. Ain't that right, Lummy?"

"That's what old Mister Wiley used to say."

We laugh as the city boy mumbles, "What are chitlins?"

I just let it lay. We slide the big door open, and the smell disappears.

The train stops every ten miles to take on water and exchange the mail. We hop off to relieve ourselves or chance a run to a store. That's risky business. A few men took their enlistment bounty and deserted. Guards now ride on the top of the cars with muskets. A man could get shot sneaking away to find a biscuit or a plug of tobacco. I stay close to the train.

It's funny how easy I find myself doing what I'm ordered to. Pretty much a loner most of my life and living under Pa's heavy hand, I never liked being bossed. Most times I bucked Pa when he bore down on us boys too hard. I guess if you don't feel bullied, you don't mind doing what you're ordered to do.

I can hear Mr. Wiley's words. "Do what you're told, and you'll do more of what you want."

The whistle blows, and the engine fires up again. Boys race from every direction to catch the slow-moving train. A long-legged man runs from behind a shack pulling up his britches, yelling, "Don't leave me!"

When we grab his hands, his britches fall down around his ankles. He doesn't have any drawers on. As we pull him into the car, we pass a small crowd of nicely dressed well-wishers waving flags. Boy, did they get an eyeful of Rebel behind! Gray-haired ladies cover their blushing faces with fans and gentlemen hope their wives don't see them laughing. Sarge just shakes his head.

We keep the big door open as we pass sandy creeks and sweet cedar breaks. I'd give anything for a drink from one of those cool fresh springs bubbling up in the woods. Next stop I'll ask if we can get water.

We stop in a larger town called Independence. Sarge shouts, "That's why we're fightin', men. Independence! To be free of the Yankee invader!" I question that.

We detrain and get water. It's good, even if it is from a horse trough. Nothing I ain't never done before.

I wipe my mouth on my sleeve. "J.A., Independence is a good name for a town. A good word, too, except everybody won't be free unless the bluecoats win. Mister Wiley told me to always be sure I know why I'm fightin' and if it's for the right reason." He doesn't say anything.

As we leave, pretty dolled up ladies wave their handkerchiefs and cheer us. Well-to-do men raise their right hands in solemn approval of men willing to die. Like generals, they're all too happy to point the way to death.

I watch Negroes load seed bags and shovel horse apples off the streets. I cringe when someone shouts, "Niggahs, niggahs everywhere. Niggahs and flies, I do despise. When I see a niggah, I'd rather have the flies." I've heard that song just about one too many times. He throws a rock at a couple slaves. I want to throw him off the train.

"We're off to fight so's you can have a home, and you don't even give a shit. If it wasn't for y'all, there'd be no war."

I start to slap the hell out of him, but J.A. grabs my arm. "Don't."

I whisper, "So why don't we just set 'em free? Those fancy town houses were built on the backs of slaves. There's too much about this that just ain't right."

J.A. squints. "I don't disagree."

Susannah comes to mind—her velvety skin, pretty face, and how we'll start a beautiful family when this war ends. My heart beats in time with the clickety-clack sound of the railroad track. Thinking about Susannah always brings peace to my soul. It doesn't last.

A man yells, "Niggah town!" Fortunately, the train picks up speed after the mail pouch is tossed on board. We pass a church with the Ten Commandments posted in big letters out front.

"Thou shalt not kill," a city boy reads softly.

J.A. asks, "So, boys, what's the Good Lord gonna say about killin' them Yanks? Will that send us all to hell or what?" Men turn my way. Some heard J.A. call me preacher. Some know me from preaching Mr. Wiley's funeral.

Sarge cuts in. "Hell no, God's on our side. We were just mindin' our own damn business, but the Yanks think they got the right to interfere." I agree with Sarge in principle but not subject.

I clear my throat. "My Uncle Silas, who fought with General Jackson at New Orleans, said that's why we ran the British off in the Revolution and again a second time. This ain't no different if that's your reason for fightin'. Anythin' else is just spittin' on the Constitution."

Sarge rolls what I said around in his head unsure of how to respond. "Lummy, you're a prayin' man. Give up some words to the Lord before we reach Camp Moore." I don't pray long.

I think about Grandpa Cloud who came from the old country. Those old tales keep my life going in a good direction as much as praying. My life never has run in a straight line. Seems it's a family trait. Uncle Silas told me Grandpa Cloud crossed the ocean in 1665 and became an indentured servant in Virginia. He worked his way free from that bond and purchased a fair amount of land. I'm indentured now, too, but for the right reason?

Those stories built strong convictions in us Tullos boys about being free from the lordship of another man. Cloud passed down the truth that, "There is no Lord, except in Heaven." There's something strangely spiritual about being free, and our family certainly is stubborn about it. Too much authority leaves a bad taste in my mouth.

Traveling deeper into this part of the South where people are even stauncher on slavery, my convictions are changing. For the better, I believe. I'm not my Grandpa Willoughby who owned slaves. Neither was Pa, thank God. We pass by the Liberty House of Prayer at the edge of town.

I elbow J.A. "Ain't that somethin'? Liberty and Independence mixed with a house of prayer in a new nation keepin' people as chattel. That don't square. Not everyone's gonna have liberty when this thing is over." I may not know where I'm going right now, but I do know what I'm leaving behind. I can see J.A.'s wheels turning.

He changes the subject as we pass a bakery. "Boy, would you smell that! Them sweetbreads sure make a man's mouth water."

Two dark-skinned beauties hang laundry on the side of the last big four-columned house. They smile. I wave. Their beauty makes my heart sing for Susannah.

J.A. pokes me. "You best quit that, boy. Some of these boys will knock you nekked and hide your clothes just for gawkin' at them girls." I don't want any trouble, but they're a nice reminder of my Susannah.

We finally reach Tangipahoa Station. Not much of a town, just a few fine homes, a water tower and fuel depot for the train, a stand for the mail, a loading dock for cotton farmers, a general mercantile, and four liquor stores. Whiskey sellers flock like buzzards to hand out little sips.

Sarge yells, "Go ahead, be a fool and get a bayonet stuck in your ass. Any questions?" The whiskey merchants back away insulted but still hold their bottles high.

The engine eases slowly up the track to Camp Moore where there's more of a town than Tangipahoa and a field of tents, but no men.

We de-board quickly. Camp Moore has a few shops, quarter master and commissary buildings, a few eatery shacks, a soda fountain shop, coffee house, and a butcher. Everything a soldier needs to spend his army pay fast. They're close by, so the smells of coffee and other delights can waft into the tightly packed rows of tents. Other than that, Camp Moore looks to be deserted. I expected hundreds of men to be here.

There's also an establishment where a man can get his likeness put on tin. I'll get two once I get my uniform—one for Susannah and the other for Ma.

"Ain't got much to leave behind if I'm killed. A picture's better than nothin'."

J.A. elbows me. "Shut up, Lummy, you ain't gonna get killed. I ain't gonna let you."

A group of men march stiffly to the train, trying to make an impression. The lieutenant waves his hand in the air. "Welcome, men. We're the caretakers of Camp Moore. We guard what's left when soldiers get shipped off to parts unknown. We'll get you settled in tents over there, and then we'll eat. Glad you boys are here."

We're the only regiment in camp and still three companies short of a full compliment. The lieutenant takes Sarge to the side to give instructions.

A caretaker says, "Damn happy to put an eyeball on you gents of the South. Ain't had no company for pert near four months. Them shops over there just closed up, that is, 'til they heard you was comin'. It's been pretty slow out here. Let's celebrate your arrivin'."

Making sure no officers are looking, he shoves a jug under my nose.

"My stomach ain't settled enough yet. Thanks just the same." He goes on down the line handing the jug to anyone who'll take it. Some do, watching out for Sarge. I want a good start as a soldier of the Confederacy, and being drunk on the first day ain't the way to do it.

I don't care much for whiskey. I ain't against taking a snort or two, but more than that is trouble. At the very least, it gums up a man's thinking. Besides, I'd probably like it too much and wind up like Ben. But I do enjoy sipping my brother Elihu's fine muscadine wine on occasion.

Officers shout orders, and camp becomes a beehive of activity. Waiting to be assigned a tent, I think about muscadine grapes hanging in big clusters high up in the trees back home. Clusters of men mill about bragging about what they'll do to the Yanks. Like ripe muscadines hitting the ground in fall, we'll soon be soldiers good for the falling, too. The blood red color of Elihu's wine makes me think it won't be long before ours is squeezed out in the Yankee grape press. I can't think on that now. I get settled in my tent not far from Beaver Creek and write Susannah a letter.

Camp Moore
March 29, 1862

My loving sweet wife, I pray this letter finds you well and in good spirits. Things are much better since we left that swamp hole Camp Walker. The land here reminds me of home, but nothin is so pretty to ever compare to you my darlin.

This ain't much of a place to look at, and there won't be much to do but fish in the Tangipahoa River. It reminds me of when we sneaked off to swim in the Big Black.

Men from cities and farms all over Looseana are here. We live in crowded tents, but we make do. The food ain't too bad, but it don't compare to your cookin, my darlin.

I found some medicine that cures sore eyes. Is Old Bart still havin problems? Tell him to ask Mr. Davis for Mitchells Eye Salve. If he ain't got it, he can order it.

Keep me in your heart and picture my face in your mind. Always have a prayer on your lips. I'll write as often as I can. It would do me good to get a letter from you soon. My heart aches for you. A few lines will revive my spirit. Love to you and all I hold dear there.

Your faithful husband,
Lummy

CHAPTER 5

CAMP MOORE

MARCH 30, 1862

Be better than your father was, whether he believes that or not.

J.A. SLAPS A mosquito. "March is gone with the cool weather." They were so bad at Camp Walker we slept close to the fire hoping the smoke would keep the clouds of pesky devils away.

The night before we left, J.A. tried to cheer us up. "Listen, y'all hear that?" He kept looking around like a wild animal was sneaking up. We couldn't figure out what he was talking about.

Finally I asked, "Hear what?"

"That tiny bell ringin'."

"What bell?"

"The little bell them skeeters ring when it's time to pick you up by the shoulders and carry you off for their dinner." We all laughed but drew closer to the fire and kept swatting. City boys who'd never slept out were miserable.

It's good we left the swamps and New Orleans. We hear the Yanks'll try to take her soon. We're not ready for a fight. Some of these boys never even fired a gun. I'm ready to face the enemy but need training as much as anyone. We're told equipment and food is already getting scarce. The Confederate war effort is strained, so we'll have to make do with sticks for muskets and no uniforms.

Officers assure us. "Just hold tight, help's on the way. They'll come through, eventually." Sarge lets us hunt for anything resembling meat. We can't go for deer or squirrels. We don't have a long gun between us, and I'm not using my pistol loads. I can get meat without a gun.

We club a hog and bring back a scrawny beef cow. We cut a pole to carry the pig and lead the cow into camp. The city boys gag as we farm boys make quick work of the butchering.

J.A. crows like a rooster. "Hot damn! Fresh meat in the pot tonight."

Bless those boys who came before us and left camp better than they found it. Nearly every tent has plank floors and mosquito bars. But camp life is no party. We drill long hours, and we're jammed together eight to a tent. But that's not the worst part. Trains pass through all hours of the night, shaking the ground so hard it rattles the bones. The brass keeps us close to the tracks to discourage deserters and thieves and in case we need to move quickly to go face the enemy.I guess it's a soldier's right to gripe, as long as an officer or Sarge isn't within earshot.

Once the day's marching and drilling is done though, we dump all our rations in the pot together and share the meal. We tell stories and bad jokes, guess at the future, and sip acorn coffee the caretakers taught us to make. We tell ourselves it's good because there's nothing else to drink but water. It's tough smelling the real thing coming from the coffee house by the tracks. Doesn't matter, we ain't got a nickel between us to spend on that. What little silver I have I hold for necessities or send home.

APRIL 1ST, AND I'm now a soldier. We receive news that Richmond will up our pay from eleven to thirteen dollars. We're happy as dead pigs in the sunshine. I guess President Jeff Davis can't let the Yankees outdo the Confederate States of America. Two dollars a month difference could cause a man to consider a blue jacket. And two dollars Yankee is worth more than the same in Reb dollars.

I'm just happy to get paid.

It's sobering to see the small but growing cemetery. Nearly every man glances at the carved wooden markers. We don't stare long. What a man gazes at too long he may become. The first man buried there was accidentally crushed by a train car the second day Camp Moore opened. What a shame.

A man comes to gain glory on the battlefield only to have his light go out for somebody's dumb mistake.

J.A. puts his elbow on my shoulder. "Sad ain't it? Bein' buried so far from home."

"Yeah, but we signed up for this."

J.A. rubs his chin. "We did."

"When my Granny Thankful died, I stood with my ma, who held Granny's hand as folks paid their respects. They said the strangest things like, 'Don't she look so good?' I wanted to shout, 'Heck no, she don't look good! What dead person ever looked good?' I just kept quiet."

A drum beats in the cemetery. J.A. sips his acorn coffee. "Another soldier put under the dirt. Wonder what it was this time?"

"Measles. Good men leave home only to be killed by an enemy they can't shoot at." The camp flag snaps in the breeze. "They'll never know what we'll do to free the South."

J.A. drains his cup. "Yeah, and I don't want all this trainin' just to be shipped home in a box or laid in a shallow grave here."

After our duties are done, several of us go to the graveyard to ponder the possibilities. The mood is quiet as death itself. Someone starts a hymn, another tears up, but most whisper they just want to go back home. I'm at ease with men honest about their fears and judge no one for theirs. A bottle is passed around. The whiskey helps us lose the worries for another night, until the sun rises to remind us we're just one day closer to fighting.

I wonder where I'll be laid under the dirt.

MOST DAYS WE get a little free time from drill and camp duties to read newspapers, play cards or dominoes, or write a letter. Reading reports of terrible battles in the newspaper makes me think about my own soul.

I kick J.A. at morning coffee. "Hey, boy, it's Sunday. Let's go to church."

"I guess I better. Hearin' you read about all them men killed in battle, I better make sure you're good with the Lord, you wicked sinner."

"I'll be right behind you at the pearly gates or the dungeon door of hell."

A Baptist pastor breathes hell fire down on us in the morning, and a Methodist preacher brings us peace and hope in the evening. The best part is we're outside and not in a church house. As we sing, birds join in the chorus. Trees sway in time as a gentle breeze leads the dance. I find some comfort in the Sunday services, but mostly I enjoy time alone with Creator down by Tangipahoa River.

J.A. and I sit by the cook fire after Sunday evening service talking about home. Isaac from Winn Parish bursts out of a shop across the tracks. "Y'all ain't gonna believe what she told me! She said I'd be home by June and…."

J.A. asks, "How much?"

"Two dollars."

J.A. throws a stick at him. "Two dollars? What a waste of damn good money. You'll wish you had them two dollars when when your brogans wear out."

I stir the fire. "Damn, Isaac, for two cash dollars, I'll tell you anythin' you want about your future and give you a dollar back."

He gives me a dirty look and runs to tell someone else.

J.A. gets up. "We got a couple hours before dark. Let's go wash clothes and get a bath in Beaver Creek, set a couple of fish traps in the Tangipahoa River."

While our clothes dry, I lie down on the soft white sand and look up in the sky. "J.A., this ain't so bad."

He throws a rock in the river. "And a few perches won't do the cook pot no harm."

Across the sandy river, the oaks drip with Spanish moss. It reminds me of ole Miss Lucille's long curly gray hair. Years ago, she lived with us and loved me like a grandson. She wasn't our slave. She lived with us because Grandpa Willoughby pawned her off on Pa when he and Ma moved north to Choctaw County. She'd cook me popcorn and put black pepper on it. She'd set me on her lap and sing "Swing Low, Sweet Chariot."

Pa taught us to respect our elders no matter their skin color. Pa gave her her freedom papers just before she died. I was only ten. I cried when they covered her simple box with dirt in the little Negro cemetery down the road. She's free now, safe in the arms of the Good Lord.

MARCHING AND DRILLING, marching and drilling. Taking orders and giving none. That's a soldier's life. I've found muscles I never knew I had with all the "one foot in front of the other" Sarge barks out. It never takes long after supper to fall soundly asleep nestled in our tent.

Most of us had good shoes when we arrived, but they weren't made for marching. J.A. found a discarded pair of boots and tore off the soles to tack on to his. The ones Mr. and Mrs. Davis gave me are holding up fine so far, but soon I'll be doing the same. I hate to spend ten dollars for a new pair of shoes. Thirteen dollars won't go far if prices keep rising like a creek after a spring rain.

We train hard and catch on quickly. In just a few days, we learn to straight line march and make turns. With new companies arriving, the 27th Louisiana Volunteer Infantry regiment looks more like an army every day. Our ranks swell to full complement by month's end.

Sunday after service, I stumble upon a wild rose bush at the edge of the parade ground the same red color as the camp flag. "Now wouldn't these flowers look good in Susannah's hair?" I know it sounds like a story in a book, but I'm determined to not forget my wife.

I turn my head and cry. "Why in the hell did I ever decide to do this?"

CHAPTER 6

TROUBLE IN CAMP

APRIL 8, 1862

Too little discipline or too much, both cause pain either way you go.

"WHAT'S IT BEEN, only a week?" Isaac asks.

J.A. wraps a blanket tighter. "Feels like a month. Bein' a soldier is dang boring."

"Yeah, but the training will pay off when we finally see the elephant."

Isaac puts on a jacket. "I seen an elephant once in...."

I laugh. "That's what they call seein' the Yanks for the first time."

J.A. shivers. "Dang cold rain, when's it gonna stop?"

Sarge stops by for coffee. "When it's hot we want it cold. When it's cold we want warm sunshine. It's just our nature to gripe, I guess."

"The rain sure beats the heat."

"You got that right," J.A. admits.

Sarge drains his cup. "Like heat and cold, there's two kinds of men in this camp—those who follow orders and troublemakers. Most want to do right by God, family, and country, but some really don't know what they signed up for and whine about it. Don't be the second kind."

The sun pokes its head out of the clouds mid-morning and dries our clothes and tents. Green sprouting everywhere makes me wish I was with Ben and Old Bart breaking ground.

J.A. looks up from mending his shirt. "Oh, hell, here they come."

Three men claiming to be of "higher status" walk by. They laugh and say things like, "I'll do no slave work. I'm above this" or, "This food is fit only for a slave." They challenge anyone to disagree as they turn their noses up at us enjoying a simple soldier's feast. Then they always make sure we see them enter a café across the tracks.

J.A. stomps the mud off his brogans when they come by. "Them boys sucked their momma's titty way too long and expect somebody else to dump their slop jars in the mornin'."

Truth be told, they probably drank from the breasts of slave women, then cussed and beat them when they got big enough. I cringe hearing them laugh about violating young slave girls. I can't think about that very long. Too late, my face is hot.

Sarge hands me his cup. "Gotta go. You leave them uppity boys alone. Their time's comin'."

J.A. pokes the fire. "We'll choose sergeants and corporals soon, and them boys think they'll get picked because they got rich daddys."

I spit. "Yeah, but them fancy hand-tailored uniforms ain't gonna make me salute 'em."

After drill, the rich boys stop at our tent like they're posing for a tintype photograph. Rubbing their chins and pointing, they act like they're conducting an inspection. They quietly mention things they don't like, but really they're searching for the weakest man.

"Private, straighten up your belongings. You there, take those plates to the creek and sand wash them. While you're there, bathe yourself. You other two do the same. In your present state, you're unfit to be in this army. Now hop to it, double time." No one moves.

J.A. starts to get up. "Damn, if their noses were any higher, they'd drown in a rainstorm."

I grab his shirt and hold him down. "To hell with them boys, we ain't here to fight them."

The biggest of the three steps up and speaks in fine English, "What's that, farmhand? You have something you wish to say?"

I slowly stand, never breaking eye contact with my adversary. J.A. whispers, "Oh, hell."

In perfect English I reply, "Please continue on your present course before my associates and I soundly pummel you three gentlemen into mindless oblivion." I sniff the air like a half-awake child smelling bacon in the morning. "Why, what is that smell you carry ever so daintily? Forgive me, your mother must have bathed you in sweet lavender-scented bath salts, and my goodness, she must have perfumed your pantaloons with rose water, as well."

The leader balls up his fists, upset that I'm stealing his show. He continues calmly. "Has something caused you to be unhappy, Private?"

"If I was any happier, sistuh boy, there'd be two of me. Problem is, it'll only take one of us."

"You sure of that, Private?"

"Damn sure. Come get some, 'cause when you're done, there'll be a helluva lot left over."

Sarge runs up pointing his finger. "Get the hell out of here. This ain't even your company."

The leader sniffs. "Just a misunderstanding, friend. But since that one started it, I'll have you put him on extra duty for his insulting nature."

My job is done.

Sarge's eyes glow red. "Let me put it to you this way, pretty boy. I'll have you washin' my drawers and polishin' my boots with your silvery tongue everyday if you don't get the hell on back to your company right now."

The leader laughs. "It appears you have forgotten who my father is. You can't possibly believe you can make me do those disgusting things." He looks around, enjoying his moment.

Sarge steps up, nose to nose. "Quicker'n shit through a goose, friend. Just try me. I'll beat you so bad your dressed-up friends standin' there'll think your face caught fire and got put out with a hatchet. Now *git*, before I report you to the captain." We move toward the three.

They bow. "Until another time, my friends, until another time." The leader's eyes and mine lock just long enough to mark each other for what will surely come later.

Sarge curses and stomps. "I'll keep my eyes on them three flower-smellin' boys. Get about your business and don't take orders unless he has bars on his shoulders or stripes on his arm."

"Yassuh, Sarge."

J.A. laughs. "Flower Boys, that's what we'll call 'em."

Isaac puffs up. "And the leader, Rosie, for what Lummy said."

I shake my head. "They're probably from good stock but ain't got the same makin's as those who fathered 'em. They've never had to work a day in their lives."

J.A. watches them cross the tracks. "They probably went to Catholic school and can quote one Bible command just as easy as breakin' another."

I laugh. "Like my brother Ben says, 'Can't be a saint on Sunday and an ain't on Monday.' They lay awake at night scheming how to hurt people. Damn bullies anyway."

The Flower Boys always stay together and keep a tent just for themselves, even though the rest of us are cramped eight or more. They believe they're invincible.

When we stretch out for the night, J.A. whispers, "Them boys got somethin' goin' on. They got cash and jewelry I know they didn't bring with them."

"Then let's go."

J.A. and I follow them, and their secret is revealed. Out behind empty supply wagons, they sucker a couple of country boys into the shadows. It's not long before a simple-minded farm boy leaves shaking his head wondering how he lost a game he was told he'd win.

I ask, "How long they been doin' this?"

"Better part of a week best I can tell."

"We gotta make a plan."

J.A. grins. "I ain't no thief, but I got no problem relievin' three mouthy bullies of their winnin's to give back to the good men of the 27th Louisiana."

AS TUESDAY PRAYER service begins, we watch the Flower Boys sneak off to Tangipahoa with whiskey on their minds. We sing loudly to make sure Sarge sees us. When the pastor drops his head to pray, me and J.A. slip into the shadows. The rest know to cover for us.

We raid the Flower Boys' tent and take gold watches, wedding rings, fine knives, two Derringer pistols, a handful of silver coins, two five dollar gold pieces, and thirty-three paper dollars. J.A. finds dice with shaved edges and a deck of cards with six aces and little colored dots on the backs. This confirms their cheating. We hide everything in a stump by Beaver Creek.

We sneak back into prayer meeting on hands and knees slowly popping up in the crowd. We nod, and all the boys smile. We give the preacher a couple of extra "amens" at the end.

J.A. whispers as we leave, "I feel like King David returnin' the Ark of the Covenant to Israel who stole it back from the Philistines."

Then all hell breaks loose.

"We've been robbed!" comes the drunken Flower Boys yelling as I compliment the preacher on his fine sermon. They tear through the tents of the men they'd cheated. We watch and snicker.

About the time Rosie sees us, Sarge and a lieutenant rush in. "What's the meaning of this? Why are you men destroying these tents?"

Sarge yells at Rosie, "You better have a good explanation, boy."

Rosie wobbles forward. "Boy? Whatever do you mean? Boy? I'm the son of Jean Pierre Demouvolet of New Orleans, and you should be very careful with your words, suh."

The lieutenant barks, "Soldier, you're drunk as a skunk. One more word and you'll be wishin' I'd call your daddy to come get you."

Rosie gently pushes the lieutenant back. "Watch your step, or I'll have you cashiered out of this army so fast it'll make your hat spin." Rosie falls into the growing crowd.

Sarge jerks him by the collar to his feet. "That's it."

The lieutenant motions for our little gang to come over. "You there— Lummy, J.A.—take this man and his friends to their tent and shackle them."

Rosie grabs the lieutenant by the collar, drawing back his fist. "You thieves aren't takin' us anywhere." He swings wildly. The lieutenant catches Rosie's punch in his hand and muscles the leader of the Flower Boys to the ground.

"Now, I'm gonna do what your damned ole daddy should've done when you was just a chap. Sergeant, get these men out of my sight. Punish them to the full extent of the law."

Sarge salutes, turns on a dime, and winks at J.A. and me. We go to our tents laughing.

WE CRAWL OUT of our tents this morning stretching and moaning about aching muscles to see the Flower Boys already at attention. The cheating bullies wear heavy ball and chain shackles on their ankles. They still drill along with the rest of us but not in their pretty tailored uniforms. They wear raggedy slave clothes that haven't been washed in weeks. As an added misery, they stand on wooden posts at evening parade wearing signs with "Thief" painted on them.

The lieutenant stops by. "I appreciate your initiative, men. It was the right thing to do, but next time bring it to me so we can deal with it before it comes to this, agreed?" We salute. "That's all, men. Carry on. You're doing well."

"Thank you, sir."

He gives us a grin. "Tomorrow they'll drill with buckets on their heads."

J.A. slaps me on the chest playfully. "So that's how *buckethead* got started."

That would have been the end of it, but Sarge hears the Flower Boys cursing the lieutenant. He has them hogtied with a bayonet tied securely in their mouths and thrown in the guardhouse for a week. They missed some very valuable lessons growing up. Too little discipline or too much, both cause pain either way you go.

After the Flower Boy ruckus, the lieutenant orders all gambling for valuables is to cease.

Sarge warns, "Boys, I know you like games of chance, but give me a listen. Do you really want to go into battle with the man behind you holdin' a loaded musket sportin' a bayonet mad as hell at you 'cause you took his silver in a damn dice game?"

Makes sense to me. I never felt I had enough money to take a chance on losing it anyway.

J.A. lays his arm on my shoulder. "The Flower Boys want to own the whole world by takin' it away from everybody else. I don't get it. They got so much but appreciate so little."

"And what they have was built on the backs of people who get no part of the rewards. Most slaves are lucky if they have a good master who clothes, feeds, and houses them decent like."

J.A. kicks a rock. "Some even brought personal helpers along."

"Yeah, I've seen too many sins against Negroes. It's happenin' right here."

CHAPTER 7

FINALLY, WE'RE A REGIMENT

APRIL 25, 1862

It's good to hear from home.

W E'RE FINALLY A full regiment ready to protect all we cherish most. We come from all over Louisiana carrying the names of our parishes and nicknames, like Winn Rebels. Other companies call themselves the Terribles, Guards, Invincibles—names that inspire strength, hope and bravado. But fancy names won't stop a bullet or get me back to Susannah.

Today the Winn Rebels are declared Company F of the 27th Regiment Louisiana Volunteer Infantry. It's sobering to be a part of something bigger than myself. The officers compliment Sarge for our good work on the parade grounds.

But today, any storybook notions we may have about this war bursts like a gallon jar of Ma's pickles dropped on a rock.

New Orleans has surrendered.

We're devastated, and the officers try to rally our spirits with yells about standing strong against the vile horde of blue devils sent to take our land and lives.

Thankfully, sometimes bad news ushers in good. The mail arrives, and I stand in the crowd excited to get a letter but anxious about possible bad news. I want a letter, any letter, but most especially from Susannah. Dog-gone it if I don't get two—one from Susannah and the other from Ma. I open Susannah's so quickly I tear the letter cover.

Winnfield, March 16, 1862

    My Dearest Husband, I miss your loving face and your sweet touch. You are always in my thoughts. See how my writing has improved since you left. Mr. Gilmore helps me, and I know that you don't mind him knowing what I write. All is well here. The ground is ready for planting. Your brother Ben puts his hand to the plow without looking to the right or left like the Good Book says. Miss Dorcas is so pretty and possesses the godliest spirit I have ever known. Old Bart sends greetings and says to keep your head down. He loves you like a son, as does Mr. Gilmore. Know that no matter how bad it gets wherever you go, you are loved by all here, and we wait expectantly your return.

    This part I wrote myself. My soul aches for our talks. My mind aches for the things we learn together. My heart aches for the comfort only you can bring. My body aches for the longings only you can fulfill. My soul searches for your soul every night. I love you, Lummy, and pray we shall be returned to each other soon.

With undying love,
Susannah

There's a red imprint of her lips at the bottom. I slip into the woods down by the Tangipahoa, and when no one is looking, I press my lips to hers and cry. I dry my tears and sit on a stump.

The second letter is from Ma, written by my niece Mary, who's attended school six years now. Mary and Emaline came to live with us after Uncle Burrell died traveling through Arkansas back in '55. Ma took them in when their mother passed not long after they returned. I miss those girls, and Ma's letter couldn't have come at a better time.

Bankston, Choctaw County,
March 23, 1862

    Dearest Son, thank you for writing me before you got on the boat at Vicksburg. I've always wanted to take a river boat ride like that, but

surely not for the same reasons. Your Pa promised me we would one day,
but he didn't stay with us long enough. Oh, how I miss him.

I got a letter from George. He's fighting with the 15th Mississippi
Infantry, but he couldn't say where. Amariah will enlist in the 1st Mis-
sissippi Light Artillery sometime early May. Henry Turner is raising
a company at Kilmichael. He'll head to the Camp of Instruction near
Jackson to be trained to shoot cannons. At least he won't be on the front
line like George. I figure Jasper and James will become artillery men too.

Elihu keeps the farm going. He'll have it all to himself come harvest
time, but the Wood family has always been our friend to help. I'm getting
a little too feeble to pick cotton these days, but Mary and I will do our best.

You should not worry about us. The hard times haven't hit us like
they have other places. You just keep your mind on what you're doing.
Elihu says to keep your head down.

Love and kisses from your Mother, Mary, and Emaline.

I sit by the Tangipahoa River, rereading both letters, soaking in the news and the sun's rays. I lay them carefully on the log beside me. Little minnows dart around like we boys did playing back home. I want to go home, but a man who takes an oath can't go back on his word.

I try to relax on the white sand, pitching rocks at the leaves floating by. They just keep coming, little boats sailing peacefully without a care in the world. There's enough disturbance in my own life to bother these little leaves. So I stop. "I'm sorry, little leaves."

J.A. plops down beside me. "You think too much. What's a leaf gonna care if you throw a rock at it. Besides, you're gonna make it through all this, I'm sure of it."

"What makes you think so?"

"'Cause that fortune teller said you and me both gonna get through this without a scratch."

"You're dumb as a keg o' nails, boy. You paid good money for that piece of nothin'?"

"I'm a little scared, and I'll take any bit of hope I can git."

"I don't mean no harm, but next time save your money. The best thing you got goin' for you when it comes to stayin' alive is me."

I push him over, and we wrestle until we roll into the shallow sandy river. We laugh, slap the water at each other, and finally just rest in the cool stream.

"Lummy, I never had a best friend, but I'd be proud to have you if you're willin'. What say you?"

"I'm willin'."

ISAAC RUNS FROM the train tracks like his head's on fire and his ass is catching. "You won't believe it, boys! Our fine new Enfield rifle muskets are here!"

Sarge proudly yells, "These rifles were saved just before the Yankees took Nawlins. It's the only one you'll get, so love her like she's your sweetheart."

We aim our muskets, checking every part, familiarizing ourselves with every feature.

Sarge announces, "That ain't all. Your new gray uniforms are here. Sorry, but you'll have to pay for part of 'em." The cap costs three dollars if fitted, a dollar eighty-five if you pick one out of the pile. I pick one out of the pile. The frock coat costs twenty dollars, but they'll take that out of my pay a little at a time.

Sarge throws me a package. "Your pants, drawers, shirt, socks, and a new pair of brogans are free this time. Take care of your equipment. You'll pay for what you need from now on."

Isaac holds up his new equipment. "I'm a soldier now for sure!"

Back at our tent, I pull off my brogans to try on my new pants when a sound like a bumblebee buzzes by. "What the hell was that?"

Young Willie Dixon yells, "I don't know, but I felt the wind go by my head!"

Sarge races to our tent. "Anybody hurt?"

We shrug and shake our heads.

"Good, but now you know what a Minie ball sounds like."

Captain Norwood marches over with shaving soap still on his face. "The dumbass who put a bullet through my tent gets extra duty."

Sarge salutes. "I'm sure it was an accident, suh."

"Accident or not, punish the man and teach these men how to handle a weapon correctly."

THINGS MOVE TOO quickly now. We're ordered to cook four days' rations and "Be ready to skeedaddle in the blink of an eye."

J.A. asks, "Where we headin', Sarge?"

"It's a secret, but be ready." We straighten up and salute. "I'm proud of you men. Remember why you're doin' this, and you'll stand tall when the shootin' starts."

Our new regimental banner flickering in the breeze fills me with pride. It's a pretty flag with two red bars split by a white one and thirteen stars, ten in a circle and three at a slant on a dark blue square background. That's the colors we'll fight under.

J.A. asks, "Sarge, what are the three stars in the middle of the circle?"

"The border states—Kentucky, Maryland, and Missourah. They're split on whether darkies should be free or not." The flag snaps. I'm torn in my soul too, like the three border states, but not about Negroes being free.

I whisper to J.A., "We're brand new soldiers in brand new uniforms with brand new muskets under a brand new flag runnin' straight at this fight with everythin' we got."

J.A. laughs. "Shut up and get your new uniform on. I want us to go get our tintype made."

We each sit still as rocks holding our Enfields as our photograph is taken.

Sarge walks up behind us as we wait in line to get our tintypes. "You boys look right smart in your new uniforms. When the Yanks see you, they'll surely turn tail and skeedaddle."

We salute, get our two copies each, and walk away admiring the first photographs ever taken of us. Back at the tent, I change out of my uniform back into my old clothes. I pack my uniform carefully and walk down by Beaver Creek to write Susannah.

Camp Moore, April 30, 1862

Dearest Susannah, my heart aches for you. Thank you for the letter. You are always on my mind and in my heart. Do you think of me often? I have enclosed a tin type for your remembrance of me. A second copy I'm sending to Ma. I put on my new uniform jacket and hat so you can see what we look like all dressed up. What do you think?

I miss spring plowin and hope there will be a good crop this year. I thank God Mr. Gilmore is your father on this earth. I sleep much easier knowin you rest under his roof of safety. It salves my heart like the Balm of Gilead to know Old Bart watches over you too.

We had some bad news. New Orleans fell to the Yankees on the 25th. They blame the loss on General Lovell, but who knows why such things happen. Trains pass through at all hours with men and supplies going north. We wave to the somber faced men and try to get any information we can. I'm sure we will be ridin the rail soon, probably up to Jackson, as rumor tells it.

Please write often for your words steady my heart. Your posts may take some time to reach me as we may be movin about in rapid fashion. In fact, I am writin this with very little time but know that God will prevail. Send your letters to the city where my shoulder got hurt back in '59. You know the place of which I speak.

I do hope this war will be over soon. When God finally has had His fill of our disobedience and we of His wrath, maybe this conflict will end. I must finish now, my dear, for there is much to do, and the quicker I do it, the sooner I may be home. Send my love to Dorcas, Ben, and the children. Express my gratitude to Mr. Gilmore and Old Bart. Kisses from my mouth to yours, dear wife.

Your affectionate husband,
Lummy

CHAPTER 8

CALLED UP TO WHO KNOWS WHERE

MAY 1, 1862

A city set upon a hill can't be hidden. That's in the Good Book. Somewhere.

EARLY THIS MORNING, we get the call. Decked out in our new uniforms, we stand ready to board a train. All dressed up and don't know where we're going. Train after train of troops pass Camp Moore. We cheer the boys headed north to who knows where. A strange excitement and fearful dread of the unknown fills the air.

I take one last look at our cemetery. Today, we leave markers for six brothers of the 27th laid to rest struck down by the measles.

J.A. hangs his head. "Why'd those men die here and not me? I guess on whatever battlefield they bury me, the next man will walk away saying the same."

I scratch where my wool uniform itches the back of my neck. "Yeah, we're fixin' to ride in a pine box, only it has wheels."

The engine strains up the inclines as we pass Osyka, the first town in Mississippi, my home state. I haven't been back since late winter of '59. Funny, I'm here to fight for my home state wearing a Louisiana uniform, under a Louisiana flag, and with men from Louisiana. I have two homes now. It doesn't matter what uniform I wear—fighting is fighting wherever it happens, gray or blue. It's just a matter of where a man happens to be born or enlist.

One man yells as we cross the state line, "Hurrah for Missip, the state and county where I was born. I'll shoot every damn Yankee ass bluecoat I see."

I ask him, "What county are we in?"

"Pike County. I was raised not far from Holmesville. Why, you know this place?"

"Sure do. My Pa's family traveled here from Georgia on the Federal Road through Creek land back in '09. Pa and two of my uncles later went north to Choctaw County. My Uncle Silas and Grandpa Temple lived in Marion County." I want to visit their graves one day.

The train pours over the rolling hills like Ma's deer gravy over stewed potatoes. Smooth. The countryside reminds me of Winn Parish. We stop only for wood and water and not for long. We hop off the railcars just long enough to get a breath of fresh air. Some boys puke from the constant swinging motion of the train.

Along the way old men lift their hats and storekeepers throw us candy and bread. Pretty lacy-dressed ladies pitch bouquets of flowers, wave little Confederate flags, and throw us their perfumed handkerchiefs. Young Isham catches a white kerchief with tiny purple flowers, instantly falling in love with the beauty who tosses it.

He yells at the blonde-haired, green-eyed girl, "What's your name, darlin'?" She blushes and turns away. We get a whiff of her sweet fragrance. We move on with brokenhearted boys who find true love quickly in a simple smile and perfumed handkerchief.

All along the way we sing "The Bonnie Blue Flag that Bears a Single Star." The young boys gather at every town and try to outsing us. We pass through all the train stations leading to the capital city of Jackson—Summit, Bahala and Hazelhurst, Terry, Crystal Springs, and Byram.

We reach the outskirts of Jackson at 8:00 a.m., Friday, May 2. Colonel Marks announces, "Take a break while the engineers switch locomotives. The one we have won't make it up the steep hills on the next leg of our ride. Gather 'round men.

"We're headed to Vicksburg, and the Yanks will soon come our way." We cheer, but Colonel Marks pats the air for us to stop. "You're now soldiers in the Army of the Confederate States of America, and I expect you to act like it. You will be mindful of civilians and be ready to give your lives for the good people of Vicksburg. Stay strong, stand vigilant."

J.A. elbows me. "I like this fella already."

"Vicksburg, like the Good Book says, is a city set upon a hill and can't be hidden. The Yanks will try to run us off, but we will make them wish they'd never seen the bright lights of that good haven of God's people. You men of the 27th Louisiana Volunteer Infantry will arrive first to defend Vicksburg, and by God, we will be the last to leave."

The whistle blows, and the engine spits steam. We cheer and return to our railcars. A messenger rushes up to hand Colonel Marks several small papers.

He holds his hand up. "Listen to me now, we'll board in just a minute. With New Orleans in Yankee hands, Baton Rouge and Memphis will be their next targets. We are to proceed onto Vicksburg and prepare defenses. That's good, but I have news you won't like. I love that song "Bonnie Blue Flag" and know you do, too. It was written and sung for the first time right here in Jackson City after Missip seceded from the Union."

We cheer, "Hurrah for Missip!"

Colonel Marks raises his hand, and we quiet down. He checks to see if an officer of higher rank is listening. "I hate to speak unkindly of a fellow officer, even if he is wearin' that blue suit. But that son of a bitch General Benjamin 'Beast' Butler ordered all copies of that song burned. Mistuh Blackmar was fined five hundred dollars for publishing the sheet music and anyone caught singin', hummin', or whistlin' it will be fined and or subject to imprisonment. Since they're bein' persecuted, let's sing loud enough for ole sour ass down-in-the-mouth Beastly Butler to hear us all the way to Vicksburg."

J.A. huffs, "General Benjamin 'Beast' Butler ain't nothin' but a bully hidin' behind sewed on gold bars on his shoulders. Put him with some of us, and he'll get his ass kicked. Then he'll run home cryin' to his momma."

Colonel Marks grins. "Well said, Private. I'll ask him to come for a polite visit."

A young boy strikes up the song with a fine tenor voice, and we all join singing so Butler can hear us. Colonel Marks motivates his men well.

After the engines are switched, our cheering, singing, and flag waving dies down. We sing until all board, and then weariness takes over. We start west for Vicksburg with the train passing through Clinton, then Bolton's Station, and over the Big Black River to stop and pick up mail at Edward's Depot. We have to tear out a few bridges so the smokestack can pass the closer we get to town. It takes two days to make the forty miles. The train is so heavily loaded the locomotive can barely pull the hills.

The crowded conditions wear on us. Some boys climb on top of the car to the hurricane deck for fresh air only to find sparks and smoke not to their liking. The extra room is good reason to stay in the railcar. J.A. comes back. He was gone only an hour up top but looks white as a sheet.

"What happened?"

He's shaking like a leaf. "I was tryin' not to breathe in that dang black smoke when I saw a shiny piece of metal comin' straight for my head. I ducked just in time, but it hit the train and left a big gash. It could've taken my head off."

J.A. sits down and passes out.

We reach Vicksburg Sunday, May 4. It couldn't have come any sooner. We make camp by the tracks about a mile from the river to get organized. We set up tents and collapse to rest. Roll call comes at 8:00 p.m., but I don't wake in time. For that, I get extra guard duty.

We make permanent camp a mile downriver and name it Camp McLauren, for our lieutenant colonel. We don't stay there long either— too many mosquitoes like at Camp Walker. Some boys have symptoms of malaria already. To make things worse, measles follow us here, and several men are sent to the hospital in Clinton.

On the 13th we're ordered to relocate camp on a bluff in a cotton field. This drier ground with fewer mosquitos catches the cool evening river breezes. We cut brush to shade the sick not sent to the new hospital in Vicksburg. I'm a bit envious of the men who get to go in town, even if they are sick. I want to see the city soon.

I stand back and take it all in. "It's a sight, ain't it, J.A.? Twelve hundred men digging earthworks, building stockades, walking post, and hauling supplies."

"It is that."

Sarge marches by. "Before you go to work, if you got any extra clothes or things you want sent home, now's the time. You'll be movin' around a lot, so totin' a bundle with you just won't do. You got ten minutes to sort through your stuff and throw it on the wagon. Don't worry, it'll get where you're sendin' it. Move it."

I didn't bring much, didn't collect anything since leaving, and want no more than necessary to carry in my haversack.

BUILDING DEFENSES SUITS me fine. The engineers use their instruments and calculating books to have us level the ground for cannon emplacements. If we're not using picks and shovels, we're guarding railroad bridges from Yank cavalry roaming the countryside. We work day and night in shifts, even Sundays, so when it comes time to rest, few men want to go in town or do anything but eat and sleep.

For oversleeping again, J.A. and I catch extra guard for a week on the road that leads south. About noon, a well-dressed gentleman stops to grease a wheel. His little girl, maybe ten, scampers over to us. She has the prettiest blonde hair and sky blue eyes. She reminds me of my sister, Saleta.

J.A. asks, "And what is your name, pretty girl?"

"I'm Lucy, and that's my father over there." He waves.

Lucy has the sound of a little bird as she shares news about the city. She's smart, mannerly, and sweet as molasses. "Father will take me up on Sky Parlor Hill after he finishes his business. You can see fifty miles into Louisiana on a clear day. Y'all should come with me some time. I'll bring some of momma's sugar cookies for you."

She smiles as the river breeze gently ruffles her golden curls. She has the face of an angel and the refinement of a courtly lady. This is reason enough to defend Vicksburg.

I smile. "We would be honored, at your convenience."

J.A. laughs. "And at Sarge's convenience."

"I'd feel safer with a big, strong Confederate soldier guarding me." She bats her eyes.

I have to know. "Where did you learn to speak so well, my little dear?"

She blushes red with a pearly smile. "At the all-girls academy. My daddy says it's not right that only boys get an education. My heart hurts, though. On my way to school, I pass by the poor children who can't afford school. I hope to be a teacher one day and help all children get an education, poor or not, and even the Negro children. It's right, do you agree?"

"I do." Maybe that's a reason to let Vicksburg fall. I keep that to myself.

Another soldier on duty asks, "What? You want niggahs to read and write?"

I whisper, "Back off."

I pick a wildflower. "A pretty flower for a prettier flower. That makes two."

She blushes again. "You are quite the gentleman, suh."

Her starchy skirt ruffles as she gracefully skips toward her daddy's wagon bounding up on the seat as he gently pops the mules with the reins.

J.A. kicks the dirt. "Sure miss my boy, Richard. Mary Jane wants a girl just like Lucy when I get back. I wish I could hug my boy's neck." He pulls me to the side. "I gotta ask, do you think them little niggah kids ought to learn to read?"

My anger flares, but I quiet my spirit. After all, he's the best friend I have here. "Damn, J.A., everybody should get the chance to learn to read, don't you think? Heck, readin' makes the world better 'cause it helps us understand each other better."

He nods.

"And about that word *niggah*. You do know what it means, don't you?" He shakes his head. "A niggah acts like he ain't got no trainin', like he's stupid, doing stupid things 'cause he don't know any better. Truth be told, J.A., there's more niggahs in this white man's army than I ever seen colored black folks back home."

J.A. rubs his chin thoughtfully. "Can't argue with that. How'd you come to that understandin'?"

"You agree the Good Lord knows what he's doin'. If he does, then he places people when and where he wants them, where they're born and to who, even what color. Knowin' that I didn't have a choice in the matter, I could've been born slave or free, black just as easy as white. That bein' true, I best treat folks like Jesus said, like I want to be treated, or it won't go well for me. Jesus came to set the captives free, not chain 'em." I let J.A. sit with that for a minute.

I whisper, "The Lord said in Psalm number twenty-four that the earth is His and everything in it, the world, and they that dwell therein. So if the Lord owns everythin' and all the people in it, it ain't mine. It's all His, especially human bein's."

I point to a slave washing an officer's shirt. "If that man belongs to the Lord, how can another man own him unless he steals him from the Lord? He surely didn't buy him from Jesus."

J.A. puts his finger to his lips.

I quiet down. Nobody heard me. They will someday.

He watches the wagon go up the hill. "I've thought about that before. Some folks back home set their niggahs free before the war. I guess that's what Jesus was talkin' about. Our Pa never had slaves. He just wouldn't have it. But what can I do to make things better?"

Here's my opportunity. "Tell you what. Let's stop sayin' niggah. Let's just call Negroes by what they are—a man, woman, or child—and by their names, what you say?"

"You're serious, ain't you?"

"Damn straight. We're better men than that."

We watch until the wagon crests the rise with little Lucy waving furiously.

"I can do that, but my reasons for bein' here ain't to set the darkies free. Nawsuh, just take a look into the sky blue eyes of a little blonde curly-haired angel like that one, and you know why you're defendin' this town."

I look into the eyes of the slave washing his master's shirt, and my reasons for fighting this war change.

CHAPTER 9

WHY WE'RE FIGHTIN'

MAY 7, 1862

Sometimes the reason you start something ain't the reason you finish it.

WE'RE ORDERED BACK to the earthworks, so we lose our easy guard duty job. Our new commander, Brigadier General Martin Luther Smith, is an engineer and makes it top priority to better the defenses of the city. With the 27th Louisiana being the only regiment in Vicksburg, that means lots of hard labor.

Sarge relieves us early at noon. "Lummy, tomorrow take ten men with picks and shovels to set them big stationary guns. Take these four hour passes and go see what you're defendin'. Ain't much time, so git." He grins and shoves my shoulder. "Don't be late for evenin' parade, and you boys keep your roosters in your britches. Don't forget, if you lie down with dawgs, you'll get up with fleas. And you best make a good showin' to the fine loyal folks of Vicksburg."

J.A. laughs. "That means be respectful and stay out of trouble."

River towns, I love them—the sights, the smells, the people, and the busyness. This is my first time seeing Vicksburg in the daytime. We get a table on a hotel porch at the corner of Crawford and Levee Streets. We drink real coffee and watch men feverishly building a gunboat. What a sight—thick timbers, pressed cotton to soften enemy cannon blows, and two inch steel plating. Most interesting is watching passengers trail up and down steamboat gangplanks—gamblers, itinerant preachers, merchants, fancy dressed ladies, families, and an officer or two.

Isham grins. "Them girls sure are pretty. Wonder what they doin' in town?"

J.A. slaps his chest. "Boy, don't you know nothin'? They're here to see us. Lotta money to be made off soldiers if you got the right parts to sell."

Isham shakes his head. "That's too bad."

I agree. "Oldest job in the world. Ain't nobody right in it, man or woman."

Travelers mostly look right through us like nothin's going on except what's in their small worlds. That'll change when the Yanks show up. We finish our coffee and wander about town to get our bearings.

J.A. scratches his ear. "People scurryin' in and out of town like rats. We must make 'em more serious about gettin' prepared for what's comin'."

I wonder at it all. "I guess some think the city will be safer, and others think the opposite. Some haul stuff to the country, and some bring stuff to town."

J.A. laughs. "And almost runnin' into each other doin' it. I guess safety's where you believe it to be, true or not."

Isaac hustles over to a candy shop. "Let's get somethin' sweet." What's not so sweet is the bitter temperament of the town folks.

"Damn Yankees'll come now with y'all here. Can't y'all go fight somewhere else?"

We assure them we'll defend them and the city. It doesn't help.

Sitting on a bench in front of the candy store, I read a newspaper. "It says here Vicksburg is the second largest city in Mississippi with five thousand souls callin' it home. New Orleans and Memphis are two hundred miles in either direction. Steamboats arrive every day to unload molasses, flour, salt, manufactured goods, and all sorts of fancy foreign merchandise. That all might change with the Yanks holdin' New Orleans and threatenin' Memphis. Merchants fear smugglers and speculators will make prices go up."

J.A. sniffs the air like a dog. "Ain't nothin' we can do about all that, but we can enjoy the smells of good food we don't have money for and pretty girls strolling beautiful streets. They smell like a spring flower garden."

Susannah's face pops into my head reminding me of God's gift.

Vicksburg is a place of culture, elegance, educated people, and luxurious living. Grocery stores are stocked full of food and clothing shops offer the latest fashions. Stores have every kind of sweet a person can imagine, and bookstores carry the latest titles. What a magnificent place—stone church-es, an opera house, hotels decorated with wrought iron lace, sidewalks, and cobblestone streets. The new courthouse rivals anything in Europe. Little blonde, curly haired Lucy was sad when she said it was built by slaves. That little lady is different. She makes me want to be different. I am different. I just haven't mustered the courage to live what I believe deep inside. That time's coming though.

We stop for a closer look at the courthouse then walk to the Warren County Jail across the street.

J.A. rubs his hand along the brick wall. "I don't want to get thrown in here."

"You don't. I was in jail for a week one time for hittin' a bully in the back with a rock."

He picks up a rock. "I guess you best leave them rocks alone, huh?"

"And the whiskey, dice and cards, fightin', whorin' around, and...."

"We get it, Lummy. We'll be good boys who go to church every time the door opens, okay?"

"Just repeatin' what Sarge told us. River towns are a den of sin for young lads like us."

Isaac asks, "You some kinda preacher or somethin'?"

"Now I ain't against takin' a snort of moonshine on a cold winter's night or of Pa's special cough medicine he made every September. He'd buy a gal-lon of moonshine from the Wood boys and put in lemon drops. It'd take the fight out of a cold and cough. Funny thing though, the jars drained just as fast even when no one was sick. Ole Mistah Wiley liked the lemon drop moonshine I made him the night he died. At least he passed with a smile on his face."

J.A. smiles. "I liked that old man. He told good stories."

"He did. But no, Isaac, I ain't no preacher. My Pa just taught us to stay away from evil places. He'd say, 'Them folks'll get you drunk, take your mon-ey, and give you a disease.'"

J.A. pats me on the shoulder. "You must've had a good father."

"Yeah, I did, in many ways."

Even though Pa was hard on us, we knew he loved us. I'll never understand why he had to be hard as nails about everything. Grandpa Willoughby must've been harder on him than Pa was on us. I guess that's the way of it. Sons should become better than their fathers. I want to shuck off the meanness Pa put in me. I don't want to pass that along to the children Susannah and I will have together. But I may need that hardness to survive what's coming.

Before heading back to camp, we scamper up Sky Parlor Hill to view the river. It's just like little curlyhaired Lucy told us. We can see for miles over into Louisiana. I wish I could see my Susannah. "Lord, I miss my darlin'."

J.A. sighs, "Me, too, brother."

Isaac points. "What's that smoke over there?"

I block the sun from my eyes. "Sarge told me Company A was ordered to set fire to cotton bales down by the river. Twelve hundred bales for twelve hundred men of the 27th Louisiana."

J.A. shakes his head. "What a waste."

I whisper, "Lord, don't let us be so easily destroyed when the Yanks bring their fire. I got too much to live for."

J.A. elbows me. "I know one dang thing for certain, that fire ain't nearly as hot as the blaze you got in your heart for your wife." I feel my anger burn about leaving.

He lays his arm on my shoulder. "She sees you, Lummy, in her heart. We both can see who we're fightin' for from up here." We make it to camp just in time for evening drill.

THE BUGLE SOUNDS too early this morning. We dress, eat, and line up for morning assembly.

Colonel Marks announces, "President Davis says Vicksburg is the nail that holds the two halves of our nation together. It's the lifeline for the whole country. Memphis will fall soon and with New Orleans already in enemy hands, all things from the west will now come through Vicksburg. Boys, we gotta hold her. We're in an impregnable position atop this great hill."

J.A. leans over. "I remember hearin' the preacher say somethin' about the

Israelites knockin' the walls of Jericho down with only marchin', shoutin', and trumpet blasts."

I whisper back, "Sittin' on top of two hundred foot bluffs with the gullies surroundin' us? Hell, ain't nary a blue army ever made can take this grand city."

J.A. squints. "Then we better build these forts stronger than the people of Jericho did theirs."

Breaking my back and sweat dripping off my face like it's raining in these earthworks and expecting thousands of bluecoats to come across the hill, I'm glad Pa toughened us up. I stop to wipe the sweat from my brow. "Am I fightin' for the right reason here? Am I on the right side?"

J.A. throws dirt at my feet. "Shut up, boy! They'll shoot you for sayin' stuff like that."

"Shot now, shot later. What does it matter if you don't believe in what you're doin'?"

CHAPTER 10

MISSISSIPPIANS DON'T KNOW HOW TO SURRENDER

MAY 17, 1862

Old men brag. Old women nag the braggers. Until the gunboats appear.

OVER THE NEXT few days, troops pour in from all over the South, besides the thirty-five hundred just in from Louisiana. Weary and sick men arrive who fought at Shiloh Church, the bloodiest battle of the war yet, the papers say.

Sarge keeps us moving, working, lifting, and digging. I'm leaner and more sinewy than if I was working on the farm. Not so for all. Some men down with measles, mumps, or a bad case of the screamers look like skeletons. They're a pitiful sight.

Sarge marches over. "Lummy, take the sick to the city hospital. The wagon's over there."

I give him an uncomforatble salute. It's a risk, but I figure if a man's going to get sick, there's not much he can do about it. I wear a rag over my nose and mouth the whole time I'm gone. Young Billy Dixon is fortunate to have the measles leave his body two days after getting a bed. Most aren't that lucky. Some don't come back from the hospital at all.

Thankfully, I've been spared any sickness, and it's not because of my un-dying good looks. Disease cares not for who you are, where you're from, or how rich your daddy is. I'm careful how I handle food and latrine issues. We each pay Doc Simpson a dollar a month to keep us well. That's quite a bit for a poor soldier, but it's worth staying healthy. It's hard to get medicine, and when he finds it, it costs more these days.

Some of the city boys whose lily-white backs have never seen the sun also don't know a man shouldn't drink water near latrines. Sarge constantly has to remind them. A drink of what appears to be cool fresh spring water can turn a stomach into a roaring fiery cannon exploding from your hind end. They call it the screamers. Their backs peel in the sun and backsides burn like fire when they go to the ditch. Not a good combination while using a pick and shovel.

The spirits of the men are high, though. Decent food, and lots of it, good honest hard work, and pay on time will do that for a man. I never mind hard work. It keeps a man's soul pure.

"Sweatin' out the ole Devil," as Granny Thankful used to call it. But the complaining increases as the workload increases.

Granville, a young boy we met from Company A, who's barely sixteen, finally changed his whining tune and is shaping into a man more each day. Some of these young boys should've thought twice before seeking glory. It's not found in digging rifle pits. The letters to his mother change from a constant moan to how he and the Skipwith Guards will fight to the last man.

Sarge walks the line to check our progress. "Step it up, boys. Tomorrow's Sunday, and I'll let you off the whole day if you finish today out real good. I know you need time to go squander your lives chasin' pretty town girls if you got nothin' better to do. But make sure you get some preachin' sometime durin' the day. Good Lord knows you need it."

We cheer and laugh. It's the only time I've seen Sarge smile since we left Camp Moore. He worries we won't be ready when the Yanks come. At three o'clock, he comes back to volunteer J.A. and me, a few others, and a young Negro for a special job.

"Don't cry. I'll get you back in time to beat the other boys to town." We all volunteer, except the Negro. He has no say. We double-time it to the south end of a long cotton field. Five hundred bales of cotton lay neatly stacked covered with tarps.

Sarge barks, "Get them tarps off, fold them up good, and claim one each for your shelter. You'll want 'em when the rains come. Then burn the cotton. Watch the fire for an hour or so after you light it. Don't let it get away from you."

We pour kerosene on the bales and Sarge lights the fire. It's the biggest blaze I've ever seen. Fortunately, the wind kicks up from the east sending choking stench across the river. What a waste. Thousands of dollars' worth of fine cotton up in smoke. It'd make a lot of cloth at the mill in Bankston.

I look down at my clothes. What I brought from home is wearing out fast. We're only allowed to wear our uniforms at guard duty and parade. So we swap out clothes, making do as best we can, but they're getting pretty threadbare. Men who sent clothes home now wish they hadn't. While we watch the fire, I write Susannah a short note asking a little help for myself.

Vicksburg, Mississippi May 17, 1862

Dearest Sweetheart of my soul. All is well here in V'burg. The work is hard but not for an old farm hand. Standing guard duty is borin, but we get to wear our uniforms. My work clothes are wearin thin. Please send pants, shirts, drawers, socks, and my extra pair of boots. I really need them. It just won't do to be naked as a jaybird around here. Send them in care of Captain William B. Stovall, 27th Regiment Looseana Volunteers.

V'burg is a very nice city. One day when this is all over I'll bring you here. We never did have a proper honeymoon. I miss and love you my darlin.

I remain always your faithful husband til death,
Lummy Tullos

WE EXPECT TO see Yankee gunboats in the river any day. With the defenses shaping up, we're pretty confident, maybe a little cocky. It's hot, and mosquitoes swarm in clouds up at our posts every night. Some men ask for passes to go home. The dismal letters they receive from family and the constant waiting for the enemy to arrive weaken their resolve. Hearing them complain makes me homesick for Susannah and the peaceful life we started before I left.

"Damn, why did I ever leave home?"

J.A. elbows me. "Shut up, boy. You'll wind up in the Warren County jail talkin' like that."

Today we hear fifteen Yankee boats are anchored near Natchez. The Yank Navy inches closer every day. I'm nervous as a cat in a room full of rocking chairs. It's not knowing what's ahead that rattles my soul. When the gunboats bombard towns like Vicksburg, people get killed standing in the wrong place at the wrong time. I don't know what to expect.

Old men come out after their morning coffee to boast how the brave boys in gray will pummel the Yanks. They spin tales of glory fighting Indians and Mexicans. Gray haired ladies bring us cold water and fresh baked bread at dinner time. They nag their husbands to get back to their own jobs. They threaten no supper if they come home late.

One old man brags, "Hell, they'll have to level this city before we surrender." Old men brag. Old women nag the braggers. At least until the gunboats appear.

Saturday night we listen to an impassioned speech by Reverend Jeremiah H. Tucker of the Dixie Rebels. General Smith believes we need a spirited word of encouragement to prepare us for the coming fight. Though he uses words most of us never heard, Reverend Tucker lays it on thick in the might of the God of Abraham, Isaac, and Jacob. A fellow next to me copied down his whole speech. I think his name is Gunnard.

"Good men of the 27th Louisiana, the exigencies of our time demand this sacrifice of us all, and like you, I willingly make it. Did I say willingly? Yes, cheerfully even. I am ready as when I left my home, as are you, to lay my life down for my country. Weak women and cowardly men may never be, but brave hearts are set on their divine course. I find often our dear ladies are more patriotic than our men. I do not see that here, my comrades in arms."

Reverend Tucker takes a deep breath. "I know you men would rather have your homes and furnishings burned by your wives' own hands rather than it give shelter and sustenance to the Yank invader. Should we hang our hallowed heads in despair? Must we tremble in fear at the sound of the Yankee gunboats? I dare say not. For did not the British take possession of all the principal cities of those thirteen fledgling colonies? Did not their all-powerful navy hem up our rivers and ports? Did they not send regiment after regiment of the reputed finest army in the world against a ragged, naked, starving, and ill-armed peasant rabble and yet were destroyed? And shall we be worthy of our fathers? God forbid, we will not yield."

With many other reassurances, Reverend Tucker outdid himself. I bet the folks in Winn Parish heard the cheering that night for such a rousing speech. I hope so, for the good reverend mentioned that the Yanks are making their way up the Red River. He assures us the farmers will block the stream with log rafts. I'm sure Ben, Mr. Gilmore, and Old Bart will pitch in. I'm glad tomorrow is Sunday. I need to hear something good about God.

THIS MORNING, WE wash our faces, slick our hair, clean our shoes, and walk to the city. After preaching, we go down to the river. We mill around throwing rocks into the stream when sky rockets shoot high south of town. It's the warning signal I've been dreading.

"They're here!" one of the boys in the Marine Battery yells. The hairs on the back of my neck stand up, and chills run down my spine like spiders crawling all over me.

Before we can scatter to our posts, the Yankee ship *Oneida* steams up fast and close. The river battery lays a shot across her bow to let her know she's close enough. The Yankee boat lowers a hack to bring a message from S. Phillips Lee, Commander of the Advance Naval Division, a high-sounding Yankee title. He's a Farragut man.

In a pee pot—which is about what his message is worth—Farragut demands the surrender of Vicksburg. *Demands?* His tone is as high and mighty as his title and worth about half as much. The officer receiving the message from the Yank sailor's shaky hand walks away, mumbling after reading the few lines.

J.A. shouts, "I'd like to buy Yankee Lee for what he's worth and then sell him for what he *thinks* he's worth." We laugh heartily, though nervously.

Commander Lee had to wait five hours to get three replies to his ridiculous demand. I hear it all, pulling guard duty as each was read before the Yank officer in the hack.

The Vicksburg mayor, the Honorable Lazarus Lindsay, wrote, *"Neither municipal authorities nor citizens will ever consent to the surrender of the city."* It has feeling, warm but clear.

Lieutenant Colonel James L. Autry, the local commander, offers a more passionate, though less tempered, response. *"I have to state that Mississippians don't know, and refuse to learn, how to surrender to an enemy. If Farragut or Butler can teach them, let them come and try."* Old Autry looks to have a high fever when he barks out those words.

The last reply comes from General M. L. Smith who exhibits no sign of feeling. In a matter-of-fact fashion, he states, *"Regarding the surrender of the defenses, I have to reply that, having been ordered here to hold these defenses, my intention is to do so as long as it is in my power to do so."* I've never heard words said more peacefully while at the same time so firmly. Smith is a professional soldier. He doesn't blink. He simply tells Lee what is and what will be. It must've struck Yankee Lee dumb. It strengthens my resolve.

Sarge grins. "Bet Yankee Lee scratchin' that ole swoled up head that got popped like a soap bubble." We taunt the Yanks in the hack as they travel back to the *Oneida*.

A man who just arrived yells, "This ain't New Orleans or Baton Rouge, and it surely ain't Natchez. This here's Vicksburg." Yeah, but the Yanks now hold New Orleans, Baton Rouge, and Natchez. Don't guess the new boys understand how that happened.

The Yankees do, though.

Colonel Marks orders F Company with a couple other units from the 27th Louisiana to march along the bluff around 5:00 p.m. It's for show, but it catches Commander Lee's attention. He's had just about enough of the defiant citizens and soldiers of Vicksburg.

The *Oneida* spits out a shell rising high in the sky. We see it coming but can't tell if it'll make the bluff or not. It just hangs in mid-air for what seems like an eternity. None of us have ever seen a cannon fire, much less be shot at by one. When it drops, there's no mistaking it.

"Run, J.A.! She's comin' right at us!"

We scatter like chickens with a fox in the henhouse. Fortunately, no one is hit by the flying shrapnel when it explodes. J. A. hands me a piece of the hot metal. I feel its warm, jagged edges in my palm. Surely would have done terrible damage if it'd hit somebody. A second shell lands near men in the earthworks, but no one's hurt.

The next day, Yankee Lee warns the mayor to evacuate the women and children. He will commence shelling the city soon.

We wait and wait, expecting the devil's fire and brimstone to rain down at any moment. It doesn't for three more days. But today, the 26th of May 1862, at 5:00 p.m., Vicksburg receives its first piece of fiery Yankee mail, with twenty shells to follow. It's on for sure now. Between shifts in the earthworks, I stay down by the river with my musket to watch. I just hope they go away. We watch Yankee gunships launch 125 exploding shells into the city in one day. Then at 10:00 p.m., Yankee Lee sends 65 more shells. Isham, J.A., and I sit on a hill above our camp.

J.A. fills his pipe. "What do you think, Lummy? Them mortar boats maybe three miles away?"

A mortar fires. We follow the red streak of their fuses until it hits somewhere in the city.

"Oh, I don't know, looks about right." My heart aches for the women and children, the innocents of this war who suffer the most.

He hangs his head. "Sure glad my family ain't in the city."

Isham hunkers down with his arms wrapped around his knees and starts rocking. "Them damn Yank shells gonna rouse the Devil himself."

I lean over to J.A. "I believe the Devil has been roused up, you think?"

He takes out his pipe. "I think." It's so loud we can hardly hear each other talk, and the incessant flash of explosions make the river like a stream of fire. But we're safe, for now.

Sarge walks to the edge of the bluff. "Sad news, boys. A shell fatally wounded the mother of three little girls. Some of our boys carried her to a house where she died in twenty minutes. Another mother, Miz Gamble, was running for her life when she was shot clean through. Her Negro carried her to our camp, but she was dead on arrival. She leaves seven little girls orphaned. Ain't it enough that they kill us men? But women and children?"

The chaplain comes by. "Damn Yanks targeted citizens watching the show near the Methodist church. Fortunately, they were all spared."

Maybe I should become a Methodist.

"At least it's over for now, Chaplain."

Sarge straightens his kepi. "Not much damage for all these damn shells thrown at us."

J.A. rubs a hand over his face. "I just can't get them two mothers and their little orphaned children out of my mind. I want to fight, dammit, but how?"

A runner comes through yelling, "Farragut's tucked tail and took his boats back downriver. Vicksburg ain't gonna be as easy as he thought."

Sarge laments, "They'll be back soon enough."

IT'S ALMOST JUNE. We choke down our morning coffee, biscuits, and fried salt pork and grab our shovels. We line up for roll call still trying to get awake.

Sarge cups his ears straining to listen. "Quiet!"

A shell screaming like a demon let loose from hell whistles toward our camp—then two, three, one right after the other.

Sarge yells. "Get down, now!"

A lieutenant with a spyglass rushes to the edge of the bluff. "It's the U.S.S *Winona,* and she's unloading on our camp!"

I grab J.A. and Isham by their shirts and yank them up. We scramble into a ditch just before the first shell explodes, sending shrapnel everywhere. I feel the heat of the red hot chunks of iron as they pass over my head.

Isham screams, "Who opened the gates of hell?"

I peek over the clods just as a shell hits a mule and scatters bloody parts in all directions. The tail lands on J.A., who shivers like a rabbit on a frosty winter morning. "Get it off me, get it off now!"

Isham grabs it and throws it.

Finally, its over. We start clean up when an old farmer drives his wagon into our camp and holds up a cannon ball. "Them bastards sent a four-inch ball through a seasoned oak two and a half feet thick and kilt my best layin' hen! Weren't nothin' left but feathers floatin' in the air. Damn Yankees."

Sarge checks with the other sergeants of the other companies. "Grape shot tore through one of Company G's tents. Not much more to report than that. Consider yourselves lucky."

Knowing death can come from anywhere, anytime, weighs heavy. Some can't stand it. They weren't trained to take a beating and not get to fight back. Most are scared out of their wits or so angry they stand out near the bluffs and yell at the Yank gunboats. My hands won't stop shaking from the constant booming. Funny, I don't feel afraid, but my body tells me to be afraid.

Young Isaac sits by the fire rocking back and forth. "I just want to kill me a Yankee. I just want to kill me a damn Yankee." He helped carry Mrs. Gamble to our camp after the last bombardment. She died in the arms of the men who bore her. Those men don't sleep well. None of us do. I wake J.A. a couple times a night from nightmares.

The shelling comes every day and night now. A boy no more than eighteen shakes uncontrollably when the shells come. He sits up on his haunches like a hound dog and howls as the shells pass over. I throw water in his face, and he comes back to himself. Often I pray into the small hours of night but with little hope of sleep.

THERE'S NO SHELLING this pretty morning. Sarge hands me a Chicago newspaper. "Here, read this out loud." Men gather around.

"On June 6, Yankee gunboats completely destroy the Confederate river navy north of Memphis. Memphis has fallen."

Sarge grimaces. "Tighten up, boys. The Yanks'll be here soon."

Isham cries. "When Sarge?"

"Don't know, but we've been ordered to move away from this damn shellin'." We make camp a mile from the river where there's good water. We set our tents in a big hollow on the back side of the city near Graveyard Road.

J.A. laughs. "They won't have far to haul us for buryin'."

Superstitious men get chills, afraid that haints and ghouls might come out of those graves tonight. For my own comfort, I write Ma a letter.

Camp Tucker, Graveyard Road, Vicksburg,
June 6, 1862

   Dear Ma, I'm doin well so far. We got shelled not long ago, but we're all right. Our camp is now by a very large graveyard. They say we will have peace soon since the Yankee boats ran like rabbits. Is the corn growin up tall? I'd give half my pay for a bushel. I escaped the measles and mumps and the screamers so far. I thank the Good Lord for that. Have you heard anythin from George or Amariah? Please ask Mary to write soon. News from home is medicine to my soul. There ain't never enough pay for what I need here. Anything I still got at home sell for your own needs. Tell my brothers I wish I was on the farm with them. How I wish I could see you all.

Your son,
Lummy Tullos.

Writing home washes the sadness out of my heart—for a time.

After we get camp in order, Colonel Marks orders a short break from all work except guard duty. J.A. and I walk to the bluff to take a look.

J.A. points downriver. "Guess old Farragut left them three gunboats within sight of the city to keep us wonderin'."

I yell, "Yeah, but we ain't wonderin'. Who's doin' the damn demandin' now, Farragut?"

Taunting does nothing to build up my spirit. I ain't got that kind of pride in my soul. I force my mind to picture Susannah's face and forget about this war. It only lasts for a moment.

CHAPTER 11

A LITTLE BOAT CAN DO A LOT OF DAMAGE

JUNE 23, 1862

Smoke rises thickest from smoldering ashes.

WHEN NOT ON picket duty, we improve the earthworks—hard work to keep worries at bay. Our batteries control the river and keep Farragut's navy from joining with the Yankee boats steaming south from Memphis. Everytime a shell flies over, we duck. It works on the nerves something fierce. With every bombardment, General Smith adjusts his earthwork plans for an assault from any direction. And it will come. Bombarding Vicksburg into submission has failed.

I wake this morning sick as a dog. Doc gives me quinine to break the chills and cool the fever. He first thought it was malaria, but that was proved wrong in just a few days. With better food and a few sips from the five gallons of whiskey we'd won in a sharpshooting contest, I'm fine now. I don't want a grave marker in the cemetery down the road.

I make it back to F Company in a couple days, and J.A laughs. "You was just fakin' so you could get some good sippin' whiskey. Always good for what ails a man." I don't argue with that.

Friday morning at roll call, our captain reads a message from President Davis that General Lovell has been replaced by Major General Earl Van Dorn to lead the Confederate Department of Southern Mississippi and East Louisiana."

I gripe, "I never liked that Lovell. He had a bad habit of torchin' perfectly good cotton even with no Yanks in sight." I know. I helped burn it.

Van Dorn has the reputation of a fighter and a lover, sometimes giving too much attention to other men's wives. Men in high positions sometimes afford themselves the luxury being above the law sometimes, civil and moral. Even so, General Smith is happy to have Van Dorn take charge but more so that Colonel Samuel H. Lockett arrived to oversee engineering the defenses.

Lockett stops by to inspect our work. He grabs a shovel and goes to work. After half an hour he calls for water. He wipes the sweat from his forehead. "Men of the 27th Louisiana, I am extremely proud of your vigorous preparations. You took an oath to defend our great Confederate States of America, and I take an oath to make Vicksburg an impregnable fortress. Spies report that Grant is bringing 1100 slaves from area cotton plantations to dig a canal across DeSoto Point. Who does he think he is, God Himself thinking he can change the course of the Mississippi?"

Now we have a West Pointer with some real know-how.

We work longer hours with less food. We're hungry all the time. I worked just as hard on the farm but always had more than enough food. Food gets scarce, and our money worth less. The going rate for a peck of Irish potatoes is four bits. The men who complain the most work the least and have bigger appetites from years of living in ease with plenty.

J.A. throws down his shovel. "You sorry, lazy no good sons o' bitches. Get up and work. You loaf around all day and eat twice as much as the rest of us."

I hand him his shovel. "You done?"

"Reckon so. I'm just tired of my guts stickin' to my backbone."

"I do understand. I wish I could put my feet under my ma's table tonight."

J.A. leans on his shovel handle. "Wonder how your lady friend across the river is doin'?"

"Probably slimmin' up pretty good, I'd bet."

"She's got plenty of men to pester with Grant bringing troops to help dig the canal."

"Reckon so." Though I don't know her well, I count Annie a friend. She makes me laugh.

J.A. licks his lips. "I wish my feet were under my wife's kitchen table, too. I'd have butter on my taters and springhouse cold sweet milk in my cup."

Isham slaps J.A. playfully on his chest. "Shut the hell up, boy. I'm so hungry I could eat the acorns out of a dead coon's ass." My stomach churns after that comment.

Sarge walks our way, message in hand. "Good news, boys. Troops from all over the Confederacy are pourin' in. Most have seen the elephant more'n once and are spoilin' for another fight. Make as many friends as you can. Every man you call friend is a soldier who'll save your ass when the shootin' starts. Bad news is all passes are cancelled. Don't matter if your momma just passed, you can't go home."

FARRAGUT'S GUNBOATS FINALLY come back firing their mortars along with General William's rifled artillery from across the river. The whistle of the shells and the bursts of exploding shells scare some men and anger others. I'm somewhere in between—scared I won't make it home and angry I have to be here in the first place. The Yanks try to weaken the river batteries on June 26th but do little more than frighten the good citizens and wound a few men. Our boys manning the big guns gave them hell in response. It was a sight to see from the bluffs above.

Before dawn, June 28th, Farragut makes a run for it. His boats steam full bore upriver. We run to the bluff to watch. Thirty-six Union ships bear down with cannon and mortar against ten guns of the Marine Hospital Battery. The river is only a half mile wide here. It's a murderous scene. The artillerists load, adjust their aim, and fire one round after another. I want to join in with each blast. I watch with my finger set on my musket trigger—a small and useless contribution if I fired at the gunboats.

Big guns belch out death flames spitting iron and shot mercilessly. When shells come too close, Sarge pulls us back, but we see enough to know those boys, both blue and gray, are having a hell of a fight.

After three hours, the last gunboat rounds the bend to safety. We crippled a few. None of our guns were damaged. Two gunners and three pickets were wounded. That's never good news.

SARGE YELLS WHILE we're eating breakfast. "Finish up! No digging to-day. We're movin' camp."

Isham pokes the fire. "Where to, Sarge?"

"Out of this damn heat and into the shade."

I reach for more coffee, and I catch J.A. staring at me. "What? I got mud on my face or what?"

He wants to turn away but whispers, "No, Lummy, it's your hands."

They're shaking. "Well, that just won't do when I aim my musket at a chargin' Yank."

"You all right?"

"I don't feel scared, but I think this shellin' is workin' on my nerves."

"It's messin' a lot of boys up. Some run off 'fore the Yanks even get here."

I'd run off too if it weren' for the oath I took. I won't. But I have turned to my anger to survive.

A boy crawls out of his tent. "Sarge, my throat hurts somethin' fierce, and it's hard to chew."

J.A. rushes to pick him up. "He's had headaches, fever, achy muscles, won't eat, is wore out all the time, and he's got a bad pain in his man parts."

Sarge points. "Isham, run get the Doc."

The doctor examines several men. "It's what I feared. The mumps have found Vicksburg. Let's get the infected to the hospital. Sarge, if anybody else complains, you send them to me."

Sarge salutes, and we load the infected men in the wagon.

J.A. shakes his head. "Mortars or the mumps. I don't know which does more damage."

A message runner trots into camp. "General Van Dorn is sendin' a big surprise to Farragut's Yankee fleet. When you see it, raise up a cheer for Captain Brown and his brave men."

Sickness and death, laughing and cheering, all in the same moment. It's too much on the nerves.

At five o'clock, Farragut gets his surprise. Enemy gunboats rumble out into the river firing cannons like there's no tomorrow.

Sarge yells, "Company F, grab your weapons, let's go!"

We make the bluffs just in time to see the Yankee ship *Queen* run full steam out of the Yazoo River as smoke billows from the *Carondelet* and the *Tyler*.

Sarge strains to look upriver. "Glory be, would you look at that?"

A ragged and damaged little boat storms out of the mouth of the Yazoo River like a hound on a rabbit's scent. The long, narrow boat with one smokestack charges the Yankee fleet straight out.

Sarge yells, "Give 'em hell, Cap'n Brown."

We raise a cheer the Yanks surely hear across the river. The gunboat hesitates. Captain Brown faces a gauntlet of masts and smokestacks, rams and ironclads on the left and gunboats, ordinary steamers, and bomb vessels on the right.

Granville yells, "He ain't scared. He's just pickin' out which one he's gonna sink first!"

Brown rams and sinks the first boat he comes to. He fires his thirty guns so quickly we think it's our light artillery.

I yell, "What's that boat's name?"

The lieutenant with a spyglass smiles. "The *Arkansas!*" All of Vicksburg cheers Captain Brown on. The *Arkansas* ducks and dodges, slips in and out of the fifty or more gunboats.

J.A. points. "Look, he's so quick they're shootin' at each other!"

The *Arkansas* passes every Yankee boat in the fleet, but their shots just bounce off.

Our captain yells, "About time you got some of your own medicine!" We yell and cheer, curse and pray for the lone brave Confederate gunboat.

Men from Little Rock shake their fists. "That's what you get when you mess with Arkansas!"

A man from Greenwood yells, "Yeah, and don't forget she was built right here in Missip."

The *Arkansas* looks like it was built from a trash heap, but she gives more than she gets.

"Here she comes!" Battered, Union gunboats chase the *Arkansas* to the riverbank but are backed off by a few bursts from our bluff batteries. We cheer her to high heaven as she docks in front of the city. Men rush from everywhere to repair and refuel her.

Colonel Marks yells, "Let's go!" We race down the hill. "Bet Ole Farragut is pukin' his guts up now. She whipped the pride of the Mississippi River Yankee Navy."

We roar, "Hurrah for the good ship *Arkansas,* hero of the Confederate Navy."

J.A. points. "Oh shit, the Yanks must've heard us. Here they come again." The *Arkansas* is ready. We take cover behind the riverbank batteries.

An old timer screams, "Look. They firin' all they got, and she's still givin' 'em hell. Whoo-hah! *Iroquois, Hartford, Richmond, Brooklyn, Wissahickon, Sumter, Sciota, Winona, Pinola,* just look at 'em all."

I shake my head. "How can you see the names on them boats, old man?"

"Old man? You tater-headed, titty suckin', cedar saplin'. Hell, I can spot a 'coon in the dark up the tallest tree and tell you the length of his rooster. I've got a good eye, son."

I like this old man. He reminds me of Mr. Wiley.

Each Union gunboat takes its turn, but the *Arkansas* absorbs the blasts and keeps firing.

Finally, the Yanks retreat.

"What's your name, suh, if you don't mind me askin'?"

The old man wheels around on one foot. "My name's Goddard. I fought with Ole Winfield Scott in the Seminole War right after the Dade massacre. Chief Oseola killed all but three of us when they ambushed a hundred Americans after we left Fort Brooke. Good friend of mine hid in a pond 'til they left. I'm the only one left to tell it. Other two died of their wounds." He tears up. "Forgive us all, Lord." Mr. Goddard grabs my collar. "Stay alive, son! That's all that matters."

While cooks prepare supper, I write Susannah. I'm shaky, and I have trouble thinking.

Camp Norwood, Vicksburg Mississippi July 15, 1862

Dearest Susannah, things are gettin worse, but I guess it's to be expected. We get bombarded every day. But we watched a little boat called the Arkansas take on Farragut's navy. The Yanks finally left with a lot of men dead. I've made good friends since I left Winn Parish. Some are sick and some dead. I wrote two letters but received none from you. Yanks across the river make the mail slow gettin here. We buy most of what we eat now. Can you believe watermelons cost a dollar? They say we might be eatin mule beef soon. Some say they won't. They will when they get hungry. Paper is 2 dollars a pound. I hope you don't mind one page letters so it will last. I know I asked you already, but please send shirts, pants, some drawers, and socks. I have no money to buy any. Just send what you can. When you need money, ask Mr. Gilmore. Pray the war won't last long. I planned to come home, but all leaves were cancelled. I want to hold you in my arms. I'm sorry to be such a burden. Stay strong my dear.

Your loving husband,
Lummy

THE MORNING SUN casts a long shadow across the river. I trot down the bluff trail for picket duty just as the ram *Queen of the West* and the ironclad *Essex* race across the river to attempt to destroy the *Arkansas.* I dive into the gun emplacements with my rifle as all hell breaks loose. The *Arkansas* surges forward to avoid being rammed. The *Essex* pulls alongside, and Yank sailors steal across the decks to capture the *Arkansas.* I curse and shout putting a cap on my musket.

I join the sharpshooters to fend off Yank sailors while the Kentucky boys fire their twenty-four pounders into the *Essex*. The fight lasts only forty minutes. The *Arkansas* sits defiant and safe under the batteries. My first real fight and I did more ducking than firing. Thank God I didn't kill anybody.

I hope.

Old Mr. Goddard steps out from behind some barrels. "How do you feel about it, son?"

"Feel about what?"

"Killin' your first man."

"I didn't kill...."

"Son, you're a shooter. When the other boys was loadin', you shot a sailor off the top deck like a squirrel out of a tree."

A heavy blanket of despair weighs heavy on my soul. "Surely, I didn't." Then I see him fall in my mind. I *did* kill him. I see his eyes.

"It's all right, son, you done your duty."

I nod as he walks away. I want to throw down my musket. "Ain't nobody's duty to kill men made in Creator's image."

FARRAGUT RETREATS AGAIN July 27th, and the rest follow the next day. The *Arkansas* is refitted, and we watch her steam south towards Baton Rouge. It was our first taste of battle, and General Van Dorn praises not only the *Arkansas* and all his brave Mississippi troops, but also the valiant men of Kentucky, Tennessee, Alabama, Louisiana, and Missouri. We're becoming a real army and proud of it. But I'm not proud of killing. I just keep my mind somewhere else and throw myself into building earthworks. The hard work is good for my heart, but my soul aches for sending that sailor to God. What else could I have done?

J.A. drives his shovel deep. "What else could you have done? You ain't gettin' out of this war unless you kill the man tryin' to kill you." He's right, but I don't have to like it.

Tonight, I lay in my tent recounting how the *Arkansas* did so much damage to so many gunboats. The crackling fire reminds me of all those muskets firing at the *Essex*. I stare into the darkness. The eyes of the Yank sailor I killed stare back. It happened all so fast, did it really happen? I saw the man fall into the brown swirling water with hardly a splash. He had the strangest blank stare on his face—a look of peace. Then I saw him no more.

My heart aches for some mother's son, some wife's husband, some child's father. I did it and without a thought until I came back to my senses. I killed a living man with a soul. "How can I live with that? How can one man do so much damage to another human being?"

I can't sleep, so I walk to river's edge.

Isham throws pebbles into the water. "I know you take no joy in killin' that man today. But we gotta do what needs doin' 'cause the Yankees ain't done with us yet." He points to a lump floating by. The body of a dead Yank bobs like a fishing cork still clinging to a log. He's too far to reach, so we let him float on by.

I shudder at the sight. "That could've been me."

Isham smiles. "Naw it couldn't. The Lord ain't done with you yet, Lummy."

CHAPTER 12

AN UNEXPECTED VISIT

AUGUST 10, 1862

"It ain't only knowin' why I fight. It's also knowin' why I want to live."

ISHAM THROWS DOWN his shovel. "Why don't the Yanks just come on and get it over with?"

J.A. pulls the weed he's been chewing out of his mouth. "They'll come soon enough."

I lean on my shovel. "The Yanks don't need no invitation. Get your mind on somethin' else."

Isham picks up his shovel. "Diggin', drillin', guardin'! Reveille at 4:00 a.m. Two-hour drill at 4:15. Breakfast at 7:00. Another two-hour company drill at 8:00. Dinner call at 1:00 p.m. Dress parade at 6:00. Dang officers got more drills than the army manual. And it's borin' as hell work in the earthworks! I'm sick of it! I wish they'd come on just to have somethin' different to do."

I thrust my shovel into the dirt. "This won't be the barn dance you think—for them or us."

J.A. swings a pick. "You'll wish you was buildin' these earthworks then."

Isham climbs out of the rifle pit we're digging. "I'm gettin' some water."

J.A. stretches his back. "It ain't easy waitin' for what you dread."

I wipe sweat from my forehead. "Especially when you're scared."

Sarge waves me over. "And bring that young 'un you got there."

I lean my shovel against the log wall. "Come on, Granville, Sarge wants us."

Sarge walks to a wagon. "Y'all take this into town with the others and pick up rations for the regiment. Think y'all can do that?"

We salute without a word.

We arrive to find more food than I've ever seen in one place. Loading the wagon reminds me of working at Davis's Feed and Seed. I'd rather be there.

Men cheer as the wagons filled with rations roll into camp. Good food and lots of it revives the faint of heart. Many things we've had to pay for now become nearly free. Harvest is in, and we get all the squashes and cabbages we can eat for a dime. Watermelons, musk melons, peaches, and vegetables are as cheap as ever. Our company fares well when we put our silver together to roast a nice fat pig. We have vegetables with cornpone for dinner. We eat 'til we nearly burst and have plenty left for supper. Heck, they even gave us buttermilk and peach pie for dessert.

Despite all the good food, only 174 men of the twelve hundred 27th Louisiana are fit to fight. We've all had some sort of ailment. Thirty Winn Rebels have died, and only twenty are ready if the Yanks came now. I'm one of the fortunate healthy few.

It's hot enough to make a man puke. Isham holds his stomach. "Everythin' I eat runs through me like lightnin'. Feels like it, too."

Sarge sips a taste from the dipper bucket. He spews it out. "Damn river water smells like an outhouse, and the spring water 'round here ain't much better. Hell, we've had to post guards to keep men from muddying up the springs."

I hold a dipperful to my lips. I pour it out. "This ain't fit to drink. Spring water gets hot so fast we can't drink it before it goes bad."

Isham rocks back and forth clutching his gut. "I just want to go home."

Sarge pulls him up by the shirt sleeve. "Let's go see the Doc. Nobody's gettin' leave time from nothin' around here, especially when the Yanks come."

LATE AUGUST, GENERAL Van Dorn orders every citizen, soldier, and Negro to have a pass just to go in and out of Vicksburg. Sarge assigns me to a check point. Lines are long, and tempers flare. That only happens if I'm paired with a man who can't read. By month's end, I've done it so much, I mostly just say, "Next," to keep the line moving. But I do look at every face.

The man I'm working with complains, "Dang, the line just gets longer and longer everyday."

"Yeah, my feet are sore."

I hand a pass back to an older man when I notice a tall, graying black man with his hat pulled down keeps peeking around the people in front of him. He acts suspiciously.

I tip his hat up. "Friend, look up, I need to see your face."

Old Bart raises his head with the biggest half toothless grin I've ever seen and bear hugs me.

And behind him is Mr. Gilmore, dressed like a farmhand.

I can hardly believe my eyes. "What... *how?*"

Sarge yells. "Is there a problem here, soldier?"

I salute. "No suh, Sergeant. This here's Mistuh Gilmore, my father-in-law and boss, and my good friend Old Bart from back home. We plowed many a row together, didn't we, Bart?"

"And caught many a catfish, too, Massuh Lummy."

Mr. Gilmore offers his hand. "It's a pleasure, Sergeant. It appears you have trained Lummy very well to do his duty as a good soldier. Thank you for being such a fine leader to prepare him for receiving the Yankee invader, suh." The silver-tongued old man knows exactly how to win over the toughest of men.

"No need to try'n sweet talk this old boar coon out the tree, Mistuh Gilmore. Lummy, take the rest of the day and visit with your friends. Be ready for duty first thing in the mornin'."

"Thank you, Sarge." I salute. I'm so happy I want to run off in all directions at once.

"Go on now, 'fore I change my mind."

We get to camp, and I hand them each a cup of coffee. "It's all we got, but it ain't bad."

Old Bart takes a sip and licks his lips. "What's it made out of?"

"The finest sweet taters you'll ever dig."

Mr. Gilmore blows on his. "Hot. The hint of sassafras is an added touch."

"I found it over in the woods this mornin'." We stare at each other for a moment. "I can't believe you're here. How'd you get through the Yanks?"

Mr. Gilmore takes a long sip from his cup. "We boated down the Black and Tensas Rivers. From there we walked fifteen miles to Waterproof and caught a steamer here.

Old Bart's eyes light up. "Lummy, a Yankee boat came runnin' fast. We just knew we was caught, but our captain hid us behind a sandbar. Never was so scared in all my live long days."

I can resist no longer. "So, what's in the packs?"

Mr. Gilmore smiles. "I figure folks back home can help you boys out just a little." He pushes the bundles over.

"Feels like Christmas. We can use just anythin' you brought." I find badly needed clothes, especially long handles, a heavy jacket, and thick socks for the winter. There are two pint jars of muscadine jelly, a small bundle of paper for letters and envelopes with postage, a pound of real coffee, a sack of lemon drops, deer jerky, and a quart jar of pickled eggs.

I can hardly speak. "I don't know what to say. Y'all risked your lives to make mine better."

Then I pull out a rubberized raincoat and hold it up. "There weren't none of these left by the time I volunteered."

Mr. Gilmore whispers, "Susannah took in lots of sewin' to buy you this bit of comfort."

I hold back tears. "It'll take the hell out of standin' guard on cold damp nights come winter."

Mr. Gilmore sighs. "I know it's tough here, son, but things are getting worse back home. A ruffian named Dawg Smith ran off the sheriff and proclaimed himself Captain of the Home Guard. They're just a band of damn devilish miscreant outlaws. Don't worry about Susannah. She's staying with your brother Ben. He'll guard her like blood kin."

"Does he know?"

Mr. Gilmore shifts on his crate. "He does. Ben was going to find out sooner or later. Dorcas already knew. Women always know things."

I rub my chin. "How'd he take it?"

"Not well at first. He got over it soon enough with Dorcas's help."

Old Bart lays his hand on my shoulder. "Lummy, it's all right. Massuh

Ben told me later, 'Lummy don't do things like other people in this damned ole world. I guess he can do what he wants.'" That's good news.

"So, how's my sweet darlin', Susannah? I do miss her so."

"Here's the best thing we brought." Old Bart shivers like a kid picking out his favorite candy.

He hands me a small leather pouch. I undo the drawstring. I carefully pull a small, silver-hinged frame from the pouch and open it to find a picture of Susannah in a beautiful dress.

My heart melts. "Thank you both. This means so much to me." I stare at my wife for a few moments. The beautifully engraved inscription opposite her picture reads,

Always.
Your loving wife Susannah Tullos
Christmas Day, 1861

"Where'd you...."

Mr. Gilmore cuts in. "A friend who makes tintypes passed through after you left. He stayed at the house for a few nights. He photographed us for the kindness. I had that one made for you. The frame is his gift for your service in the army. Susannah said you'd like the inscription."

"This is my most treasured possession—a portrait of my wife no longer the property of any man. It's only because of men like you. I love you dearly, my brothers."

Mr. Gilmore reaches into his coat pocket. "Almost forgot, you'll want these, too." He hands me a stack of letters from Susannah, Dorcas, and one from the kids.

I dry my eyes on my shirt sleeve. "This is better'n gettin' back pay."

Mr. Gilmore and Old Bart stay two more days to walk around Vicksburg. Mr. Gilmore visits old friends and business associates. Old Bart plays the part of a slave for the sake of the circumstances. I look forward to the day he'll be free of that.

"You play the part so well, Bart. You should take up actin' after the war."

"Lummy, one day I just want to be myself, the Bart who lives deep inside. He just wants to be free, and he's got a plan when that time comes. For now, I just wants to help Mistuh Gilmore."

Every break I get, they're waiting for me in camp. I catch up on home news and tell them about my adventures since leaving Winnfield. I introduce them to my friends, and some ask to have letters, small items, and money carried back to their families in Winn Parish.

They leave early morning September 2nd. It's hard to watch. I send letters to Susannah, Ben and family, and one to Mr. and Mrs. Davis. I try to put money in one of the envelopes, but Mr. Gilmore won't have it. Instead, he slips me twenty dollars.

"Ben sent it to you along with a piece of his heart, he said to tell you."

I nearly burst out in tears again. Their visit renews my hope for the future. I have a life waiting for me back in Winn Parish, and I want to live it.

Later at supper, I tell J.A., "It's not just knowin' why I fight, but why I want to live, too."

J.A. puts his arm around my shoulder. "What you thinkin', Lummy?"

"If I had a choice, I'd be on that boat with them." There's something they're not telling me about Susannah.

CHAPTER 13

WAITING FOR
WHAT WE DON'T WANT

MID-SEPTEMBER 1862

*The prophet wrote, "It is good that a man should both hope
and quietly wait for the salvation of the Lord."*

IT RAINS SO hard and for so long, the catfish are using flatboats. Hills
and roads are slicker than a greased wagon wheel. Isham was returning
from picket duty last night with a few others and got too close to the
edge of a gully. It caved, and they slid forty feet to the bottom. We pulled
them out with ropes this morning.

Sarge stops by the cookfire before we head to the earthworks. "Cool weather's comin'. Most of the sickness will leave when the first big frost comes."

J.A. laughs. "Can you order the mosquitoes and redbugs downriver with
the Yankees?"

Sarge points at his arms. "Stop scratchin', or they'll get infected."

All kinds of thoughts race through my mind waiting for the inevitable.
Some boys drink whiskey, some run with whores, and some gamble pay
they haven't received. Few seek the stillness of the Lord within. Nothing on
the outside a body can bring peace like the Creator inside. Granny Thankful
said, "Let those Holy Ghost dove wings flutter in your soul and your mind'll
stay straight, your heart'll be full of joy, and your body'll walk in obedience."

Reading the little Bible Mary gave me before I left and hearing church
music comforts my soul. As the organ plays, I clear my mind to all but the
music. Sounds fade and so do I into a peace that soothes my nerves, relaxes
my body, and strengthens my soul. Still, I find God's presence best sitting on
a log in a quiet place under some willows down by the river.

The twenty dollars from Ben came at a good time. Prices are up, and rations never keep a man fed very well. Two dollar watermelons, four bits for a dozen peaches small as a man's thumb, two bits for a dozen apples, eight dollars for smoking tobacco, four bits for a peach pie, and forty cents a dozen of the sweet cakes I like—who can afford such? I squeeze every bit I can out of Ben's gift.

MID-SEPTEMBER, COOL rains settle the dust clouds rising from all the comings and goings. It's good to sit by the fire after a long day in the earthworks.

Sarge gathers the company after evening roll call. "We're gettin' paid! And backpay, too." We cheer. "A word to the wise. Don't gamble it away or waste it on whores." Some will come begging a nickel in less than a week when they lose it all.

We relax by the fire, drinking coffee. J.A. pulls a newspaper he's reading closer. "Says here, President Davis is proclaimin' September 18th a day of fasting and prayer. It's in thankful praise to God for our recent victories."

I can't help myself. "Huh, that's somethin'. Offerin' thanks for killin' other human bein's."

J.A. shrugs. "I guess it's all right. They did it in the Bible."

I wonder how long the Lord will put up with our wickedness.

Sarge lets us attend special preaching. We trail into town to hear a fiery preacher rail on about how God Almighty of the angel armies will smite the wicked wearing blue.

I lean over to J.A. "Enough of this talk about who's got God on their side. Only thing will get us through this—how the inside man fares with God."

"Whatever do you mean, Lummy? You go to church, hear the preacher, pay your tithe, pray, and do your best to stay away from cussin', too much moonshine, and whores, right?"

I don't intend to, but I whisper a short sermon. "Yeah, but that's all them long-winded blowhards say nothin's know to preach. 'Be at church and be a good boy.' Teach me to talk with God like you and me talk, not that He's out to get me everytime I fail. Jesus came to show us how to walk in the cool of the day with Creator like Adam. If we learned that, hell, we wouldn't even be here." I cover my mouth for cursing at church service.

J.A. rubs his chin. "Yeah, I'd rather be home with my pretty wife than here."

"There ain't one good man amongst us. If so, it ain't you or me. It ain't about how good I am. It's about how good Creator is. God knows us the best and loves us the most, good and bad. So if I know Him like I know you, I'd treat Him better. I'd treat the man next to me better, too."

"Makes my head spin like a top, but it sounds right."

"Think about it. Creator didn't make us to be hard on us. I know a man can't just do what is right 'in his own eyes' like the Book of Judges says. God just wants us to be friends again. I don't need some Bible quotin', looney loud mouth, two dollar Bible thumper who can't find God even if he was in a jar like a lightnin' bug tellin' me how I'm supposed to know my Creator."

I'm drawing a crowd. It's time I shut up.

I wave my hand. "No preacher here, boys, just a man seekin' his God where he was told to, right here." I point at my heart. "You boys'll do well to follow suit. See you Sunday. I'm sure Reverend Tucker will have another good'n for us."

Sunday I listen to Reverend Tucker, who tells us that, like the Israelites who looked on the bronze snake were cured of snake bite, we should look to Jesus to be saved.

He forgets to tell us it won't stop a well-aimed bullet. The world works. Stick your head up, and a minie ball will find it.

I've had enough and slip out to visit Sky Parlor Hill to talk with Creator. "It's hard to wait on you sometimes, Lord. The Yankees are comin', and my heart is gettin' hard. Don't let anger take my soul." I pull the small silver frame with Susannah's picture inside. She's waiting for me back home. I can't lose my heart, or my soul, with what's coming.

Granville comes trotting up the hill. "Have you heard, Lummy?"

"What?'

"Nobody can go home, at all."

"They already said that."

"Yeah, but I was hoping I could be home for my birthday next month. Sarge said we're spending the winter here."

"How old you gonna be?"

He puffs out his chest. "I'll be seventeen." Like my younger brother, James, just a bright-eyed gullible child. Granville should've stayed home.

"Written your mother lately?"

"Yeah, she's making a personal appeal to General Smith to get me home. I miss my mother and sister. If I'd listened to them, I wouldn't be here."

"That's just you bein' heart sick talkin'."

"Don't think so. I'm better. My mother worries about me all the time. She's heart broken."

It hurts my heart to watch him suffer.

GRANVILLE'S MOTHER SENDS a notarized paper advising General Smith of his age and that he enlisted without her permission. She requests a discharge. They deny it and never give a reason. Jeremiah's words ring true. *"It is good for a man that he bear the yoke in his youth."* It don't make it easier to bear, though. The yoke is getting heavier in the waiting—and not just on young Granville, neither. Some think the war will be over by Christmas. Others say we'll be sent up to Corinth.

Rumors—worthless as our Confederate money.

Sarge tries to comfort us. "Hell, Yanks ain't gonna attack in winter. Everybody shuts down when the cold sets in." That's comfort for neither the soul nor body.

OFFICERS COME AND go, but we still do the work. October 14th, General John Pemberton, a Pennsylvania man turned southern to please his wife they say, takes command of the Vicksburg defenses. What can I say? I became a Louisiana man to please mine. It's worth it.

Pemberton makes General Earl Van Dorn his cavalry commander and orders Stephen Dill Lee to command the 27th along with the 17th, 28th, and 31st Louisiana regiments. Lee has battle experience. Maybe he can keep us alive when the fighting comes. I'll sleep a bit better tonight.

The 27th is assigned Patrol of Police guard in town. Isham's name is called, and the first night back he says seventy-five of the men are French Creole and can't speak a lick of English.

"They call out orders in two languages every morning. But let me tell you, we tried cooking our own food, even hired a cook. It was all just terrible, until we smelled the delights drifting from where the Creoles are posted. It's good 'nuff to make you stand up and slap your granny. We pitched our rations in their pot after that."

Our turn comes around for town duty. J.A. yells, "What in the hell is all that racket?"

"The hawgs are comin' to town!"

Isham picks up a rock. "Watch this."

I tell him, "Don't do it, son."

Isham hits a big sow with a couple piglets in tow. She snorts and lights out after Isham. I beat the others to a tree and go up it like a bear.

Isham squeals louder than the hogs. "Hurry, let me up that tree!"

"Can't go no faster."

The momma hawg bites Isham's leg. "Yeow!"

"It's your own damn fault! Run!"

Men run like lightning in all directions, hogs snapping at their legs and backsides. A farmer doubles over laughing. "If you run from these hawgs, what the hell you gonna do when the damn Yanks come?" He howls like a redbone hound dog treeing a coon.

We get back to camp after duty, and the Doc takes care of Isham's wounds.

Johnny Bond of C Company passes by, taking papers to headquarters. I lean on my shovel. "Well, looky what the cat drug up and the buzzards won't eat. Johnny, how the heck are you? Your momma finally get you well?"

"Yeah, I've been back a couple weeks. Hate I missed the train from Camp Moore. It's been hell gettin' here. Damn Yanks are everywhere. Took a riverboat to a point opposite Waterproof and walked the rest. Damn Yankee gunboats were patrollin' everywhere. Wasn't sure I'd make it. I never got the chance to thank you and J.A for gettin' my daddy's watch back from the Flower Boys. I appreciate it." He shuffles on like an old man.

J.A. yells after him, "Whoa, hold up. What's got your tail draggin'?"

He tears up. "We buried Isaak Jennings this morning."

"That's a damn shame."

"Doc says he died of neuralgia or some blamed fool thing like that."

I chime in. "Men die, you know that."

Johnny rubs the back of his neck. "Yeah, but I knew him before we enlisted. He was a good man, but he became as wicked a man as I ever did meet."

"What do you mean?"

"He was as fine a Christian as you ever did meet, loved his wife and kids, worked hard. He got here and turned to gamblin', drinkin', and whorin' around. He never would've done all that if them shells hadn't busted up his nerves."

J.A. shakes his head. "Damn shellin' broke many a good man down."

Johnny kicks the dirt. "Lummy, you're a prayin' man. What do you say about a good man losin' his soul fightin' for his country when if he just stayed home, he'd been all right?" He coughs and sniffs. "Worst part was, not forty feet away men were gamblin' and cussin' durin' the service. I'm tired of tryin' to figure it all out."

I don't know what to say to ease his soul. "Johnny, ain't none of us good. Isaak might've done more wicked stuff, but only the mercy of the Lord'll get us through this. Sometimes the wickedest man has the deepest wounds. The Lord don't judge a man for the few wrong things he's done. Preachers make God out to be an angry Pa waiting to whip your ass for every mistake. That ain't in the Book. Just be glad we don't make them judgments."

Johnny shakes his head. "Reckon it ain't my place and nobody else's to judge. Thanks. Don't forget me in your prayers tonight."

I realize now I don't have to be a preacher in a black suit with a white collar standing at a pulpit in a church house on Sunday to help people know God.

CHAPTER 14

DON'T RUN OR
THEY'LL SHOOT YOU

NOVEMBER 2, 1862

*Only way to get discharged from this army is be dead
and buried five days. Then your papers come through.*

T HE COOLNESS OF the fall air lifts the spirits of men drained from
incessant heat and slow recoveries from sickness. It's nice to watch
the leaves change across the river from green to yellow and orange
to red. The gumball trees are the prettiest. When they fall, it'll be easier to
spy on the Yanks camped on the DeSoto peninsula. Morning frost covers the
ground like snow but is gone within minutes of the sun shining.

Granville turns seventeen today, November 2nd. We pitch in to get him
a cake and a new hat. The cake lady brings her daughter along, and Granville
thoroughly enjoys his birthday dance with her. And of course, Granville falls
head over heels in love with a girl he's just met and has danced with once.
When the party breaks up, Granville pulls me to the side.

"I got my papers back, and they weren't signed."

"You expected them to be?"

"I don't get letters from my Ma no more. I'm cold and sick. I just don't
know how long I can do this."

I don't know what to say.

"I'm gonna get killed, I just know it. I'm scared as a cat dropped in a dawg
pen. I'm thinkin' about runnin' away." He scratches the back of his neck.
"Come with me, Lummy? I'll wait 'til Christmas if you come with me."

I shake my head.

Granville sits on the ground completely defeated. "Word is a man can't get a discharge 'til he's dead and buried five days. Then his papers come through." He sits, head down, shoulders slumped, breathing heavily. I lay my hand on his shoulder. He shrugs it off.

Isham, carving a set of dominoes from scraps of wood, mumbles, "They'll shoot you for desertin' if you run." I put my finger to my mouth, and Isham keeps whittling.

Granville knows he can't run. Yank cavalry swarm these parts and would love to put a Reb away before the real fighting starts. If he escapes, the home guard will catch him and send him back to the army or shoot him straight out for being a coward.

I grab him by the shoulders. "You gotta stay strong, son. Don't give up. Find somethin' to do to keep your mind off the bad things. You got some artistical talent, don't you?" He nods with a weak grin. "Then carve me one of them chess sets out of minie balls. A few won't be missed."

"I can do that. It'll be your Christmas present."

Sarge marches up. "Party's over. Get packed. General Pemberton has ordered us to build winter cabins. Pick eight men whose stank you don't mind bunking with."

I'm fortunate to be with J.A., Isham, a few others, and a young fella we all like, Edrow.

J.A. throws his pack and musket in a wagon. "I'm glad to leave these leaky tents. They got more holes than bumblebees burrowing in a rotting barn."

There's a good feeling around camp until we realize the wood they give us isn't any good. There are so few tools, some men have only one axe between them. In a few days, we have crude cabins built that will at least keep us out of the wind and maybe the rain. I stop to write Susannah.

Winter Quarters Vicksburg, Mississippi,
November 9, 1862

    Dearest Susannah, sorry I failed to write for some time. We don't get much free time, and post is hard to come by. I pray your health is good. We built cabins for winter that will keep us warm and dry. I thank the Lord Mr. Gilmore and Old Bart brought clothes and the rain slicker you sent.

All the boys envy me. It keeps me safe from the pneumonia goin around. A
Lootentant from C Company died of it yesterday. I fear hardness of heart
is the worst sickness we have here. Pray that this war don't make us like
beasts in the field. Pray I don't change from who I was before I left your
sweet arms. I know that when I see your face again all this will disappear.
I miss you darlin. Your picture keeps my heart beatin. Please write. I have
received no letter from you in three months. I must go now.

Your affectionate husband,
Lummy Tullos

I don't send Susannah any hard news. I do complain about our cabin
to my friends though. We all complain... too much, and it gets back to the
officers. Colonel McLaurin finally gets so fed up with the whole regiment's
mouthing off that on November 16th he assigns the 27th Louisiana all the
worst duties as punishment. We dig latrines, muck mud out of the earthworks, and cut down heavy timber in front of the breastworks as obstacles
when the Yanks attack.

Even so, with steep gullies and high ridges, the forest cut back half a
mile, and treetops and rotten logs scattered about, we are well barricaded
against the Yank attack. That's some comfort. A better comfort comes when
Sarge says we might get paid soon. The Confederate government is only five
months behind. It'll be a great payday if we get it all at once.

Finally, we're allowed to move into our winter cabins November 24th.
We gather anything available for bedding and wall covering to keep the wind
out. Our first night is wickedly cold. When Edrow sneaks in from visiting
the latrine, he takes too long getting in the one room shanty.

Isahm yells, "Shut that damn pneumonia hole. Heat's gettin' out and rats
gettin' in."

Edrow pulls the door tighter and pushes the half-rotted blanket against
the bottom. The room finally warms up again, and we sleep.

CHAPTER 15

IT COULDN'T BE? COULD IT?

EARLY MORNING, NOVEMBER 30, 1862

Passing like ships in the night, unless both finally tie up at the same river port.

I CATCH THE midnight picket out by the rail station—worst duty a man can be assigned in this army. To make the midnight to six shift I get ready at ten and leave camp at eleven. A man gets no sleep if he pulls midnight picket.

Sarge whispers, "Somethin's comin'. Can't say what, but pack your stuff for a trip. Just be alert. The officers'll be watchin' you." I stick a couple biscuits and salt pork in my shirt for tonight—my rations I'll cook by the tracks.

It's a frosty night and looks to rain. I make a tent covering from a cotton bale tarp. That and my rain slicker keep me warm and dry, even standing in the rain. I walk my line, back and forth ten times, and then stop under my tarp to watch for fifteen minutes. I stir my little pot of acorn coffee and taste if it's ready. My rations cool, and I store them in my haversack.

A lieutenant stops to compliment my ingenuity for avoiding pneumonia. "Colder'n a meat cutter's ass in the icehouse, huh, Private?"

I salute. "Yassuh."

It rains hard, then sleet falls, but I stay dry. I walk down to one of the big fires to warm my hands but really to catch any news from the men gathered there. My hands suffer most. We have no gloves. None are issued. The rags I wrap around them help some.

By 2:00 a.m., I'm having a waking dream about Susannah when a train comes barreling down the tracks at full speed. It jolts me awake, and I jump back thinking it might be a runaway. But it slides right into the station, pretty as you please, stopping on a half dime. Another engine is steaming up preparing to leave. Men scatter like chickens at feeding time. Everyone seems to know his job and why. This must be what Sarge couldn't say anything about.

Soldiers bail out of boxcars like cattle as officers exit passenger cars like gentlemen. Light artillery is rolled down ramps as fast as men can unload them. Cannons are hooked behind wagons, horses and mules with chains, and also pulled behind eight men with leather straps on their shoulders. Company F marches my way fast.

Sarge barks, "Pick them feet up! C'mon, Lummy, you're goin', too. You do what I said?" I nod and fall in at the end of the line.

As I wait my turn to climb up in a boxcar, two artillery men with leather straps strain to pull a Napoleon with six other men. I squint. One has long shaggy hair that needs a cut and the other a long raggedy beard that needs trimming.

I wipe the rain out of my eyes. "Can't be. How could it?"

Sarge grabs me by the collar and yanks me on board. "Get your snail's ass up in here, Lummy Tullos, the train's movin'." I'm as dumbstruck as that Yankee Lee must've been when Vicksburg didn't surrender quick as he wanted.

Sarge yells above the train noise, "What's wrong with you, boy? You want to get your leg taken off by a train wheel?"

"I think I just saw my brothers. Ma wrote they were in the artillery."

Sarge pops me on the shoulder. "So sweet, Lummy boy, like ships passin' in the night. This ain't no love story unless you love to kill Yanks, 'cause we're headed to Grenada, boys! Possum's out the sack. Set your caps, top knot now, muskets when we get there, 'cause you'll need both when we meet the blue-bellies." The train picks up speed.

J.A. yells, "Who's that runnin' like a scalded dawg screamin' like a hysterical woman?"

A man wearing a jacket with a red collar and cuffs runs after our car waving his arms.

Gasping, he chokes out, "Help me up!"

I grab him by the collar like Sarge grabbed me and swing him up in one motion. Building earthworks produces some fine sinews.

He straightens his jacket. "Whew. Thanks, friend. Captain Turner'd nail my hide to the barn door if I didn't make this train." He shakes my hand. I let him catch his wind, but after a couple minutes I can't stand it.

Before I speak, Sarge butts in. "You best be goin' where you're supposed to, or I'll have you in chains."

"Nawsuh, I'm supposed to be on this train. Here's my papers."

Sarge looks them over. "Looks good. Go on, Lummy, ask your question before you bust."

"You with that artillery company just rolled in?"

"Yep, 1st Missip Light Artillery, Company C. I enlisted in Choctaw County then went to the School of Instruction at Jackson. I'm good with numbers, angles, and figurin's, so they put me to instructin' new men, how to place and sight in a gun. That's why I'm on this train, but I'll be back here quick as lightnin' when I'm done."

I'm almost too excited to ask. "Choctaw County, you say?"

"Yep."

"Know any Tullos men?"

His eyes light up like a kid handed a new toy at Christmas. "Sure do. Two brothers who joined the same day as me, Jasper and James. Fine artillery men. We jumped off this same boxcar a few minutes ago unloadin' those cannons you saw go by. You know 'em?"

Sarge pats me on my back and turns away.

"They're my brothers. I'm Lummy Tullos, in Company F, 27th Louisiana."

"Well, any brother of Jasper and James is a brother of mine. Glad to know you, suh. Now all we got to do is survive what's comin' and get back so you boys can have a big ole reunion. They're gonna be happy to see you."

I yell louder. "Do you know anythin' about Amariah Tullos?"

"Yeah, I knew Amariah." He shifts from one leg to the other, hesitating. "Good man."

"What do you mean, *knew?*"

"Amariah joined up before we did. He got sick, and they sent him to the hospital at Edward's Depot and then to Pensacola near where y'all are from. Don't know after that."

My mind drifts back home to the farm. Amariah would chase us around the yard, thumping our ears, rolling us around on the ground, laughing and playing. If my brother was sent home from the hospital, he probably didn't survive.

He offers his hand. "Put her here, brother. I'm Will Stern from Columbus. Don't worry, you'll see Jasper and Jimmy soon."

We never called him Jimmy, but okay. It's my first time seeing Jasper and James since leaving Choctaw County. It's the first time I hear of Amariah's condition. It's the same night I ride to Jackson in search of the enemy.

CHAPTER 16

A FALSE ALARM THAT GETS US THE BEST JOB IN TOWN

DECEMBER 1, 1862

War never makes sense until you're in it. Then it doesn't have to.

THE UP AND down motion of the train ride turns my stomach. I hope we'll stop before we go north to Grenada and get our guts back. I try to get my mind off my rolling stomach.

"J.A., we couldn't have gotten into our new winter quarters any sooner."

He laughs. "Yeah, that tent was holier than all the apostles, saints, and angels put together."

It's been cold and windy, but our little cabins keep us dry at night. Our captain suggested we dig into a bank and construct the walls, floor, and roof with three sides protected by dirt. With only the front exposed to the wind, our new home is warm. I'll be ready to hunker down in new issue wool blankets when we get back from fighting Grant at Grenada.

Adding to the misery of the pukey train ride, Sarge says we won't be paid. We're six months behind, and some boys threaten to desert. I try not to complain. I don't, except under my breath.

Sarge announces, "Grant just don't seem to run out of plans for takin' Vicksburg. He's like your Ma checkin' the henhouse for new chicks hatchin' or eggs for your breakfast every mornin'."

I hate to hear that. Not the part about the Yanks, but Ma's breakfast that sends a man out the door ready for a day's work. I lay it on thick for the men.

"Yeah boy, hot buttered bi-i-i-scuits with blackberry ja-a-am, sugah cured ha-a-a-m, red-eye gravy, fried eggs, hot coffee with fresh cream."

Isham yells, "Shut up, Lummy. That's enough to make a man run home!"

"Yeah, but the tellin' is almost as good as the eatin'. Almost."

A short, stocky man grumbles, "I ain't had a bite since yesterday. We didn't get to cook rations before we left."

Grumbling disappears when Colonel Marks comes by at our first water stop. "We're finally gonna get at them boys in blue. Anybody want to take a shot at ole General Grant?"

We yell, "Hell, yeah!"

Corporal Willy Miller boasts, "I'd like to shoot that big ole cigar right out of his big mouth."

Another man laughs. "Willy can pluck a fruit fly off a twitchin' bobcat tail at a hundred yards."

Big talk hopefully builds big courage. Those who are the most scared do the loudest talking.

Sarge pulls the boxcar door closed as we take off. "Just get him some fine moonshine. That'll keep 'em goin' in circles. Yank papers say he stays drunk all the time, anyway."

We pull into Jackson, cold and shivery but ready to go to Grenada. We jump off the train cars to walk around and warm up. A captain from G Company reports, "Don't know the details, but we got a change in plans."

Colonel Marks gathers us up. "Wouldn't you know it, false alarm. We got counter-ordered. Better to be sharp and ready than good and deady, huh?" We laugh half-heartedly.

Sarge barks, "No sense whinin' about it. You'll eat when we get there. No spare rations here. The supply train will sit tight in Vicksburg 'til we get back."

The weather worsens as do our spirits waiting in line to board. We're hungry and cold. Everyone's grouchy, so it's best to keep quiet. I share the food I brought. Others do the same.

Edrow chews on a piece of bread. "Heck, Lummy, you bein' the preachin' kind and all, do a miracle and feed the five thousand like Jesus did." I laugh, but I'm in no mood to joke.

We roll back into Vicksburg, cook our rations, and retire to our cabins to dry out. It's never as bad as we make it out to be once it's over. We're way too wet, cold, and tired to complain. Sarges gives us the morning off to rest.

Colonel Marks stops by our cookfire. "Who in the hell would know what a good soldier is if he ain't got at least one good gripe?" We all half laugh, mostly out of respect.

Marks squats beside our fire in the misty rain. "Boys, let you in on a little secret. With Grant pokin' around this close, the 27th Louisiana Regiment has been assigned police duty in town for the next few months." We lean closer.

Marks whispers, "You men will stay in the Prentiss House Hotel down by the river. Spread the word, but don't let it get outside our regiment. Just thought you boys could use a little cheerin' up."

We thank the colonel as he goes to the next gathering of men down the way.

Edrow rubs his hands together. "Ain't never stayed in no hotel and never been a policeman neither. What's it gonna be like?"

I wrap my rain slicker close. "Pretty borin' standin' guard all day. But at least we'll get to see the pretty girls, huh, Isham?"

"Damn straight, a damn sight better than what these eyes have had to look at lately."

It takes two days to finally get dried out. Some men get sick from the cold train ride and go to the hospital. Others get simple colds, but it adds to the misery. Sitting in my cozy little cabin nestled in a new woolen army blanket, I write Susannah a letter.

Winter Quarters, Vicksburg December 15, 1862

Dearest wife, things are so slow here now. We went on a train ride lookin for the Yanks but turned out to be a false alarm. We been ordered to move in town to guard military supplies and the town folk who fear the Yanks comin. They run and hide every time a gunboat sticks its nose out from behind a willow tree. I have had no letter from you in a long time. I pray for your good health and that no misfortune befalls you. There's not much to eat here now with the Yanks squeezin us like a snake. President

Davis and General Johnston will visit soon. Hope we make a good showin. Susannah, please write. This picture only comforts a soul so much. I send my love and devotion to you on wings of angels. I hope you get this letter. I love you.

Lummy

FOR BEING THE first regiment to arrive in Vicksburg and having done more than our fair share in the earthworks, we receive the honor to serve as provost guard for the city. We'll serve as military police with Colonel Marks as our Commandant of Post. Staying in town will certainly beat tree cutting, trench digging, and stockade building. We pack our meager belongings for the march into town.

Colonel Marks announces before we go, "Because of your faithful work, the earthworks just west of the Stockade Redan on the Graveyard Road will be named the 27th Louisiana Lunette."

I whisper to J.A., "Sounds good now, but it won't when the Yanks rain shells down on our heads, charge with bayonets, and shoot minie balls at us."

He elbows me. "Shut up, boy, if Colonel Marks hears you, Sarge'll give you extra duty."

"What's that, soldier?" Sarge yells.

I pipe up. "Oh nothin', Sarge, just sayin' how nobody best not say a dang word about that fine piece of earthworks."

Sarge nods his head with a jerk. "Damn straight. Now get your stuff."

J.A. bumps me with his shoulder and sticks his tongue out.

IT'S A COOL crisp day this morning, December 19th. We line up to march in good order on the Graveyard Road. You'd think we're headed to a firing squad with all the complaining. While some men are happy to go into town, many are disappointed about leaving their comfortable little cabins. They've become home to us.

Down in the mouth Johnny Bond marches by, squawking like a jaybird. "Why don't they move them regular troops who ain't got no cabins and let us stay here? Heck, we gonna lose all our quiet and hear nothin' but Cajuns jabberin' who can't talk English."

A wagon master sergeant cracks his whip on the back of a mule. "Shut up, boy, or I'll jerk a knot in your ass. Move on and shut your damn mouth."

"Yassuh."

Sarge barks, "Company F, at the quick step. Make a good impression on the citizens."

CHAPTER 17

FROM CABIN
TO HOTEL

DECEMBER 19, 1862

One man's cabin is another man's castle.

THE COMPLAINERS STOP once they see the beautiful buildings, brick streets, and pretty girls waving on every street corner. The sounds and smells of the city bring possibilities of new experiences. I pray that I do well in my new assignment to watch over the souls of this great city.

By one o'clock, we stand by the river in front of the Prentiss House Hotel on the corner of Crawford and Levee Streets. It's the largest hotel in Vicksburg—an imposing three story, thirty room establishment within a rock's throw of Hall's Ferry where I crossed the river back in '59. They put us on the third floor.

Sarge gives us an hour to get settled into our rooms and then calls for volunteers for first watch. I take it and march off with J. A. to our post up by the courthouse. We're positioned across the street by the wall of the Warren County jail. I rub my hand along the brick wondering who's on the other side wishing he'd done things differently.

Town folk compliment us on our professionalism and smart uniforms. Our four hour watch ends and we take our time getting back to the hotel, enjoying the sights as we go.

I've never stayed in a hotel before. It's much more than I expected, except they jam us fifteen to a room no bigger than our cotton house back home. Company F gets rooms that open to the balcony where we enjoy the river view. I try to see Annie Fanny over in DeSoto, and I do once. She's hard to miss, even that far across the water. I wave, but it's too far for her to see me.

The hardest part about staying in the Prentiss House is the smell of restaurant food but not getting to eat it. There's no money for that. We cook our meals on the street, such as they are. I carry my personal eating utensils with me each day to post. Some boys make fun because I clank when I march. That changes when theirs get stolen. Now, more of us clank.

Another advantage to being on the third floor is we enjoy the heat rising from the first two floors. There's no fuel for a fire in the little grate chimneys in our room. The only good thing about close quarters is the body heat it provides, until some of the boys with no manners let out farts smelling worse than a hog pen.

The humor does break the monotony, though.

Some of those boys sound like women tearing pieces of cloth for bandages. So I figure to have my turn. One night after a supper of beans and more beans with a slab of bacon nearly turned sour, I lay on my side and began passing gas that goes so long and gets so loud, I get a little concerned myself.

One of the boys across the room cries out in the darkness, "Da-a-ang, you are a *god*. I bow down and worship you. Who was that?"

I answer quickly, "Dang, that was a good'n, Edrow. Smells like a big ole hawg farted."

Everybody laughs and someone yells, "Way to go, Hog Fart!"

Edrow whispers, "Damn you, Lummy. Now you done it. I got blamed and a new nickname."

I roll over, feeling better. "Shut up and go to sleep, Hog Fart."

After a few nights of this, I'm ready to go back to our little cabin. Still, city life's not so bad. I'd rather be in Winn Parish under warm blankets with Susannah. That makes my heart ache.

Reports of Union troop buildup in Memphis, supply stockpiling in Holly Springs, and more gunboats on the river raise our concerns. Shelling remains a constant, though not much damage is done. We assure the good town folk we're ready to whip the bluecoats when they arrive. We know they're coming.

So does President Davis.

We get word that President Davis and General Joe Johnston will visit any day. Security has to be tight when they come. We don't want them getting assassinated on our watch. We steadily watch for suspicious looking characters. Who would've thought this backwoods boy from a nowhere county a hundred miles from here would see the great president of these Confederate States of America? As the coonass boys from down on the bayou say, "Not I, frog eye."

Their visit is short but boosts morale both soldier and town folk alike. I write Susannah about it while standing guard near the courthouse.

Vicksburg,

December 21, 1862

Dearest Susannah, love of my life forever.

I pray this note finds you well and in good spirits. I don't have much time to write. More will come later. We now stay in a hotel called the Prentiss House, and we guard the town. President Davis and General Joe Johnston came yesterday. We were all dressed and a sight to see. They cheered us on with the Yanks comin closer ever day. I went to preachin this mornin. The songs cheer my soul. We had a prisoner exchange this afternoon. Our boys came back to their companies happy like they was goin home. We expect a fight soon, but don't worry. I pray for you Susannah and wish for the day when we will be together again. Say hello to Mr. Gilmore and Old Bart. Give special love to Ben and Dorcas and the children.

Love in my heart for you til death,

Lummy

CHAPTER 18

ME, A POLICEMAN?

DECEMBER 22, 1862

The Lord uses the least likely to do his will, I suppose.

COLONEL MARKS ORDERS us to stay close to our posts. And though we're out in the weather most of the time, it's nice to have the pretty lace covered girls bring sweets or a blanket for the evening's chill. Occasionally, we get invited by a good family to enjoy a true home cooked meal. Ma would be proud of these ladies making us feel like sons and brothers.

More than one pretty girl winks passing by, and it grabs my attention. I'm as red blooded as any man, but my mind is always on Susannah. Though far away, she's close in my heart. J.A. feels the same about his wife and family. "Good company keeps good morals," Granny used to say.

J.A. complains, "I don't get it. So many of these boys got pretty wives waitin' on 'em back home. How can they talk about their wives like whores, or worse, women they had before they married? They got such a bad case of red rooster they can't talk about nothin' else. I don't want to be around them." I nod. "I guess that's why I cotton to you, Lummy. You try to stay right with the Lord, includin' your rooster."

"Makes me glad I ain't the only one bein' true to the most important things in life."

J.A. hangs his head. "When you been with more'n one woman, I guess it's like whiskey. The more you drink, the more you want. I'm glad I ain't been with no one but my sweet wife."

"Me, too. A man who can't control his rooster can't be trusted with important things in life."

I was a little afraid of girls growing up because they were so different. My sister, Rebecca, is so much older than me, and Saleta passed about the time I noticed girls were made different. But when I met Susannah, I instantly knew things. God taught me how to be with her. I am glad we waited, but there was many a time I wanted to roll her in the sack. I can't think on that very long.

Standing guard beats the boredom of the earthworks, though I do miss the hard work. We watch over army property, guard deserters, report shirkers and drunks, make sure everyone follows military laws, and keep a watchful eye for Yankee spies. Not much action but important work none the less. It's still strange being a policeman enforcing the law. Heck, as a young man I tried to break as many laws as I could, that is, the ones that didn't really hurt anybody.

I get a kick out of the little boys standing guard with us with their carved wooden pistols and stick rifles. They march so seriously in formation when we shift from street corner post to picket down by the river. I hope these young saplings never have to do this. Maybe it'll all be over soon. I really don't believe that.

It isn't all fun and games though. Standing on our feet for hours, guarding the train depot and supply warehouses, and watching the streets and civilian homes is taxing. We occasionally get a bit of excitement if men from other units start a drunken brawl. It happens more often than it should. I had to knock a couple in the head last week to get them to the Warren County jailhouse. Sheriff Platner back home would be proud.

With the Yanks closer, suspicious people lurk around town. Colonel Marks warns, "Watch deserters. They have valuable information about our defenses, whether they sell it or get caught and the Yanks beat it out of them. Either way, Grant'll have his information."

A few deserters get caught, but I'm glad to say I haven't had to shoot a gray coat yet. After shooting that sailor from the *Essex*, I find no satisfaction in killing a bluecoat, either. I'd hate to be part of a firing squad. But a spy is different.

Jed, from Company C, noticed a well-dressed man with a fancy top hat and nice overcoat acting strangely. "Somethin' ain't quite right about him." Most of us were just enamored with the man's fancy duds for which we'd have shot him. Not Jed. The man wandered around like he was conducting business, asking about our defenses, number of soldiers and cannons. He claimed to be a wealthy New Orleans merchant whose questions seemed legitimate in finding out what he could procure and deliver to the army. It didn't fool Jed. After we arrested him, one of the colonels knew him to be an actor who played in the theaters of New Orleans and a Yank sympathizer. I'm not sure what happened. We just didn't see him anymore.

Jed got promoted to corporal for that and crowed like a rooster, "Boys, I'm in the money now!"

J.A. laughs. "And when was the last time you got paid, Corporal, suh?"

Jed stopped crowing.

I never imagined being a law officer. Grandpa Temple told us Grandpa Cloud served as Constable of Chicacone in the Colony of Virginia back in the 1680s. I guess it's only fair I take my turn keeping the law. Some lawmen never seem quite square to me, like some county judges back home. Often their judgments were based on if they had a good breakfast, were in a bad mood, were offered a bribe, or if they had a good roll in the sack with their wife the night before. A bit too slimey for me.

Crooked is the word.

Late one night back in '58, I sneaked out to meet Susannah. I went through the back alleys of Bankston trying not to wake the town dogs. As I rounded the corner of the shoe factory, I heard glass break. Two sheriff's deputies were carrying armloads of stuff from a mercantile. They drove off in a wagon when a third deputy threw a drunk inside. The owner ran downstairs yelling just as the other two deputies who'd hid the wagon came to the rescue and caught the thief. That sealed my beliefs about most lawmen. The law isn't bad, just the crooks who claim to uphold it.

The next day, Pa came from town with the story of how "one of those damn vagrants who wander from town to town" broke into the big general store and got arrested for drunkenness and thievery. I couldn't tell him what

I'd seen. My secret about Susannah was greater than the need to tell him. But I felt bad for that man.

Pa leaned back in his chair after supper. "Serves him right. Three months in the Jackson prison doin' hard labor will straighten him out." The only salve for my conscience was that maybe the poor man would dry out, have food and a place to stay, and no whiskey.

I was ashamed of the law, my Pa's attitude, but mostly of myself for being a coward. Funny, nobody asked how the goods got out of the store when the man was caught in the act.

The reverend preached last Sunday about how the locust and honey eater told soldiers to be fair and just. John the Baptist must've seen city guards misuse their power to fill their pockets. Sheriff Platner was different, even when I had a run-in with his nephew, Lester.

Lester was a devil around town but an angel to his momma at home. In her eyes he could do no wrong. It's easy not to see what you really don't want to in this world. She'd defend him to the death, like he was Jesus on the cross.

When we were around ten, my friend, Poole, and I had picked up empty whiskey bottles Mr. Wesson at the Bankston general store would buy. He'd give us a penny for every five we brought in. We collected twenty-five each and went to get our nickels. A boy could buy a good sack of candy for a nickel back then. We stepped up on the store porch, bottles clanging. The door swung open knocking Poole down and breaking a couple of his bottles. It was Lester and his half-pint punkish, loud-mouthed weasel of a cousin, Kneehigh.

Lester growled, "Dirty rotten son of a bitch. Yeah, Tullos, I said it."

"Lester, don't cuss me no more."

"Why, bitchy boy? You gonna go cry to your niggah mammie? You like them black mammies, don't you, bitchy boy?"

My ears pinned back, the hair on the back of my neck stood up, my eyes became narrow slits, and my voice got deeper. "I said, don't cuss me no more." Poole held onto my arm.

Lester and Kneehigh ran across the road in front of a wagon, upsetting the horses. Lester turned and grabbed his crotch. "Come get this, bitchy boy." They started running.

Poole tugged on my arm. "Let it go, Lummy. It ain't nothin' but trouble."

"I've had enough." I picked up a rock about the size of an apple and let it fly. The stone hit Lester in the back knocking him to the ground.

He got up crying and spitting dirt. "I'll get you, Tullos, just wait and see, you bastard."

Poole howled, "Great shot! Didn't know you had it in you." Poole kicked the dust on the porch floor. "He's goin' straight to his witchy momma who'll find his uncle, the sheriff, quick as lightnin'. I'll wait for you at our fishin' spot on the Big Black. I hope you make it, but I bet that sheriff will be out to your place pretty quick." I went home, and Poole went to get his cane pole for the fishing trip we'd planned for the afternoon.

I'd just finished leftover peas and cornbread when a horse rode up. I thought about bolting out the back door like a rabbit but figured I didn't do anything bad enough to run. I'd have to face it sometime anyway.

Sheriff S.C. Platner knocked on the door. "Anybody home?"

Ma answered, "Just a minute, Sheriff," looking at me with a worried expression on her face. Thank goodness Pa was in the back pasture checking on a new calf.

Ma opened the door, and Sheriff Platner removed his hat politely. "Hello, Mary, I'm sorry to trouble you. Is Lummy around?"

Ma looked back at me and said, "Yes, come on in and have a seat. Would you like some coffee or maybe some buttermilk, S.C.?"

He wiped his forehead with a kerchief. "Cool water sounds good right about now, ma'am."

Sheriff Platner eyed me. "Lummy, you know why I'm here, boy. Tell me what happened."

I told the truth because there was no need to lie.

Sheriff Platner rubbed his chin. "His momma showed me the bruise on his back. It looks pretty bad, but not enough to take him to the Doc. She says Lester never would do anythin' like what you said he did. She wants to press charges."

My face got hot. "Lester is a damn bully, suh. Sorry, Ma. He takes the little kids' pennies for candy when nobody's lookin' and threatens to beat them if they tell. He's bullied me for years. He came out that store cussin' me for no cause, knockin' my friend, Poole, down, and breakin' some of our whiskey empties. His momma don't know the devil that boy is!"

Sheriff Platner held up his hands.

"Sorry, Sheriff, I asked him politely to stop cussin' me, but he did it again in front of the store. I told the boy again to stop. Ask the clerk or Poole. They saw it all. We just wanted to sell our bottles and get some sweets." I was so mad I was shaking.

"Take it easy. I know my nephew and his momma. She believes that demon is an angel. But I gotta do my job and won't make it too hard on you, son."

Ma asked tearfully, "What you gonna do, Sheriff?"

Sheriff Platner scratched his head. "Lummy, come to the jailhouse in Greensboro for a week, and we'll call it square."

Ma jumped in, "But S.C...."

"He can bunk at the jail. I'll make sure he eats good. Mary, he ain't bein' put in jail. It'll just look like it. I won't even write it in the record. How's that?"

"I understand. And I appreciate it."

"Lummy, Lester's gonna poke at you, but that's part of your punishment and trainin'. He's a rotten egg, that's plain to see. You got promise, son. You need to get a handle on that anger, boy, or it'll be the death of you one day. Maybe this'll help you."

"Yassuh."

He thanked Ma for the cool water. She thanked him for the kind judgment.

"See you Monday mawnin' early, Lummy."

"Yassuh."

After the Sheriff left, Ma let me fish with Poole. We caught enough for a good fish fry that night. The only thing Pa said as he finished his third bream was, "You can't let the weak-minded of the world rule and sometimes you gotta nip it in the bud." He grinned and winked.

Jasper and James laughed singing, *"Lummy is a jailbird. Lummy is a jailbird."*

I raised my hand to swat them.

Ma cleared her throat. "There you go, boy, lettin' somebody else get you all riled and watch you get the troubles for it."

Pa snickered. "Hard head, just like his ole Pa." Too much like my ole Pa.

I made it through the week without seeing Lester, but Sheriff Platner didn't let me out much either. I learned a few things about law. He answered all my questions.

"Lummy, you interested in the law? Maybe you can turn this into somethin' good."

After that, I knew I'd never be a lawman. Too many rules and too much trouble I don't need.

The meals at Elkins's tavern across the street were good, though. Mr. Elkins's Negro lady cook rivaled Ma's cooking. Sheriff Platner even paid for mine and Poole's when he came to visit.

Poole just had to see me in jail and laugh. "Yeah, Sheriff, it's about time this wicked outlaw got his just reward for everythin' he should've been caught doin'." He meant it as a joke.

Sheriff Platner saw it as an opportunity. Poole sat up slowly as he asked, "So, Poole, just what have you two miscreants done I should know about?"

Poole stood up. "Better go. Pa has an order at the store. It'll be lashes if I get home late. Thanks for the fine vittles, Sheriff."

"I ain't done with you, Poole. I'll see you soon."

Poole tipped his hat, winked at me, and got out the door in a flash. I waited for Sheriff Platner to start in on me. He didn't. Just the possibility was enough to curb more foolishness out of us.

I walked patrol with the Sheriff every day. When we passed the blacksmith's shop, Mr. Ayers would rattle chains. "About got them leg irons ready for your new prisoner, Sheriff. Bring him by anytime, and I'll get him fitted." He laughed and waved. "Be good, Lummy boy."

The best part of my "imprisonment" was when the new schoolteacher, Lamech Edwards, came by after class to lend me books—history, poetry, and some with good stories. It was the most reading I'd ever done, and my skills sharpened up with his help.

Finally, Saturday came. Sheriff Platner said, "Lummy, it was good havin' you, but next time on better terms, you hear?"

That night at supper, I held up a shiny new silver dollar the sheriff gave me for helping about the jailhouse. I handed it to Pa. The family could always use an extra dollar.

Pa laughed, "And they say doin' wrong never pays."

Ma popped his shoulder. "You know better'n to say that."

We tried to hide our snickering.

THE NEWNESS OF serving as provost wears off soon enough. Standing post in town is nothing short of boring. Colonel Marks keeps us in tip top shape though. So much so the town men comment how safe their ladies feel with us around. Older gentlemen say they don't even need to lock their doors or windows.

One sweet grandmother stops to chat one sunny afternoon. "Thank you, men. Why, I can set a fresh baked blackberry cobbler in my window and nobody'd dare take it."

She reminds me of Granny Thankful. "Now, sweet lady, if you put that pie out there under our noses, you'd ruin our fine reputation."

In her slow as molasses voice, she says, "Young man, I'm Granny O'Neil, and that was no temptation. That's an invitation to supper tonight. Bring just four 'cause that's all the room I have, all right? Come at 5:30 this evenin'. I could only find an ole rooster tough as shoe leather, but he'll be good dumplin's."

"Granny, how'd you know that's when our duty is over?"

She points up the street. "I watch everythin' goin' on around here, boy. Mine's the white one. See you later on this afternoon."

"Thank you, ma'am."

Edrow shakes like a kid handed a piece of cool red ripe watermelon in the summertime.

"I see you grinnin' like a mule eatin' briars. Yeah, you can come along." He jumps up and down like he just got paid. Just the thought of having a home cooked meal can do that to a man.

CHAPTER 19

CHICKASAW BAYOU BATTLE

DECEMBER 24, 1862

And the angel said unto them, "Fear not: for, behold, I bring you good tidings of great joy, which shall be to all people." Where's that angel now?

IT'S THE NIGHT before Christmas, and peace is hard to find in the hearts of men. The Yankees are coming like the Mississippi surging south, and there's no stopping the raging current of blue and death. We hear steamer engines north of town safe from our batteries. We expect an attack any day now. I shiver but not from the cold.

I've heard nothing from Susannah or Mr. Gilmore for some time. I'm disappointed and worried. I'd hoped for packages to celebrate the holiday season. None came. I wanted a note from Susannah on our one year anniversary. I know if it was possible, it would be in my hands now. I'm pretty sure my letters aren't getting through to her either. Damn Yanks.

It seems like only yesterday Susannah and I became husband and wife. It was only a year ago that Mr. Gilmore gave us Susannah's freedom papers. It was only a year ago we talked and loved the night away in our marriage bed. I savor those happy thoughts standing picket down by the river. I wish I was home presenting Susannah a Christmas gift. Maybe a catalog ordered dress to adorn her shapely body or a locket to grace her smooth silky neck. I wish I was sitting by a warm fire in my own home sipping Mr. Gilmore's special eggnog, preparing a roast goose with all the trimmings, and being with the people I love dearly. I wish....

J.A. kicks the mud from his shoes. "No gifts or holiday party except solid shot, exploding shells, screamers, and firebombs."

"Yeah, Merry Christmas, J.A."

As Sherman makes his way downriver, Grant will try to draw off the bulk of our forces again to Grenada. It makes us nervous to be one of the few regiments left, leaving us lean on numbers if attacked. Sarge shifts us to different posts to keep us warm and awake. He positions J.A. and me on the corner of Crawford and Levee Streets between the Prentiss House and St. Paul's Catholic Church.

A messenger races through the streets. "Merry Christmas, boys! General Van Dorn destroyed Grant's supplies at Holly Springs, and General Pemberton is headed back this way!"

I turn to J.A. "There's our Christmas gift."

"Gettin' your supply depot destroyed must throw a cold wet blanket on a warm Yankee Christmas celebration tonight."

"Bet that cost them a pretty penny."

"Merry Christmas, Lummy Tullos."

Spies report Sherman's troops are disembarking by the hundreds near the mouth of the Yazoo River west of town. Pemberton sends the returning regiments to Walnut Hills, stretching the line all the way from Vicksburg to Snyder's Bluff on the Yazoo. Sherman wouldn't attack with Grant's supplies destroyed. He must not know. The Yanks don't know the ground, and our boys are very well dug in. To our disappointment, the 27th Louisiana is ordered to stay in town.

Colonel Marks stops to encourage us. "Stay alert, men. The Yank invader is near. While there's time, write a letter home. It's Christmas, and your people need to hear from you. Write a good one, and we'll send them all out tomorrow. Send a little of your pay home, too, if you got any left. I'm sure they can use it. Don't dally. It might be a while before you get another chance."

What he really means is, *This may be your last letter home, and you'll be dead before you can spend the last bit of your pay.*

I take out one of the two envelopes I have left. Thankfully, the postage is paid on them. We haven't been paid now for seven months. I hope Ma likes the envelope I picked that has our flag and a picture of Jefferson Davis printed on it. The letter will explain my choice. I find the stub of a pencil in my haversack and go to writing.

> *Vicksburg,*
> *Christmas Eve, 1862*
>
> *Ma, I hope things at home are as pleasant as you always made them for me. I think of you often and know the good Creator watches over your soul every day. Not much to tell except that we are on city guard duty now. We got that honor for bein first in Vicksburg and havin built a lot of earthworks. It was hard labor but not bad for a boy raised up on his pa's farm.*
>
> *You're never gonna believe it, but President Davis and that tough old bear General Joe Johnston came for a visit. It had all the fanfare of a Jackson City parade. We dressed up in clean uniforms, and people came from all over. Ladies brought all kinds of sweets, one even a batch of chocolate fudge like you make. I'd rather had yours. Bein provost, we were inspected personally by these two great men of the Cause in front of the Prentiss House Hotel where we stay.*
>
> *We waited six hours, but when the President and General finally arrived, oh how proud we was to show ourselves true loyal southern soldiers. We all laughed when a man said President Davis was the ugliest hatchet-faced man he ever saw. General Joe was a picture perfect soldier.*
>
> *President Davis walked the line sayin encouragin words. Then he stopped right in front of me and straightened my gun. He asked where I was from. My chest swelled up. I told him Winn Parish, with the 27th Looseana Winn Rebels, but that I was born near Greensboro Missip. He grinned. I said I heard him speak back in May of '51 when he ran for governor. I said Pa voted for him and the States Rights party.*
>
> *President Davis grinned, "So you must know I'm a Mississippi man and got a place just south of here." I was nervous as a schoolboy recitin poetry at school. He popped me on the shoulder. "Ready to fight Missip boy turned Looseana man?" I yelled, "Yassuh! Ready to kick some blue coat Yankee ass, suh." The President slapped me on the shoulder again and said,*

"That's the spirit son." The boys howled til Old General Joe growled like a bear. "Attention in the ranks."

President Davis nodded at the General but winked at me. "Glad to have you with us son. Give em hell when they come." Pa would have been proud. Sorry I cussed, but it fit the occasion, me speakin for all the boys of the 27th Looseana.

The best news I saved for last. Jasper and James are here in Vburg somewhere. I saw them get off a train back at the first of the month. I haven't got to be with them yet, but it'll happen soon. I'm glad we here together. I ain't got paid all these months, but I hope this little bit helps. I pray for you Ma, Elihu, and the girls, and George in wherever he's fightin. Tell the folks makin boots at the shoe factory in Bankston to send us brogans. We need them bad. Say lots of prayers, the Yankees are close.

Stay strong, Ma. Don't ever think any of us won't come home after this is over.

Your lovin, obedient son,
Lummy.

I don't expect Ma to get this letter for some time, if ever.

EARLY CHRISTMAS MORNING as the sun rises, I step outside to breathe in the cold, foggy, fresh air. Somebody whispers, "Shut that damned pneumonia hole up."

I slip out quickly to help keep the heat in the room. Getting out of that cramped, smoky room is a good shock to wake me up. I lean on the rail. Granville sits on a boar's head smiling.

"C'mon down, Mistuh Sleepy Head, got somethin for you."

I pull my pants on over my long handles and ease down two flights of stairs. I meet Granville perched on the rail by the steps.

"What's got you grinnin' like a possum this mornin', Granville?"

He proudly holds out a small wooden box that has squares checkered in black and white, top and bottom. "Merry Christmas, big brother."

Then I remember. "The chess set? When did you find the time?"

"Told you I'd have it ready for Christmas, didn't I?"

I unhook the small latch to open the neatly hinged box. I find thirty-two carefully carved minie ball chess pieces in the box.

"Lay the box open and flat. You can play your game on it."

I turn away, tears spilling over my cheeks.

Granville puts a hand on my shoulder. "Lummy, you kept me from doin' somethin' really stupid. Makin' this chess set kept my mind off of my troubles. I'll never forget what you did. You'll always be my big brother." He bear hugs me.

"But I ain't got nothin' for you."

"You like it, that's enough for me. You already gave me yours." He turns on his heels like in a marching maneuver. "I best get back to camp before my sergeant thinks I run off. See you soon."

I hold the most precious gift I've received since leaving Winn Parish, save the tintype of Susannah. I ease back up the stairs to the third floor porch and sit on a box. J.A. steps out of our room scratching the back of his head with one hand and his privates with the other.

"What was that all about?"

I hold up the chess set.

"Dang, boy, who brought you that?" I tell him the story and he whistles. "That boy's got some talent. Can you play?"

"Mistuh Gilmore taught me. It takes a fair amount of thinkin', but it works your brain good." I admire the chess set and count my blessings.

Sarge lets us have Christmas Day free. After a party the officers put together, General Smith calls all regiments to arms and alerts those guarding Walnut Hills to be ready. We're ordered to evacuate the good citizens after General Pemberton urges all non-fighting folks to safety. The 27th Louisiana is ordered to protect the city in case of a breakthrough and guard Yank prisoners taken in the battle.

With the leaves off the cottonwoods and willows, it's easy to see the

Yankee troop buildup on the banks of the big river where Chickasaw Bayou spills into the Yazoo River. I want to join in the coming fray, but we are the provost, and we have a job to do.

THREE DAYS AFTER Christmas, the Yanks shell the earthworks seven hours. Colonel Winchester Hall of the 26th Louisiana sends a reconnaissance team to locate the enemy. They send the bluecoats running like scared rabbits.

But today, December 29th, Sherman attacks with fury. They face the wrath of men in gray but also confront God's creation too. The Yanks try to trick our boys by bombarding the left end of our line to push it to the center. It doesn't work. Our men are dug in along the bluffs. The Yanks cross ditches with water up to their chests and climb over felled trees. The land defeats the Yanks as much as the rifle. The 26th Louisiana men bring us prisoners.

A young private cries. "They just keep on comin'. It's awful. All them Yanks died without firin' a shot. When they can't run back to their lines, they hide behind stumps and under logs."

The Yanks make a valiant attempt, but when they get pushed back, General Stephen D. Lee orders the 17th and 26th Louisiana regiments to counterattack. They capture twenty-one officers, 311 enlisted men, and four battle flags. It takes all of Company F to walk the prisoners to the Warren County Courthouse, feed them, and allow the doctors to tend their wounds. We move those with no wounds to the Warren County Jail. They sit dejected.

One keeps repeating to himself rocking back and forth, "Never should've tried it, never...."

I grab his hands. His fingers are bloody. "What happened to this man?"

Another Yank, chewing on a piece of bread, says, "He got left after his company retreated. He tore the meat off his fingertips diggin' in the frozen ground tryin' to hide. He lost his mind." Nobody says anything.

The Yank with the bloody fingers finally comes to his senses. "I just want to go home to my wife and three little girls." The batteries fire off again, and the Yank prisoners duck.

I hand him a cup of hot water. It's all we have to offer. "We all wish this damn thing was over. But it ain't. Good boys like us and those layin' out there in the mud and the cold ain't got no choice." I've never talked with a Yank before. He's not the evil dark demon newspapers make him out to be. He's human enough.

"Sherman told us we'd just have to raise our rifles, and you'd scamper away without a shot. You boys sent us scurryin' like rats out of a burnin' barn."

I lean forward. "We heard the shouts of the 26th Looseana, their rifles, your screamin', and Porter's gunboats shellin' our boys on the bluffs. We were just too ready for you, I reckon." I stand straighter. "And the 27th Looseana are just itchin' to get in this fight."

The Yank looks up and stops chewing. "You don't want that. It's like Hell busted open, and all Satan's demons have been set loose. I don't care which color you wear—you don't want it."

The Yank chews on his bread and starts to say something, but hesitates to see if it's safe to ask his question. I nod.

"I want no trouble, Reb, but why don't you just let the damned darkies go? Most of this would already be settled. All of you can't want slaves. Heck, you wouldn't even be here if you owned slaves. And besides, blacks are as human as you, even if you don't want to believe it."

A guard slaps him on the back of his head. "Shut up, niggah lover, or I'll swat your ass again."

The Yank shakes his head, whispering, "Lord, open their eyes so they may see." My anger flares—not at the Yank, but at the Reb who hit him. I glare at him. He was wrong for that.

Am I wrong wearing the gray suit? Damn Yank factories are just as happy to buy slave-picked cotton as the South is to sell it. That dog won't hunt. Reasons for this damn war have gone way beyond men in fancy suits smoking expensive cigars so greedy and so willing to sell their souls for worthless trinkets of this world. It's not about profit. It's about human beings. They just don't know it.

I want to be on the side that sets Susannah free to be the human being God created her to be. I want Old Bart to have the right to come and go as he pleases, just like me. I want poor departed Lucille to be able to buy her own pepper for her popcorn with her own money.

Am I fighting for the wrong cause? I've never felt this strong about it. But why shouldn't I, loving my Susannah, black as coal? Tonight the gray uniform looks different. Is gray the darkness blinding my eyes though my heart has changed?

Colonel Marks makes sure we treat the Yank prisoners with respect. They're just human beings now, beaten and discouraged, worrying about what we'll do with them next. I'm sure they think the worst. I would.

The battle is over two days before New Year's. Colonel Marks reports the Yanks lost 1776 men besides twenty-one officers and 311 enlisted men as prisoners of war. We capture 500 rifles and four battle colors. Colonel Marks begged to let us fight, but General Stephen D. Lee refused.

We lost only 187, but that's men who won't see spring plowing. What a damn shame. I've only fired a few shots at the enemy, killed one Yank sailor, and already understand the futility of believing this war will solve the gray and blue disagreement. I'm glad General Lee turned us down, but it only prolongs the inevitable—I will kill more men if I want to stay alive. I'm not afraid to fight, just of losing my soul in it.

Granville sits down on the bench beside me. "Lummy, I ain't goin' home 'til this war is over. If I get killed, it'll be facin' the enemy, not gettin' a bullet in my back from runnin'. Before this war is over, I want to kill just one Yankee and be done with it." Big talk for a naïve young man.

"You'll get your chance soon enough. Ole Shermy will be back."

The young man squirms. "Really, he might come back?"

I feel his fear. "Just do your best to stay alive. There's a big fight comin', and we're all gonna be in it. When you shoot that first Yank, don't look him in the eyes. You'll see him every night when you close your eyes to sleep if you do. Believe me, I know."

Reports come in that Sherman wants to try again, but fog and rain stop him. God's good creation is at work for us once more. I bet he's fit to be tied after losing the battle. The Yanks fall back to their boats, and who knows what their next half-baked plan will be. They'll be more determined now than ever to take Vicksburg. A captured captain said Grant vows there'll be no turning back until Vicksburg is under his control.

The battle being over brings little relief to poor widows and orphans who lost husbands and fathers. I sit on a bench outside a prisoner's cell in the Warren County Jail trying to stay awake. It's just after midnight, and though I'm glad the battle is over, I hurt for so many wasted lives.

"Glad tidings? Hell, is victory over men lyin' out there rottin' in the swamps anythin' good to tell? Ain't no joy in that. Where's the Christmas angel now? I've only seen the Death Angel."

A small voice whispers from a dark corner. "Amen, friend."

The man wears a blue cap.

FOR A DAY or so, there's little action around Vicksburg except for an occasional steamer passing our big guns. The 26th Louisiana guards the port on the river in case the Yanks try a frontal attack. They assure us that no amount of Yank infantry will get to shore.

One yells, "And besides, the 27th Looseana is right here behind us, sleepin' in that warm hotel." They give us good natured hell about that. Anyway, we feel fairly safe for now. Still, we're watchful as a momma doe over her newborn fawn.

Grant tries running supply barges down river. Our batteries open fire, and the Yanks return with blasts from their decks. Smoke, flames, shot, and shell fill the air in a tremendous fireworks show. The 26th Louisiana men just keep their heads down. Rifles can't do anything against that shower of death.

We watch from the safety of barricades we'd built in front of the Prentiss House. Sarge sends men across to DeSoto to fire the houses to light up the river to help our batteries shoot more accurately. The blazes make the river like daytime. Our artillery boys disable some boats but only sink one tug. The Yanks cut the barges loose, so we capture prisoners and grab supplies from the boats scuttled near the 26th position.

Running to the water's edge, I find one of the boys who'd just returned from firing the shacks in DeSoto. I throw a blanket around the shivering soldier. I ask about Annie Fanny.

"Naw, didn't see nobody. They either run off or been killed." His teeth rattle as I rub his shoulders to warm him up. He thanks me for the blanket.

"That house over there, sure you didn't see nobody there?"

"Yeah, now that you mention it. A big ole gal was hidin' under a porch. We tried to get her out, but she was stuck, too scared to move and too big to budge. Before we could get her out, a shell caught the house on fire. Nobody could've gotten out alive, especially her. You know her?"

"Just a friend from way back, that's all."

Annie Fanny is dead. A part of me dies, too.

I slip around a corner and cry.

CHAPTER 20

THE BEST AND WORST NEW YEAR'S DAY, EVER

JANUARY 1, 1863

New Year's ain't always a good day to leave the past behind

THE FIRST DAY of 1863. Though the recent stormy conflict has passed, the greater battle begins. Many a good soldier's life, in blue and gray, has ended. While the town sends up rousing victory hurrahs for the valiant men in gray, preachers kneel to pray for the fallen. For some, New Year's Day brings new life. To others it brings grim realizations.

Both fight for my soul.

We march the Yank prisoners to the rail station to board cars for prison camp. I hate to see them go to those horrible places of death, but we can't guard or feed them.

The Yank with bandages on his hands nods. "God bless you, my friend. Pray I survive." A corporal pushes him on with the butt of his musket. I just let it go.

After the prisoners are loaded, we get the rest of the day free. As I check for mail, I wonder if Jasper and James were in the battle. It's been a month since I caught a glimpse of them. I guess it's a big brother's right to worry. I pick up two letters—one from Ma and the other from Mr. Gilmore. I shiver with excitement. That means one from Susannah. It's been too long. I have mixed feelings. For some reason, I expect hard news.

I sit on a log by the river where all is quiet. I take a deep breath. "Lord, help me take whatever news I get." I open Ma's letter first since it's dated more recent.

Bankston, Choctaw County, Mississippi,
December 5, 1862

   Son, I miss your face at breakfast every morning. I leave empty plates
waiting for you boys to come home. I pray that the angels who sang the
night of our Lord's birth protect you.

   I must tell you Amariah passed from this earth November 30 due to
some ailment. Doc operated on him on our supper table but to no avail.
I shed many tears for him and his sweet wife Amanda who passed right
before he left for the war. Too much death and too much sorrow. You must
stay alive and come home when this is all over.

   Mary and Emaline say hello. Mary and Elihu keep the farm going. I'm
so glad he stayed when Ben and Dorcas went west. I know he thought about
going with them. I'm glad Ben and Dorcas found a good life in Louisiana.
Maybe they'll come visit one day.

   I hope you find Jasper and James soon. Firing those cannons must be
hard work. I know they'll make us proud.

   Lummy, take care of yourself.

I love you,
Ma

My goodness, Amariah died the very night I boarded the train for Grenada, the same night I saw Jasper and James. And Amariah's sweet and pretty wife Amanda must've died of heartbreak just before he left for the war. They were such a lovey-dovey couple, calling each other "angel" and other sweet names all the time. I thought it was silly, but now I understand they just tried to keep the sweetness in their marriage.

I reread the letter, and my heart hurts. I want to be around family. I feel homesick, heartbroken, and alone.

"Lord, bring my brothers to me soon."

Now Mr. Gilmore's letter. It took a long time to get here.

I take a deep breath.

Winnfield Louisiana,

September 18, 1862

My Dear Friend Columbus Nathan Tullos,

I hope this letter finds you well and in good spirits. We hear little, but what we do is always a good report of your noble stand. Be strong in your present trial. The Lord will deliver you from the Philistines. Now, I must ask you to stand even taller in the midst of a greater trial.

There is no good way to tell you this, my dear son, but your sweet Susannah has taken the journey to meet her Creator. It was measles. A man from Camp Moore came home sick. Susannah ministered to him as she did others and caught the deadly disease. She has received the Lord's reward now for her faithful service.

Her last words were for you, son.

"Tell my blessed Lummy I love him dearly, and I'll wait for him on Jordan's other side." I cannot imagine the pain you must feel in this moment, except when my own darling wife's passing came without warning. They both died before their times. The few short years you had together brought Susannah an eternity of happiness. As you reminded me often, I now encourage you. The resurrection is true. You will see her again.

Pray for us, Lummy. The home guard, led by a bushwhacker named Dawg Smith, brings terror to these parts. He leads the Home Guard, claiming direct orders from President Davis. He makes old men unable to enlist pay a $100 exemption. Otherwise, they are executed. Men not eligible for war service are shot down or dogged to death by Smith's brutal hounds. Husbands and fathers hide to escape him. Even a song mocking his exploits is sung around the parish. Smith sends secret agents to persuade slaves to run away promising to help them escape north. Then he returns them to their owners collecting bounties up to $100 each. I don't mean to trouble you son, but he's raping, pillaging, robbing, and murdering. We're gathering up now to go after him. Pray that St. Michael, the Protector of God's people, leads us with his sword.

Lummy, stay alive. Do what is right in your soul, what brings peace. Follow your path, even if it's against what others preach. Make your own

*decisions and follow them. I miss our talks and your prayers, my friend.
I'm closer to God because of you.*

*Come back when this is over. A good life awaits you. Old Bart prays for
your soul. Again, I'm so sorry, my son. May blessings cover you from head
to heel, my friend of friends.*

*Forever your servant,
James T. Gilmore*

I fall to the ground. Memories of Susannah flood my mind. They leave
me shaking. My heart feels like it will explode and collapse at the same time.
I can hardly lift my head. My soul sends out deep guttural wails. I cry endless
tears. I stretch out before the Lord on the sand. Ma's right. There's just too
much death in this world. I'm ready for mine if the Lord brings it now. I lay
on the soft white sand, sobbing like a young child. I want to jump in the river
or start running as fast as I can. And I hope I get shot in the process. This is
too hard.

I push my head into the sand. "Lord, this is just about more than I can
bear." My head pounds and body wretches. I'm hopeless. Helpless. I don't
know what to do with myself.

I sit up to watch fish jump in the river. I'm so very tired. And the worst of
it is yet to come. I calm myself, watching the gentle stream pass by. I sing my
favorite song like I'm in church. "Oh, Susannah, Oh, don't you cry for me,
For I come from Mississippi with my banjo on my knee...."

I sing until I no longer feel the brisk wind, hear the birds, or see the willows swaying. I become a part of all that surrounds me.

Susannah appears, pretty as ever, walking to me like fog drifting on the
river. She keeps looking around, like she's lost. Then she sees me sitting on
the sand. She's barefoot, and her legs show from under her glowing dress.
She walks to me with arms outstretched, smiling and saying something I
can't hear. The sound of the river rushes loud. I try to get up but can't. Susannah keeps walking but can't reach me. Her smile glows in the fog. *"My darlin'
Lummy, you will come to me one day, one day, one day...."*

A splash ends my vision. And another, like a fish jumping. I shake my head to clear my glassy eyes. I blink, hoping Susannah is still there on the sand. I wipe tears from my eyes. She's gone. Another rock hits the water, then another. I'm still dazed, but a third skips across the smooth water twelve times before it sinks into the muddy stream. Then a high-pitched laugh bursts out a few feet away.

"I know that laugh!" I jump up like a cat after a bird. "Jasper? James? That you? Tell me you ain't no haint like Granny used to say."

Jasper yells like a hound howling at the moon. "Well, if Granny Thankful was here, she'd make us bow so she could kiss us on the back of our necks. No haints here, big brother."

I plow into them, and we tumble on the ground like schoolboys. We hug and rub each others' heads with our knuckles. We check each others' arm muscles and slug each other in the shoulder. It's what brothers do. For a moment, I'm home. Finding my two brothers brings life back into my soul. Susannah's death cast a deep shadow. It's the best and worst New Year's Day ever.

We trade news. I ask, "Amariah?"

Jasper wipes his eyes. "It was terrible, Lummy. He took sick and was sent to Edwards Depot Hospital 'tween here and Jackson. Then, they sent him home. Ma wrote sayin' they didn't know why he died." We talk about missing Pa, and though he was hard as a rail spike, we each pointed to something he taught us that keeps us alive. I tell them about Ben and Dorcas, their sack full of children, and working in Winn Parish.

I'm not ready to tell them about Susannah yet.

Jasper throws a rock into the water. "Ma says the farm is doing well. Elihu keeps meat on the table and the fields in good shape with the Wood brothers' help. They're rough but loyal men."

James acts like he's turning up a jug. "That Aaron Wood's spring has the sweetest water around and makes the best damn moonshine." We laugh, wishing we had a jug. I could use a drink or two.

Jasper punches my knee. "Our battery done good in the battle a few days ago. We wasn't close to the fightin', but me and Jimmy did our part. You'd been proud of us."

I rustle Jasper's hair. "I'm just proud you're alive. And what's this Jimmy stuff? I heard him called that by a man in your company."

"They started calling me that right off, but I'd rather be called James."

I throw a rock. "Well, I ain't callin' you Jimmy. Ain't your name."

"Good." James tells about their travels, being stationed at Grenada and seeing action at Coffeeville. James squirms like a freshly dug night crawler. "And guess what? They got us stationed at First Water Battery just below town. We can visit most anytime."

"Good."

Finally, I tell them about Susannah's passing.

Jasper puts his arm around my shoulder. "Ain't only bullets takin' away our loved ones. At least she's safe in the arms of the Lord." I take the consoling, but I want to scream.

The sun starts to set. "I best git. I'm sure Sarge is lookin' for me." We walk back up the bank. I point at the Prentiss House Hotel. "There she is, my home in Vicksburg."

Both hit me, one on each shoulder. "No way, you rotten son of a...."

Sarge yells behind me. "Lummy, I've been all over Hell's creation lookin' for you, dammit. We-e-e-ll, ain't this a pretty picture out of a sweet romance storybook. Three little princes lookin' for princesses, or maybe one of you boys is the princess. So sweet."

"I'm sorry, Sarge."

"Private, your free time ended an hour ago. Get your slow ass up that hill, get your musket, and get to your post, dammit."

"Yassuh, Sarge."

"Who'n the hell are these varmints? Crawled out some hole called Choctaw County I'd imagine?" Jasper and James freeze. Sarge plants his feet and stares them up and down.

"Artillery, huh? Never knew them boys to be worth a shit."

James steps up. "Now hold on. I'll get my sergeant over here, and we'll see about that."

"Down, son, just razzin' your young ass and glad to see that mean streak runs in the family. Put 'em here, boys, Lummy told me all about you."

James cools down, embarrassed he got so riled up.

Sarge turns. "Sorry, boys, we gotta go. Work it out, and I'll make sure you get a proper reunion. Which regiment are you in?"

James puffs out his chest proudly, "1st Missip Light Artillery, Company C, suh."

"Wouldn't be ole Henry Turner, would it?"

"You know him?"

"We worked together in Bankston at the tannery by McCurtain Creek. We even made a couple visits to Bucksnort years ago. Y'all don't know about Bucksnort, do you?"

Jasper grins. "Buck who?"

He belly laughs. "Uh-huh, right, just fine good church goin' lyin' bastards, ain't you?"

"Wesson's factories still goin'? Cheap son of a bitch never paid us what we was worth."

James proudly says, "Them factories is the best kept secret in Missip."

"Hope it stays that way. I wish I could get my hands on a pair of them fine boots right about now. Anyway, you boys get on up back to your company and let Lummy get to his post. Look forward to seein' more of you boys real soon."

We shake hands and go our way. A little bit of home. It helps, but it ain't nearly enough.

As soon as Sarge and I get back to the Prentiss House Hotel, he orders twenty of us, "Get your gear. You got guard duty at Four Mile Bridge. Can't let them Yanks capture that crossin'."

We march the entire way on the slick roads, slipping and sliding, some falling down and rolling around in the mud. I'm ashamed when Sarge commandeers the Negroes' cabins. They have no place to go. Some of our men curse at them. One kicks a young boy in his backside as he walks away. I restrain myself from kicking the soldier.

We build fires, but our clothes and blankets don't dry. We don't have time to cook rations before duty, so they bring us some half-cooked beef and cornbread.

No complaints here. It's become the common meal.

EARLY MORNING JANUARY 4th, the rain stops, making for a beautiful Lord's day. I wander into the woods to find a stump near a trickling creek. Though I meditate, I keep one ear open for any unusual movement in the brush, especially anything blue. The quiet reminds me of Bowie Creek back home where I sat with God many times. I can't get Susannah out of my mind. Her death overwhelms me. I ask God for peace. I find none.

I get back to camp around noon. Sarge holds open a sack. "Found these potatoes this morning. Each man gets four. They're little but taste good."

I roast mine over the fire and eat slowly, enjoying every bite. I'm strengthened after that. I sleep out by the fire until J.A. nudges me before daylight.

"Get up, boy, your hair's done turned white."

I shake the frost from my head. My nose is stopped up. My body aches.

Sarge warns, "You don't sound so good. Get on over to the cook fire and drink some coffee. There's food, too. Thanks for lettin' the other boys have their turn under a roof."

By nightfall I have chills and a fever.

ON THE 6TH, we're ordered back to town. Sarge immediately sends me to my hotel room and tells me not to come out. I collapse on the pallet. "Sarge, I'm weak as a popcorn poot."

J.A. piles blankets on me. "I'll bring you somethin' to eat."

The next few days, I hardly sleep. My body aches all over, and I can't get comfortable. The doctor says it's no use giving me medicine. "Just sweat it out and let your body do its work."

J.A. watches over me like kin. He feeds me eggs and a little milk as my stomach can take it.

Jasper and James bring me a few ounces of butter and a small flask of whiskey which I'm thankful to get. Just having my little brothers close cheers my heart. Though I'm advised to talk little, those two have plenty to gab about, often taking advantage of my disadvantage to gig me with jokes and old stories.

After a week, my fever finally breaks. I volunteer for guard duty down by river's edge. I need the time alone.

CHAPTER 21

FAREWELL ISN'T FOREVER

FEBRUARY 26, 1863

You gotta get through this conflict to be ready for the next one.
There's always a next one.

THE LETTER ABOUT Susannah's death sends me into a sorrow I'm not sure I can climb out of. Though I haven't told them yet, J.A. and the boys try to cheer me up. I spend most of my free time in St. Paul's Catholic Church just up Crawford Street from the Prentiss House. It may be the only place I can find my soul again with such misery and heartache as I'm bogged down in now.

I like the paintings, stained glass, and statues of the saints. Granny used to say, "Folks gone to be with the Lord are just on the other side of a sheer curtain. If you get real still, you ju-u-u-st might see them through the thin veil. So why not talk with them from time to time?" Honoring and treating the departed like family and calling on them for help? Why wouldn't those once alive, who loved and cared for us for so long, not love and care for us now just because they're dead? Yep, I'm sure of it. I got a little Catholic in me.

As I sit with the saints in this beautiful place, I think about Susannah. If there ever was a saint, it'd be her. I remember when I first heard that President Lincoln planned to free the slaves, North and South. Some in Winn Parish freed their slaves before war broke out. Mr. Gilmore's slaves were already free. Susannah was free, but she couldn't leave the safety of his farm.

I clinch my fists. "Lincoln, you're just too damn late. My wife is dead because of your war."

The priest pokes his head out of his confession box. "You all right, my son?" I nod. "If you'd like to talk, I'm here." I shake my head. He makes the sign of the cross. "Bless you, my son."

Mr. Gilmore does the best and right thing keeping his slaves. If he frees them, they'd probably get caught, killed, or wind up who knows where. He set people free long before Lincoln's proclamation. The man is a visionary. He saw Susannah and me getting married long before it happened.

But why couldn't she have been free from birth? Why did it take a good man like Mr. Gilmore to steal her away to free her? Why did it take this damn war to force white people to realize they never owned another human being in the first place? Why did that soldier, doing what he thought was right, go off to fight for his country and then bring home the measles that killed my Susannah?

I rub my eyes. "If there was no war, Susannah would be alive. And I'd be home with her."

Don't slave owners know they could've just as easily been born black as white, slave as free? No one gets to choose where or what color they are when they come into this world. Too many whys and not enough becauses.

"God, is it okay to scream in your church house, in front of all your saints and the priest?" I don't have the strength to yell. I sit still. I empty my nearly wasted soul. I need something, but I don't know what. "Lord?"

My surroundings grow dark. The stained glass windows no longer allow in sunlight that make the multi-colored Bible scenes come alive. I sink into the depths of my soul, and a tiny light in the far off distance wanders my way. Someone walks with a very small candle. She has fiery red hair and wears a flowing white dress covered with pink and purple flowers, though not flowers. They're lights glowing like springtime azaleas in full bloom. This lady is young, and though I don't recognize her, she is very familiar.

She places a stone in my hand.

"Who are you?" The red-haired lady points at the sparkling gem that changes color as I turn it over and over in my hand.

"I bring light to your dark soul, my son. You must trust the river for it flows without end, and we all are blessed to rest in its current. You must join us in the stream of life, Columbus Nathan Tullos, for you cannot stay in the place you have assigned yourself. You will not live. Go to the river. You will find the reminder of what you now hold in your hand. It will teach you that we are never apart from those whom we love so dearly. We all flow together in this river of time." The red haired lady turns to walk back the way she came.

"Wait, I want to know about my Susannah."

The red-haired lady turns and grins. "She waits for you."

"But who are you?"

"One who has known you since you were born and walked this earth for a time. You know me, Grandson. I live just across the thin line between this life and new life."

"Granny Thankful." She melts into the darkness from which she came. I watch until someone speaks, shaking my arm.

"Son, are you all right?" It's the priest.

Two words pop out of my mouth. "I'm thankful." I go to the prayer garden with the priest, and we talk for hours. I tell of my experiences with God, my struggle with anger, my love for Susannah, talking with Granny Thankful, and my change of heart about this war. He listens patiently. He finally speaks when I finish.

"Son, your Susannah is not gone forever. She is not far away somewhere in the stars. No, she's right here, right now, with you still. Those of us still alive are surrounded by a great cloud of witnesses, the Bible says. Susannah now lives in that crowd. This great crowd is not present to witness to our every mistake. No, that sort of belief only strikes fear to keep us children when the Lord wants us to mature as healthy spiritual adults. The cloud cheers us on our way and helps pick us up when we fall in this life." The priest leads me back into the sanctuary.

"Remember this, my son. A piety towards God fostered in leisure rarely proves true in the trials of life. Let the Lord flood into your soul and be mindful of what he gives you."

I study the statues of the apostles and paintings of Bible story scenes, thinking of my friends and loved ones gone on—Grandpa Temple, Granny Thankful, Saleta, Pa, Amariah, Amanda, Susannah. Annie Fanny could be painted on these holy walls as easily as Mary Magdalene. Kindness comes in all shapes and sizes and just maybe with a snuff juice stain on a chin. Peace covers me beyond anything I've ever felt before.

A door slams. Mrs. O'Neil walks in the back. She smiles as she makes the sign of the cross and then kisses me on the cheek as she passes on her way to the confession booth—another saintly woman whose picture should be painted on these walls.

I close my eyes for just one moment more in the silence, stillness, and solitude in this place, emptying my soul of all distractions. I am not alone. And I have no fear.

I trot down to the river and walk along the bank until I find a rock bed. The first stone I spot is a beautiful agate like I've never seen—blue, green, and red wavy lines in a swirl of designs. This is the reminder Granny Thankful sent me to find. What I find is peace.

I walk along the sandy bank watching the water roll by. There are so many things I don't understand, so many things I can't get my soul around, things that probably won't become clear for years or until I reach the other side. I let the sun shine on my face.

I clear all thoughts. A faint voice like Granny Thankful's speaks. *Faith is standing firm where there's little to no understanding.*

I walk back up the hill and thank God I don't have to figure it all out. He holds me in the palm of his mighty hand.

SHERMAN STAYS UPRIVER waiting on Grant. The constant rain and cold make us miserable, but they keep the Yankee troops and gunboats away. We need the peace, and it offers opportunity for me and my brothers to have a few good times together. They come into town, and I get them a place in the Prentiss House for the night. We drink a little, as weary soldiers will, talk of home and joke a lot, and eat everything we can get our hands on.

I take Jasper and James to Mrs. O'Neil's for more of those rooster dumplings. She's happy to meet my brothers. We know our time together is short with the Yanks creeping up closer every day. We make the most of it.

JANUARY PASSES BY relatively quiet, except for shelling and the noise of steam-powered digging machines working on Grant's canal behind DeSoto.

I grin. "Pretty high minded to think he can change the course of the Missip."

"Must think he's God Almighty himself," J.A. crows. "Still, I'd like to see those machines."

"Look at all those Yankee tents across the river."

"Yeah, they're dug in like ticks on a dawg."

"They got us hemmed in pretty good now."

"I wonder if they know over a hundred of their troops in the Warren County Jail want to take the oath to fight for the Confederacy. Yank deserters come in nearly every day now."

Some of the officers speculate the war will be over by March. That talk usually has little to back it up. I'm content with whatever the Lord brings or allows. What choice do I have anyway?

The townspeople are in good spirits, watching the Yanks work hard and getting nowhere for their labor. Regiments from Tennessee and Georgia pour into our defenses, raising morale, until the smallpox plaguing the Yanks crosses the river into our ranks. Talk about wasteful death. Good boys leave their homes, wives, and sweethearts to fight for the Cause only to be struck down by an enemy they can't shake a stick at. It's like one of the ten plagues. Several men of the 27th Louisiana die from the dreaded disease. I want to blame God, but I know the pox spares neither Reb nor Yank. Truth is, ain't none of us right in this war.

The worst is the screamers. Men dwindle down to nothing, trying to eat, staying away from water like the doctors order. Screamers, dysentery, the flux, whatever you call it, is when a man runs to the ditch as the watery, sometimes bloody mess screams right out of his backside. It's hard to watch men die.

SHELLING IS SLOW but steady now. The Yanks remind us they aren't going away.

I huddle up with Sarge while getting ready for picket duty. "Where you want me tonight?"

"Go stand guard up at the city hospital. Check on our boys while you're there. They should be upstairs."

It's a peaceful walk with a light snow falling. I enjoy the quiet, alone with my thoughts.

About halfway through the night, a shell screams our way. I duck behind a big tree. The house next to the hospital catches the exploding shell and burns like they poured coal oil on it.

I rush inside the hospital. "Get them boys out of here. A fire's blazin' next door."

We work like bees in the hive getting the sick and wounded out. Some boys who are so weak they can't walk. Those who can help those who can't. All we can do is lay them in the snow, a recipe for pneumonia. Better than being burned alive. Thankfully, the blaze settles down when the house collapses in on itself away from the hospital. I sit after we get everyone back inside, smelling of smoke, but thankful my friends are unharmed.

A doctor pats me on the shoulder. "Just another tale to be told about the brave 27th Louisiana Volunteers. Thanks, son, you did your duty well tonight."

I look into the clearing sky. "Thank you, Lord. It's by Your hand these men were saved from the flames and me from measles, mumps, pox, and the screamers." I want to say it's because Tullos men are tough, but I know better. I've watched stronger men than me waste away from disease that eats their bodies down to nothing. And not a damn thing can be done about it. Disease respects no one. It's killed more men than bullets ever will. It killed Amariah.

TOWN FOLK AND troops cheer Grant's failures. He gives up on one project to start another one. It's all too comical until the Yanks target the hospital with their shelling. Pretty low down, even for a Yankee. Grant tries to cut the levee at Lake Providence to make the Mississippi bypass the batteries at Vicksburg, Warrenton, and Grand Gulf. Doesn't work.

Grant's newest plan is to cut the levee at Yazoo Pass and let the Mississippi run into the Coldwater and Tallahatchie Rivers, then into the Yazoo. That'd flood the whole Delta and allow the Yanks to get behind our defenses without having to run the gauntlet of batteries at Snyder's Bluffs. But the Yanks forget about Mississippian ingenuity. Pemberton sends soldiers and slaves to fell trees blocking the narrow river channels upstream that flow into the Yazoo.

A man with an axe wound comes in on a wagon. "Grant's gunboats ain't gettin' nowhere. We felled eighty trees a mile if one!" Good men with sharp axes can do it. "Them sharpshooters are wearin' 'em out, too. But the best part is hearin' them Yanks scream like schoolgirls fightin' off snakes fallin' out of trees." They give up on that big plan, too.

BY MID-FEBRAUARY, the weather feels like spring. Train cars arrive daily full of guns and ammunition. Wagons bring corn and provisions from the depot as drays haul barrels of sugar and molasses and all sorts of government stores.

The Yanks hurl mortar shells in the city up into the evening. Town people scatter like chickens hearing a red-tailed hawk whistle when a bombardment starts. Little damage is done, except a cow is killed. One man had his arm torn off by shrapnel late this evening. Most soldiers pay little attention to the constant barrage. I think the Yanks are simply amusing themselves or are mad as hell that none of Grant's plans have worked. Damned devils, anyway.

IT'S THE END of February, and I stand picket by the river. My brothers race down the street. James falls and slides on the wet cobblestones right up to my feet but springs up like a cat.

"We're headin' out tonight to Grenada. Grant's found a way through to Greenwood. We're goin' to Fort Pemberton, big brother!"

I place my hands on their shoulders and pray. "Lord, watch over my brothers, Jasper and James. Keep the train on the tracks, the fort secure, and their aim straight and true when they face the blue invader. Amen."

Jasper and James whisper, "Amen."

I shake them. "Look at me. This battle's comin' for you, but don't fear it. Listen. You gotta get through this conflict to be ready for the next one, 'cause there's always a next one."

James lays his head on my shoulder. "Thanks, big brother."

Jasper grins. "See you soon, Lummy dummy."

I sling a rock at him. "Go on now. I'll be right here waitin'. Keep them blue-bellies off of us."

Jasper yells, "We'll blow 'em all to hell and back, big brother."

Young men boast, and so many die before their time. I look out over the river at the Yankee fleet—death waiting to pounce like an owl on a cotton mouse. I don't care if Jasper and James fight Yanks. I just want them back here, close, alive, where I can watch over them. I know that's the Lord's job, not mine. Truth be told, I'm the one needing him to watch over me.

Prentiss House, Vicksburg,
March 1, 1863

Dearest Ma, it's been a while since I wrote. We've been busy with the Yanks comin back. Good news is I have escaped the pox and other diseases. Pray we escape the shells and bullets. Jasper and James left for Grenada to meet the Yankee foe. I sent them off with a prayer. There'll be some heavy fightin soon, but worry not for sons who love the Lord. The Yanks send shells into the city all day. We don't sleep well. I'm still in the hotel by the river. We're ready if the Yanks try us here and will pay dearly if they do. I have bad news. My wife of just a few short months died. Measles took her life. I'm heart broke. That's all I can say right now. Pray for me about that.

Tell Elihu, Mary, and Emaline hello. Here's half my pay to help out on the farm. I miss you Ma and hope to be restored to you one day.

Your affectionate son,
Lummy

CHAPTER 22

PAYING THE BIG PRICE

MARCH 6, 1863

The only good thing about payin' the big price is you only have to pay it once.

T HE WEATHER CHANGED to frosty overnight, and I have the shivers. It's not as cold as the chills creeping down my spine at the spectacle I'm not looking forward to later this morning.

The Yanks must be happy the cottonmouths retreated back into their dens. It's the big blue snake creeping toward us that has our attention, except one of the boys at Four Mile Bridge had an encounter with a rather large rattlesnake.

Day before yesterday it was so hot we had to strip down to our drawers to sleep. Granville complained that his company did the same at Four Mile Bridge taking turns at picket and sleeping. They slept in tents because the cabins sequestered from the Negroes were full. Sequester. Just another word for stealing what belongs to another. Anyway, Granville took his turn at picket relieving Pete Lipscomb, who they simply call Lip. Granville had the midnight to 6:00 a.m. watch.

Granville laughs. "I noticed Lip rolled around and mumblin' about somethin'. He got up rubbin' his back sayin' it was the worst night's sleep he ever had. Said it was like a tree root sprouted underneath him in the middle of the night. Everywhere he moved, the root followed him. Said he checked for roots before he spread the tarp on the ground."

Granville digs in his pocket. "Y'all ain't gonna like this part. Lip pulled back the tarp to see what ruined his sleep and you know what he found?" Granville pulls out a broken rattle with seven buttons from a rattlesnake.

I take it from him. "Lemme see that thing." I ain't afraid of snakes, but I've got a real healthy respect for them. I shudder, thinking about how large that snake must've been.

"Lip said he'd move and that ole tree root would be under him when he woke up. Guess that ole rattler found him a warm spot under ole tater belly Lip." I hand the rattle to Hog Fart, who stares at it like it's the devil himself.

"Not me. I ain't touchin' nothin' to do with no snake. Oh, hell no. Besides, my grandpappy said the dust off that rattle will blind you."

I shove it towards him. "Tell the truth and shame the devil. Why you crawfishin'? Can't get bit by a rattle."

"Keep it away, dammit. It might not bite, but my Pappy said the smell will bring another."

I pitch the rattle back to Granville. "Do tell." After Granville leaves, I casually saunter down to the river to scrub my hands in the muddy water. I'm takin' no chances.

J.A. steps out on the balcony of the Prentiss House. "Ain't scared of snakes, you say? Get your ass on up here. Sarge said we gotta put on uniforms for dress parade." It's the spectacle I had hoped was called off. We gather in front of the Prentiss House at the sound of a bugler.

Sarge holds his hat over his chest. "Men, it's a sad day. A young feller deserted from the 1st Looseana Heavy Artillery. They found him wearin' a Yank uniform. Get your hearts set. You have to watch this man die."

Today, I'm ordered to witness a scene I wish I'd never be forced to endure. We march past the train depot to a clearing at the edge of town and line up so all have an unobstructed view.

A firing squad marches in a weeping boy in a Yank uniform with a sign hung around his neck that reads, *I Deserted My Country.* They push him hard against a post. Before they tie his hands behind him, he dries his eyes and stiffens up straight. They try to blindfold him, but he refuses. A last effort at courage, I reckon.

Men who know him sob. Older men cry because he's so young. My heart aches for life needlessly taken. I want to scream, "Just whip him and let him go." The brass can't let it go. They won't. They can't.

The determination of the military court is read by his captain. "This man knowingly, willingly placed himself into harm's way by deserting his family, his regiment, the defense of Vicksburg, his country, and his God by breaking his vow to serve in this army. His punishment is death. Let it be a lesson for all. May God have mercy on his soul."

The captain asks, "Any last words, deserter?"

He stares into the eyes of his former comrades and then up into the sky. "Lord, I left the gray suit for the blue 'cause fightin' to keep people as chattel ain't what Jesus would do. Set 'em free, Lord. I'll see you directly." He lowers his head and looks straight at the general. "I got a clean conscience to meet my Maker, do you?"

The general presiding owns slaves and treats the ones he brought along worse than animals. The general doesn't blink. I shudder like when I heard the story about the rattler under Lip's tent.

This man is dying for his convictions. I should be standing with him for the thoughts I've had lately. The lieutenant readies the men chosen by lot. They aim. Just before giving the command, he looks at the general as a last chance for a pardon. None is given. The general stares at the prisoner without compassion. I don't want to be in his shoes when he faces the Lord one day.

I've never witnessed anything like this before. Pa took us to a hanging once. He told Ma, who was against it, "It'll keep 'em from doin' somethin' to deserve it."

This is different, though. Those men were hanged for raping and killing a young girl outside Bucksnort. They yelled and kicked, cursed and pleaded. But to no avail. They deserved to die. This young man has good reason to stand so solemn, steady in the courage of our Savior, willing to face the muskets. With such resolve, those bullets might just veer off, and he won't die.

The lieutenant barks, *"Fire!"* The bullets strike him hard in the chest. He slumps over and dies. A little of me dies with him. When we break ranks, young Granville pulls me aside.

"Lummy, thanks for keepin' me from runnning off. That boy's eyes scared me. He was set for what was comin', but his knees trembled somethin' fierce. That could've been me."

I look around to see who is listening. "I told you nothin' you don't already know. I just held you to it, that's all. But I'll say this, and then I'll leave it alone. No doubt that boy had a good reason for puttin' on the blue suit. I just hope it was worth dyin' for. If you gonna make a hard decision like that, you best make sure it's the right one. There are two prices to pay in this war. One is for the Cause and the other for doin' what you think is right when nobody else understands. Think on it. We'll talk again later."

The execution weighs heavy on my mind. Why did he exchange his gray suit for blue? I've had similar thoughts but not his courage to do it. I'm ashamed.

THE WEATHER WARMS, and the woods turn green. Sunshine brings our hearts back around. After that rattler story, I watch out for snakes everywhere I go.

March 20th, the gunboats edge closer. Hearing little from Winn Parish makes me think the worst for friends who have family there. Some worry more about rising floodwaters, livestock drowning, and their families having nowhere to go than to the Yankees. Some receive letters like I did on New Year's Day. If I survive what's coming, maybe I'll try to gather up the pieces with Mr. Gilmore and Ben. Right now, I walk with the depressed. I walk by the river, take off my shirt, and soak in the last bit of sunshine. My soul is low.

THE RISING RIVER and smallpox ourtbreak forces Grant to give up his canal project. I'm sure the Yank troops and Negroes are glad to leave the mud, mosquitoes, and swamp water. He tries other bayous and rivers to get his army in position for his attack on Vicksburg.

Admiral Porter, Grant's gunboat man, attempts to get by our river batteries March 25th. They float smoothly across the waters like a wedding processional. Pickets on the bluff tops fire warning shots, and when the gunboats come even with the shore batteries, fireworks erupt. Major Ogden's battery sinks the ironclad *Switzerland,* and another is rendered useless.

As the *Switzerland* sinks, men jump overboard. Some drown. Others jump into skiffs to escape. Ogden bears down on one of the small boats with his Columbiads and blows it to high heaven. We let out a great cheer.

Johnny Bond runs up, shaking his fist. "You ain't never gonna take this place, damn you. Send more, and we'll send them to the bottom of the river." The whiner comes alive.

Young Granville grabs me around the chest from behind. We fall on the ground happy for the victory. He's in much better spirits now, talking about pretty girls and how he wants to kiss one.

Grant's diversions don't work very well. We hear that my brothers and the 1st Mississippi Light Artillery gave the Yanks hell at Fort Pemberton earlier this month, hiding behind cotton bales covered with dirt with carefully placed cannons where no ground forces could attack. Colonel Marks says it's the only time the U.S. Navy has been defeated by a land force.

I crow like a rooster in the chicken yard when I hear the news. "And dang it if my brothers weren't there holdin' the fort." I just hope they survived.

J.A. pushes my shoulder. "You Tullos boys are sure proud of each other, ain't you?"

"Damn straight!"

CLOTHING HAS BECOME a valued item, and most of the men's clothes are worse for wear. The good ladies across the river in Louisiana sneak in clothes, but some of the regiments are issued white uniforms made of wool. It's all the ladies had to sew together. The men hate them.

J.A. whispers as the 26th Louisiana marches by with disgusted looks, daring anyone to say a word, "Da-a-amn, they look like the conscripts brought up after we volunteered."

A smart mouth from the 46th Mississippi yells, hiding behind a shack, "Lily white church goin' angel boys! How you feel 'bout wearin' slave clothes?"

A sergeant with the 26th Louisiana barks back. "Better white than a damned yeller streak painted down your sistuh boy back. Come with us, and we'll drown your ass in the same brown muddy ditch we're gonna dye these in, you bastard." Nobody says anything else. When those men get their uniforms back on after they dry, the officers call them butternuts.

THE NIGHT OF April 16th finds me on duty down on the levee. I listen, walk a bit, check with the next soldier on the line, turn, and make my way to the soldier in the other direction. I've done this too many times. It's boring, until tonight. I throw a rock at J.A. dozing at his post.

"I hear splashin', do you?"

He quietly runs over, musket in hand. "Yeah, sounds like water splashin' against wood." The dark shadows loom large as the current brings the boats closer to our position.

Corporal Nelson of Company K yells, "Here they come. Light the fires."

J.A. and I rush to the water's edge with others assigned to light barrels of pitch. They flame up quick as a match strike. A few pickets dash over to DeSoto and fire the houses.

Nelson screams, "Porter's whole gunboat navy is runnin' the gauntlet. Give 'em hell, boys."

The sky lights up like daytime as fire and shot rain down from the batteries atop the bluffs and in front of Vicksburg. We steadily fire our muskets at anything moving on the decks. They're so close we can read the gunboat names.

J.A. yells, "You ain't sneakin' past us Looseana boys, damn you!"

A sailor on the *Henry Clay* throws water on a fire creeping up the side of the armor plating. I follow him with my musket. He stops, turns around, and looks me dead in the eye with the most frightened look I've ever seen. He's so caught up putting out the fire he forgets he's being shot at. He jerks a pistol, but I fire first. He tumbles into the river.

It seems like thirty minutes, but the battle is three hours of non-stop cannonading and sharp shooting. Their boats make it through the gauntlet, but they pay the price. The *Benton, Lafayette, General Price, Carondelet, Pittsburg,* and others pass that we couldn't see the names, besides coal barges—they all got hit, many times.

The *Henry Clay?* She paid the biggest price. She lies at the bottom of the river. So did another, but we didn't get the name before she went down. One transport drifts downriver, burning as it goes. The cotton bales and logs Porter's men lashed to the sides of their boats for protection against our batteries didn't work. Cotton burns hotter than hell.

Now that the duel is over, I want to give that sailor back his life. I don't want to look, but I have to. He drifted fifty feet from where I stand. I feel terrible killing him. But it was his life or mine, and I won't hand mine over so easy. I probably saved him from a more horrible death of burning or drowning when the boat sunk. That doesn't make it any easier.

Sarge hustles down the line checking on us. "You done good, Lummy. You saw the elephant tonight but didn't pay the price. Did your duty and made them damn Yanks pay. You did that man no favors, but you did for us. Good work." He pats me on the shoulder.

"We lose anybody, Sarge?" He doesn't hear me.

J.A. hangs his head. "Remember old man Elsey from K Company? He played dominoes with us durin' the smallpox outbreak."

"Wasn't he a little deaf?"

"Yeah, he didn't hear a picket guard during the fight yell halt, and Elsey got it in the chest. And the damnable misery of it all? He was already discharged to go home in two days."

I shake my head and moan. "I liked that old man. Shot dead by one of your own. I hate it, dammit, I just hate it."

Sarge comes back by. "What's that soldier? You hate what?" I say nothing. J.A. whispers to Sarge about Ole Man Elsey getting killed.

"Oh, him and Lummy was friends, weren't they?" J.A. nods.

Sarge rubs his chin. "Try not to take it too hard, son. Go down the bank and fish out the Yank you shot off the *Henry Clay.* Take his belt buckle. Keep it to remind you why Ole Man Elsey died." Sarge is trying to console me the best way he knows how, but it ain't working.

"Yassuh, headed that way right now, Sarge."

He leaves me alone.

I walk to the river's edge where debris washes up on the muddy shore. The sailor I killed bobs facedown in the ripples. I pull his body up the bank. Sarge watches my every move. He's genuinely concerned about me despite all the grief he dishes out on us.

The sailor is about my age. When I pull his belt off to take the buckle, I notice he has a wedding ring on. I check his pockets to find an oiled leather billfold. Inside are letters from his wife and a tintype of her and their two little boys. The letters are damp but readable. I remove the ring, check for anything else of value, finding a few coins and a pocketknife. I carefully wrap it all in my sweat cloth and put it in my haversack. I remove the buckle. I keep the belt.

"I know what you're doin', but I ain't sure it'll help, son. If you want to get those things to his family, I'll pull some strings for you." I nod. "First time killin' a man?"

"Nawsuh, but this is the first time I looked into a man's eyes as I shot him. Seein' his family in the picture, it's like I could've known him." We're both silent for a moment. "Damn the Union gunboats and Porter, too. This man paid the biggest price of all."

"So did Private James Elsey. Only good thing about paying the big price is you only gotta do it once." Sarge squeezes the back of my shoulder like a vise.

"I feel lower'n a snake's belly in a wagon rut, Sarge."

He looks up into the sky. "Believe me, son, I know the feelin'."

He walks on. I cry.

Prentiss House Hotel, Vicksburg,
April 17, 1862

Dearest Ma, the weather has warmed. It's good to see things turn green. I pray the farm does good this year. Will Elihu plant corn? Don't plant cotton. Either we burn it, or the Yanks steal it. Grow food Ma. You can't go wrong doin that. We had a terrible fight here last night. We sunk some boats and burnt others. Ma, I don't like telling this, but I've shot two men. I feel so bad about it. Man wasn't created to kill other men. Cain should never have killed Abel. The killin has gone on for too long. My heart breaks for them. God forgive me. Pray my heart doesn't turn to stone. I have to go to work cleanin up after the battle, so I have to make this short. I hope this five dollars helps. I will write again.

Your son,
Lummy

BESIDES OLD ELSEY, two artillery men die when a shell explodes prematurely as the shooting started. The train depot is set on fire, and one shell kills seven mules nearby with one shot. We took a beating this night. Thankfully, we move up behind Sky Parlor Hill in case another gunboat barrage comes raining down on us. We need the rest from the constant bombardment and sharpshooting. The officers know rest is just what the 27th needs. We do miss our hotel accommodations, though.

I roll over on my back, staring out into the darkness. I close my eyes. All I can see is the surprised look in the sailor's eyes the moment I shot him. My eyes are shut so I can rest to fight another day. His eyes are shut so he can rest never to fight another day. There's peace in that, somewhere.

For him, that is.

CHAPTER 23

THE SECOND DIVERSION DID WORK

MAY 1, 1863

It ain't all bad, gettin' fooled.

W E WORRY ABOUT the Yankee threat to the Red River region. Little is heard from our families, and we wonder if the Yanks control the area. If so, it could cause plenty of good and loyal men to desert.

Our officers keep us busy improving the earthworks, and in our free time two West Pointers teach us to play a game with a ball and stick. It's good for morale at a time when we're uncertain about what lies ahead in this war. Also, Capt. Norwood of Company A left for Mobile to bring back a band for the 27th Louisiana Regiment. He hopes it'll cheer us up. He asked Granville to play an instrument upon his return.

"I can learn good as anybody. What do you think?"

I laugh. "You can do anything you put a mind to, son." Granville's gonna make it.

Grant tries everything possible to lure our forces out of the defenses, but he just can't do it. He sends Sherman to fake an attack on Haines Bluff, just north of the city. General Pemberton orders the 27th and the other regiments to guard the city if Sherman breaks through. So we wait, and rumors continue to fly like a flock of scared birds escaping a storm.

Yankee Colonel Benjamin Grierson's cavalry sweeps down from Tennessee through middle Mississippi destroying depots, telegraph lines, and railroad tracks. General Forrest takes off after him, but Grierson's three regiments are reported to be everywhere at once. He destroys Newton Station with all its ordinance and supplies slated for Vicksburg.

Sarge curses, "Damn, I guess Grant has his revenge for Van Dorn's raid on his supply depot in Holly Springs last year." I just hope he steers clear of Choctaw County.

Things don't look good, and the fighting hasn't even started yet. Grierson pulls Pemberton's eyes and ears away from Grant's real plan. It works. Sarge overheard the brass saying we're blind as bats because our cavalry runs all over the countryside but sends few reports of the enemy's location. Our spies report Grant wants to cross the river south of Vicksburg. So we wait.

IT'S MAY 4TH, and I've been in Vicksburg a full year. With the pressure of the upcoming contest, our officers snap at us, overwork us, feed us less, and give little praise. It's too much tension for men pent up like hunting dogs. Edgy men want to fight—even if it means fighting each other. The Yanks are coming, and the 27th Louisiana may be the first to meet the blue-bellies when they arrive. That's all right. We're loaded, toughened by all the hard work, and can find the necessary rage when it comes time to defend the city—better to direct rage at the enemy than each other. We try not to lose our heads waiting.

Scouts report a large Union force marching south on the west bank to Hard Times, Louisiana. They watched Union gunboats bombard the Grand Gulf fort "like God rainin' down fire and brimstone on Sodom and Gomorrah." They report a large buildup of troops and barges to ferry them to our side of the river.

The diversions work. While we're gallantly holding the line against an attack from Sherman that never comes, Grant crosses the Mississippi at Bruinsburg with 24,000 men. They do it without a shot fired. I bet it makes that whiskey drinking, cigar smoking general happy. He may be happy now, but the 27th is ready for a fight when Grant turns this way. It ain't all bad gettin' tricked. We're still alive because of it, at least for now. And we wait.

PEMBERTON SENDS MOST of our regiments to meet the Yanks at the Big Black. But that's not where Grant goes. The Yanks hot foot it east to strike Jackson. It will look good in the Yankee papers if another Confederate capitol city is captured. Raymond falls. Then Clinton is taken. And now Jackson is securely in Union hands. In two short weeks, the tide turns and doesn't favor the gray. Soon the big blue snake will turn our way and try to swallow us whole.

The wounded and doctors tell us the Yanks are close. My heart aches to see the wounded limp using rifles as crutches. The cries of those suffering under the surgeon's knife and saw are unnerving. I'm angry at the waste of good men for worthless causes.

One soldier, ordered to destroy supplies hid when the Yanks raced into Jackson, tells us, "A kid in a fancy dress uniform ran to the capitol building to take the Confederate flag waving on top of the dome, but an officer beat him to it. The boy was quite upset. When they raised the Yank flag, the boy embraced Grant standing on the capitol steps. What a catch that'd been! Takin' Grant's son prisoner would sure make his momma mad."

The Yanks come our way. I hope General Johnston will hit them hard now their butts are exposed. Grant's not stupid. He'll protect his rear. They're coming to Vicksburg, and we're the welcoming committee to receive guests. It'll be a cold reception.

The Yanks move swiftly like a cottonmouth after a frog. I once watched a snake squirm about, having fun with its captured prey. Suddenly, the frog leaped six feet in the air. I've never seen a snake move so fast. I heard a tiny peep and then silence. Is my namesake, Nathan the prophet, coming out? Is our army a frog escaping just to get caught again in a death grip here?

The wounded trickle in telling of a terrible battle on Champion Hill. They say we were champions for a moment, but the blue storm pushed through. Grant keeps up the chase, and General Pemberton throws up a wall at the Big Black. That too fell apart. The snake nears its prized prey, but Grant will get more than a peep out of this frog.

Wagons and beaten soldiers steadily stream into our lines, and the Yankees aren't far behind. I just want to do something. Anything. We all do. But holding this line at the edge of the city is our job. So we stay put.

The sun rises like any day today, May 18th, but the call comes. We rush forward to protect men driving cattle up from the Yazoo bottoms into town. Pemberton stockpiles as much food as he can. The growing stream of defeated and distraught men dragging back into the city makes herding the cattle a problem. No one says anything to them.

Once the cattle get into the city, Colonel Marks marches us to the 27th Louisiana Lunette. We're a half mile east with the city behind us. We take position in the breastworks ready to meet whatever comes down the Graveyard Road. Graveyard Road? Am I guarding my own grave?

We expect the blue snake to pour over the hills any minute like a busted Mississippi River levee—unstoppable. Colonel Marks announces, "Men, the 27th Louisiana Lunette just may be the best damn fortification in the whole ring of Vicksburg defenses!"

J.A. yells, "It ought to be, we built it!"

Marks laughs with us. "Damn straight you did! Keep a sharp eye and your muskets ready!"

J.A. elbows me. "Damn, if we ain't ready for this fight...."

Marks turns. "What in the hell is that?"

A crazy-eyed soldier with his hat blowing off races down Graveyard Road riding a light grey horse like a bat out of hell. "Yanks are comin'! Yanks are comin'!"

Hog Fart wets his pants. "I'm scared, Lummy don't tell nobody."

As men crowd around the messenger, I push Hog Fart down. "Roll around and cover your pants with mud. Nobody'll know the difference."

J.A. watches. "Lummy, you're a damn good big brother, that's all I can say."

General Shoup quickly calms the man down, asking which Yankee regiment is in front of the 27th Louisiana. The rider falls off his horse, but the men catch him. Someone brings him a dipper of cool water, and he points back down Graveyard Road.

"They're comin'. The whole damn Union Army. I was leadin' the 29th

Louisiana to that there hill when a bullet whistled by my head. I stood up in my stirrups and hollered out, 'What the hell are you shootin' at?' Then it was like a whole company of Yanks laid down fire on me. I hauled ass down the hill and advised Colonel Thomas to spread out skirmishers. They were only eighty yards away." The man catches his breath. "It looks to be Sherman comin' up, General, suh, and they'll be here directly."

Shoup sends the rider to report that valuable piece of information to Generals Smith and Pemberton. The low rumble of the blue army sounds like hog killing day, only we're the hogs squealing knowing the butcher's knife comes for us. There's a mass scramble. Men pour in to fill the rifle pits. J.A., Isham, Hog Fart, and I stand shoulder to shoulder in the 27th Louisiana Lunette.

The big blue snake has come to get its frog.

Hog Fart shakes like he has the death chills. I check his rifle for a percussion cap. He hasn't put one on, but the hammer is cocked back. I take one from my pouch and seat it on the nipple. He smiles through dirt-stained tears. I fear for him. I'm shaky myself but don't let it show.

I elbow him. "You'll be all right." We stand ready, muskets trained on the hills before us. I line my sights on a bluecoat squatting on a hill in front of us. I touch the trigger.

Sarge whispers, "Want to try it?"

"I dunno, Sarge. Looks to be a couple hundred yards."

J.A. elbows me. "Go on, Lummy, take his head off."

I narrow my focus, tune out the world around me, make small the target, and squeeze. I wave at the powder smoke. "What happened? I can't see a thing."

Sarge pats me on the shoulder. "Sorry son, but you missed him." Everyone laughs. "But you took the hat right off his damn head! Flew ten feet up in the air! He ran like a cottontail scared out of a burnin' brush pile!"

J.A. slaps my back. "He ran holdin' his britches up in the back. He shit all over himself."

We laugh hard, and men keep congratulating me.

Sarge finally stops laughing with tears rolling down his cheeks. "What a way to start a battle. Damn, ain't never seen nothin' like it."

I joke it off. "Must've aimed a hair too high." I'm glad I didn't kill the man. I'll have plenty opportunities soon enough.

Wheels roar down the line behind us like thunder. Eight men pull a cannon with straps on their shoulders like oxen. They move fast as lightning.

My heart leaps. "It can't be!"

J.A. whispers, "What?"

I grab a strap before my brother Jasper sees me. He huffs and puffs like a steam engine.

"Thank you, friend, I'm just about give out."

"You would be, you lazy, no good sack a horse shit."

"Lummy, that you? You're stationed here?"

"Right here in the 27th Looseana Lunette. James?"

"Over there, big brother. Damn good to see you."

I squeeze his shoulder. "Glad you boys are here. When you get settled, I want to hear all about Fort Pemberton."

James bear hugs me from behind. "Lummy, we beat the britches off of 'em."

Jasper pulls James by his jacket sleeve. "We will, Lummy. Right now we gotta get back. Company C is stationed just across Glass Bayou this side of the 3rd Looseana boys. We'll be back to get this one situated directly."

Colonel Marks sends out flanking skirmishers two hundred yards to meet the Yanks. A few picket shots are fired, but no assault comes.

Sarge chews a straw while staring at the Yanks. "With no more men than we got here, why don't Sherman attack? He could just waltz right into Vicksburg to the tune of "Yankee Doodle," and we couldn't stop him. With all the tricks the Yanks tried gettin' into Vicksburg and not take advantage of our weakness? Don't make no sense."

J.A spits. "Hell, he's so scared he's pissed his britches and havin' to change 'em." The whole company laughs.

Sarge yells, "Shut the hell up, and eyes to the front." He winks. "But that was funny, J.A."

In a half hour, Jasper and James return with six other men. We help them settle the gun on a level defensive position with a good field of fire in all directions. I'm glad my brothers are here. I can keep an eye on them.

We work all day and long into the night improving the earthworks. The heavy work was done earlier, but anything we can do to make the defenses better helps.

The 27th Louisiana Lunette lies west of the Stockade Redan and east of the Graveyard Road to block Sherman's approach. A lunette is a five point shaped star the engineers call a pentagon with a deep ditch in front and a wall made of timbers set some seven to nine feet high. The dirt from the ditch forms the parapet and the chest-high rifle pits we stand behind now. The lunette and the redan have artillery pieces capable of throwing large amounts of grapeshot and shell when the enemy advances.

We finally rest about midnight, exhausted. A lone shot is fired here and there, but no one comes. I have one envelope left, so I write Ma by firelight. Don't know if it'll get to her, but I do it for my sake. It might be my last.

Vicksburg,
May 18, 1863

Dearest Mother, flowers bloom everywhere, and you know I like honeysuckle the best. I pray all is well at home and the men left behind in this struggle are gracious to help get the crop planted. Are the Wood boys helpin?

We expect serious trouble soon. Grant took Jackson and burned most of it. It was such a lovely city. I remember travelin there for the big Independence Day celebration back in '54, fireworks and all. It was quite a different kind of fireworks there four days ago.

Ma, the Yanks are just over the hill. There'll be a big fight tomorrow. We hope General Johnston will come soon. Jasper and James are just down the way and set their cannon not far from my spot on the line. I feel better with my little brothers here. You must believe that we all will come home from this terrible mess.

I pray for you, the family, and George, wherever he may be. Please tell all hello for me. Jasper and James send their affections. I wrote a little song thinkin about you the other day. I have a little tune to sing it by, but I guess that'll have to wait til this is over. I hope you like it.

Ma's Song

No one knows, the love of my mother, she cares so much for me.

She knows my heart, and though we live apart,

She prays every day that I walk in the Way.

Through thick and thin, when I leave and come again, her love never fails, she waits.

She knows my heart, and though we live apart,

She prays every day that I walk in His Way.

No one knows, the love of my mother, she cares so much for me.

Your son,

Lummy Tullos

Muskets bark in the silent dark. I sing my song to Ma. There'll be little sleep tonight.

CHAPTER 24

THE ATTACK

MAY 19, 1863

And blood dripped like soft falling rain.

T HE MORNING IS unseasonably cool but appreciated. It'll heat up soon enough and have nothing to do with the weather. We stand at our stations along the line at the crack of dawn. The barrage on our earthworks begins promptly at 10:00 a.m. and doesn't let up until noon. It's the worst shelling yet. We hunker down, but it's hard not to take a peek at the mass of cannons firing from the hills in front of us.

Sarge yells, "Anybody dumb enough to stick his head up, if a ball don't get you, I'll shoot you myself." No one says anything. We simply obey.

By 1:00 p.m., the heavy smoke clears just enough to see the wide blue lines marching our way. Yank sharp shooters and skirmishers break for cover when the 26th Louisiana fires a volley. Then all is quiet. A mockingbird sings. It's the last best sound of the day.

The Yanks make their way through gullies and hollows, crossing the small spring-fed ditches before forming up into a single unbroken line six men deep. The blue snake looks invincible, almost frightening. Almost.

Young boys whimper, but Sarge shores them up. "You better shoot when the command to fire is given. There's too many blue-bellies to cry for your momma now. Bow your necks and be men. Fight for your mommas back home, for the man next to you."

At 2:00 p.m., the Yank cannons fire three volleys in the fury of a spring tornado. The barrage does little more than stir up dust to blind us. That's the signal. The blue line comes at us without resignation. They're banking on recent successes at Champion Hill and Big Black River. Muskets gleam bright in the burning sun as company colors fly proudly over brave men who want to plant those flags atop our parapets. They don't know the resolve of our men.

The front lines take the brunt of grapeshot, our cannons are belching without mercy, devouring huge gaps in the blue snake with each blast. The blue wave pushes hard up the hill under the cover of dust clouds. Men stumble and crawl over abatis—fallen trees laid in rows, sharpened limbs laced with telegraph wire to slow their progress. Their lines break up when they have to squeeze between the barriers. They slip and slide in the very dirt their cannons made into baking flour like powder. Not a single musket shot is fired from our lines.

A Yank sergeant yells, "C'mon boys, they done run off. I can't see a single head pokin' up."

We wait an eternity of fearful patience.

Down the line, Sarge whispers, "We'll shoot when we smell their stinkin' Yankee breath and can count their nose hairs."

The men next to me, J.A. and Isham, Hog Fart, and even Sarge, fidget as the blue line winds through gullies over fallen timbers through scattered brush to within seventy yards of our position. I swallow hard. Hog Fart leans his rifle against the earthworks, drops to his knees, and twitters around like a nuthatch on a shagbark hickory. The fear of death is in his eyes.

He rises to shoot. "They're too damned close."

I grab his shoulder to keep him from spoiling the plan. "Give it one more minute, boy."

He nods with tears rolling down his cheeks. "They ain't scared. They beat the hell out of our boys since they crossed the Missip, and they mean to run us over."

"Say another word, and I'll swat you like a fly."

Blue sharpshooter's bullets whistle overhead. The blue snake rumbles up the hill to the Lunette, but no one moves. Our cannons rip holes in their lines, killing twenty or more men in a swath. The gaps are filled in seconds with more bluecoats. I want to raise my head to see Jasper and James. I don't dare, but their cannons across the gully fire as furiously as ours do here.

The Yanks march the double-quick step with glistening musket bayonets high and banners higher. They make a mad rush, but we stand still. A lone sentinel peers through a sharpshooter's peephole. He lifts his hand for us to rise, and we throw our muskets across the top of the earthworks. A thousand heads rise as one man to aim a thousand rifles at the advancing blue line. We level down a concerted flash blasting the struggling Yankees with the weight of a sledge mall on a wedge to split a stump—heavy and hard.

It must look like a belching volcano of fire to Sherman and his staff watching from the hills in front of us. The smoke burns my eyes and chokes my throat. I cough but send my ramrod down the barrel to seat a bullet for another shot. I put the cap on quickly, and my Enfield is ready to shoot in seconds. The Yanks are cut down like a scythe cutting hay.

Thousands of men in blue have encircled our defenses. Sounds of this assault come from every direction. There are only six roads into Vicksburg with one railway all heavily fortified with redans, lunettes, cannons, and long lines of rifle pits. Ravines and deep gullies flank their narrow pathways. The Yanks must approach us on our ground we know all too well. Our 31,000 man army will make the blue snake wish it returned to its northern den.

The Yankee lines stall in the continuous fire. They buckle like the knees of a boxer knocked silly by his opponent. The firing is appalling, and the destruction is fierce. Men fall everywhere like so many toy soldiers knocked down by rocks thrown by young boys. They fall like cornstalks cut down after harvest. Their solid lines give way to pandemonium—some men trying to take the earthworks and others just trying to survive.

I see their faces—wrenching, struggling, and fumbling to make it up the hill. Two men try to establish a foothold. Every time a clump of blue gathers with any sort of effectiveness, one of our boys launches a grenade that scatters them—whole bodies or in many parts.

It's worse than the blood, guts, and skinning at hog killing. That day in Winnfield with Old Bart flashes before my eyes. The screams of the wounded and dying remind me of the squealing pigs herded into town that morning. The hogs seemed to know it was their time. These men do, too.

I call on my anger to make this fight bearable. Bearable becomes survival. They just keep coming, Ohio farm boys and ridge runners from West Virginia—some too young to shave, others have gray in their beards. They're hardened men who've seen action at Corinth, Shiloh, or on the road from Bruinsburg here.

Hog Fart ducks. "Look out! They throwed my grenade back over."

A blast burns my face, scaring the daylights out of me. We're stunned from the force of the explosion. Some men bleed from shrapnel in their backs and buttocks. I can't hear anything. I shake my head and help the other men get up.

Five bluecoats surge over the dirt bank and kill three of our men before we can get our senses. We fly into them. They're tough men, and I respect them. But I want to live. More Yanks press through a small breach, but we push back. A soldier near me falls into mud with a bayonet lodged in his ribs a Yank can't pull out. I hack at the bluecoat with the knife Pa made me like a farmer chopping vines. They both go down. A Yank grabs my arm, but my pistol blows a hole in his neck just below the chin.

A loud whistle knocks me against the back wall of the rifle pit. I feel a terrible pain in my chest. "Susannah, I'll see you soon." I'm dizzy and dazed, expecting to die any second.

Isham falls from the parapet where sabers slash and short swords clang, pistols fire and men club with rifle butts. It all grows quiet except for Isham laughing almost hysterically with relief.

He slaps my shoulder. "It's over, Lummy. They're goin' back down the hill!"

"I ought to be hearing angels sing about now."

J.A. jumps down from the parapet. "Get up. They may come back." He jerks me up by my jacket collar, and I sit up. I check my body. No blood. I'm happy but shocked. And then I find it. That dang Yankee minie ball struck me square on a button over my heart. The letter "I" for Infantry on the button isn't recognizable anymore. I open my shirt, and there's an apple-sized mark turning purple fast.

"That'll be black tomorrow." J.A. laughs.

"Thank God for brass buttons." I find the bullet flattened at the nose. "This was meant for me. Thank you, Lord."

I put it my pocket, feeling for the Yank belt buckle, gator tooth, and brass cannons. I don't believe in luck, but charms remind me of times the Lord spared me.

All falls quiet, and the silence of a tomb and the stillness of the grave surrounds us. It unnerves some of the men. No cannons, no sharpshooting, no screams, no rebel yells. No noise. An occasional groan rises up from both sides like animals licking their wounds. I guess the Reaper has that effect on people. I lean on the rifle pit and faint away for a minute.

I awake to Isham whispering, "Get up, boy. They're tryin' to slip up on us. Get your smoke pole ready." I ready my rifle and thank the Good Lord I'm still alive.

It's times like this you either believe God is real or he ain't. "Lord, forgive my thoughts and my deeds not of you. Forgive the anger I'm about to display before you. Forgive me, Lord, I'm about to kill human beings you created in your image."

Isham leans over. "Good words, Lummy. I claim that prayer with you. Here they come."

Crows flock everywhere, not to watch the battle but to wait for the feast soon to follow. I cock my rifle and find a button on the chest of a blue jacket.

"Forgive me, Lord." I pull the trigger with hundreds of other grays and butternuts. Smoke blinds us for a minute, but the blue snake squirms like it fell into a fire pit. They come at us in a storm of smoke and lead. The second volley doesn't stop them, either.

Smoke burns our eyes as the wounded scream and cry. I grow weary on the line. I'm no quitter. I'm tired and hungry, weather beaten and mosquito eaten. I keep loading and firing, and then I see them.

Some Ohio boys lay quiet as others charge. Over the top they hurl themselves in a screaming frenzy like demons hell bent on devastation. I fire my pistol point blank into the face of a captain whose head splits like a ripe melon. The Yanks grab for me, one stabbing at me with his bayonet. I'm alone on the parapet for just a moment when an awe-inspiring guttural rebel yell wreaks fear in the faces of the Yanks.

The boys behind me rush forward, pushing hard to throw the Yanks back over the embankment. I'm caught in the middle, shoved face to face with a big Yank whose breath stinks of bad coffee and moldy hardtack. For a second, all stops. The equal force from both sides presses me and the Yank together so close we can't move our arms or legs.

We're lifted off the ground with feet dangling underneath. We both look down and then up into each other's eyes. We grin like two schoolboys at the comedy of it all, forgetting we're enemies for a moment. Then the light goes out of his eyes. A ball enters the left side of his head and exits the right clean as a whistle. His stare is one of disbelief. His last mumbled words are "I don't deserve this."

His look strikes me as if that same bullet had struck me square in the heart. That feeling disappears as the rebel yell boils loud and forces the wad of mangled blue men over the edge and into the ditch in front of the 27th Lunette. I grasp at my comrades, and they hang on to my belt. I slip in the bloody mud, dodging sabers and a grenade exploding nearby.

I fall into the pit in front of the lunette with the Yanks.

The attack stops, and the Yanks pile up unable to climb into the lunette. Here I am, in this pit filled with dying men like a dungeon of writhing snakes. Some even hiss and can still give a death blow. I lie still, hoping the bluecoats think I'm dead. The battle rages over me, black brogans stepping on my chest, head, and legs as the Yanks try again. I pull a bluecoat over me when no one's looking to avoid grenade shrapnel.

Lying with death all around, slowly moving in the dark smoky pit, I conjure up the memory when Hiram, Poole, and I skipped school one cool early March day to shoot gar fish spawning in the creek. I'd taken my turn with the squirrel gun, killing four or five. It's easy to do when they're all bunched up like that. We'd heard they didn't taste bad once you got past the greasiness of the meat. So we gave them a try. I laid the meat on a flat rock in the middle of the fire and went to look for deer tracks.

It was cool but not so that we couldn't take off our shirts and shoes to keep them clean. We didn't want any mud as evidence of our playing hooky. I stood in the shade of several tall oaks on a small mound with a number of holes in the ground. The clouds parted, and the sun broke through the trees. The woods brightened like turning a coal oil lamp on in a dark room, and the sun warmed the air. The rays felt good on my face, chest, and back.

I closed my eyes, enjoying the slight breeze, when I heard a slight rustle in the leaves. Inching its way between my bare feet was a cottonmouth. It was too cold to move fast. I froze like a dead man in a coffin. I shuddered like a man with the malaria shakes.

Fortunately, his flicking tongue didn't find me. I breathed a sigh of relief until I heard hissing. I'd stumbled onto a cottonmouth winter den. I couldn't run and didn't want to yell. I had to be still but also knew as it got warmer the snake's senses would become keener.

When the sun went behind the clouds, I tiptoed over eighteen large cottonmouths and a few small ones. There wasn't two feet between each snake. I got clear and collapsed to my knees. Hiram and Poole laughed, thinking I'd tripped on a tree root. I pointed. They gasped at the mass of creeping snakes. They took me to the fire.

I didn't want to make more of it than it was. "Y'all gonna let the gar burn or what?"

I shudder as I wake from a dream whispering, "Oh. Susanna, oh don't you cry for me, for I come from Mississippi with my banjo on my knee." I must have dozed off. Maybe I passed out from exhaustion. I don't know. I'm fully awake now, and I'm in a blue-coated snake pit.

Other men sing with me in low voices. I don't know what to do except keep singing. The Yank next to me sings with a raspy voice. Blood oozes from his chest wound. He sings one more line, and his eyes fade into a death stare.

The fight rages on, men screaming, gasping for air, calling for their mommas and wives. Some pray for God to save them, others for Him to take them. Something trickles down on my neck. Its blood from the Ohio boy I was pressed against. I pray for him. Out loud.

I have to get clear of this mass of blue "cottonmouths" before they realize

I'm a Reb. I'm exhausted, too tired to think straight, and haven't even tried to get clear of the pit.

The last of the Yanks slides down the hill ducking the steady fire of the 27th Louisiana. Killing a soldier in retreat is like shooting ducks on the water. But a soldier killed retreating today is a soldier who can't kill you tomorrow. A duck shot sitting on the water is still meat in the pot. My soul is not that hardened. Not yet.

As the smoky sun retreats over the hill, so do the bloodied Yanks.

When it gets dark, I whisper, "J.A., you up there?"

Dirt spills over the parapet, and a small voice falls from above. "Lummy, that you? Just knew you was a goner. Grab this rope, and when we say go, get up this hill quicker'n a bobcat with a dog on its ass, 'cause them Yanks surely gonna put a bayonet in it if you don't."

I hope the Yanks are too tired to shoot me.

A sergeant whispers, "I heard you prayin' over that boy. We need more men prayin' no matter the color they wear. Go on now, nobody'll shoot you. Do one thing for me."

"Sure, Sarge, anythin'."

He folds his hands together. "Pray for me tonight. Larkin's my name."

"I will, for you, Mistuh Larkin, and the rest of these fightin' men." Calling him by his Christian name is the human thing to do.

As I crawl over dead and dying bodies, I quote a Psalm, "O Lord, thou hast brought up my soul from the grave and thou hast kept me alive that I should not go down to the pit."

"Thanks. Keep your head down and hands folded in prayer. God's blessin' on you, son."

I don't look back. I can't. If I make him a friend tonight, then I won't shoot him in the morning. The 27th Louisiana boys pull me back over into the lunette without a shot being fired.

J.A., grinnin' like a possum eatin' a sweet tater, says, "Boy, you're a sight for weary eyes!"

I start shaking and collapse, like the Yankee assault.

CHAPTER 25

AN EARLY MOURNING DOVE

MAY 20, 1863

*"And lo, the heavens were opened unto him, and he saw
the Spirit of God descending like a dove and lighting upon him."*

I MUST'VE SLEPT soundly through the night. I wake early. No one's moving around. It's quiet, except for the moaning of our wounded and theirs. I'm lying flat on my back in the same spot where I collapsed.

J.A. hands me a cup of acorn coffee. "Come take a look."

Through a sniper's hole I see the battlefield. The first thing I look for is an old hickory we decided was too beautiful to cut—still standing but with fewer limbs and half its bark missing. I guess men aren't the only living things wounded here. But I'm still standing, with a few bruises and a saber cut on my arm. Doc cleaned and bandaged it while I slept. It stings something fierce.

Blue-covered bodies are scattered everywhere the eye can see. The Yanks haven't come for their wounded or dead. They stay where they fell. Strange. Inhuman. Wrong.

Isham pulls at my jacket. "Don't look too long, Lummy. They'll shoot your eyeball out."

I sit, still exhausted from battle and weakened in soul from the killing. Isham wipes a tear from his face covered with mud and spent black powder.

J.A. takes a quick peek, too. "Them boys sure got a Holy Ghost baptism of fire yesterday."

"Yeah, where's the Holy Ghost now when you need him?" I hear fluttering before I see it. A dove gently lights on the nose of Jasper's and James's cannon. The bird looks around, then settles slowly like a momma bird on a nest of eggs, fluffing her feathers.

Hog Fart grins. "Look at that. The Lord is with us after all, Lummy. That's how the Holy Ghost came down on Jesus when he came up out of the water."

"God's bird of peace. Ma wouldn't let us shoot 'em. I ain't ever tasted dove. Never will."

J.A. cleans his rifle. "A mourning dove sittin' on a cannon that caused the mourning, huh?"

The dove fluffs her feathers and begins its mournful call. She cries for the dead and the living. Other doves around the battlefield join the chorus of gray coated mourners.

I mourn, too, for blood dripped like soft falling rain through the night.

The boys catch me up on what happened while I was stuck over in the pit yesterday.

J.A. starts. "Isham pulled a Yank into the lunette kickin' and screamin' like a wildcat."

I pat him on the shoulder. "Caught you a prisoner, huh, boy?"

He puffs out his chest. "Provost should be by anytime to get him."

The Yank wakes not too long after the dove lights and rocks back and forth like a scared child, sayin, "Grant said it wouldn't be like this. Said we'd take Vicksburg without a scratch."

I whisper, "They should have, no more than we were ready for them."

He counts on his fingers. "We beat you boys at Raymond, Clinton, Jackson, Champion Hill, and even Big Black River. They said Vicksburg'd be a Sunday cake walk. Arrogant bastards—drunk Grant and scared of his own shadow Sherman. I got good friends dead and dyin' out there right now because of their damn assumptions."

I hand him a rag to wipe his face. "Like Grandpa Temple used to say, 'You know what the first three letters of the word assumption are?'"

"Yeah, ass, and you're right, Reb. Only I'm addin' a jack to the front of it." He hunkers down like a rabbit hiding in a briar patch. "Can you spare a cup of that cool water for an enemy like it says in the Good Book?"

Hog Fart smiles. "It ain't cool, but you're welcome to it."

So this is what it's like to be captured. I give him the dipper, and he nearly chokes swallowing it so fast.

I try to change the mood. "The 27th Looseana gave 'em hell yesterday, didn't we, boys?"

The mourning dove flies off about the time the words come out of my mouth. *Who's the arrogant ass now, Lummy Tullos?*

I repent. "Sorry, Yank, that was uncalled for."

"Don't matter. It was just our turn to get whipped, anyway." His shoulders slump, defeated.

This first attack gives me pause. I've never been shot at before or scrapped with men either. Anger ruled my soul in those hours, but now I want to give it back to the demon that conjured it up in me. The bullets whistling around our heads weren't like getting peppered with rock salt when my brothers and I ran after stealing watermelons from old man Prewitt. Here, I could die.

I could've been killed being on the wrong side of the deer musket or like a boy who fell and a plowblade gashed his side before his daddy could stop the mule. I could've been snake bit on Big Sand Creek, and my head could've been split open crossing the Mississippi back in '59.

"Death's comin' for us all."

J.A. pushes my shoulder. "Shut up, Lummy, you're talkin' out loud again."

"It'll be a Jesus miracle if I make it out of here alive."

He walks away. "Sometimes you talk too much."

I wander down the line. I think about my life, where I've been, and if it's going anywhere. As the bullets whizzed by my head memories flew through my brain. I steadily prayed. Not the "crying for your momma" kind of babbling, but like the disciples must've done when Jesus was asleep in the boat when the storm came up. They were scared, and they weren't weak men. Neither are the men in this lunette.

On the way, I peek at the Yanks. I want to yell, "Go home, ain't this been enough?" Won't happen. Can't happen. There ain't been enough dying yet.

I'm not ready for this. Who could be? We had less than a month's training and only a few shots practice with our muskets. My few scrapes down by the river gave me some experience, but a full frontal attack that turned into a hand to hand brawl is different. Mr. Gilmore warned me about the close fighting. The pistol he gave me saved me. I hate what I had to do with it, though.

The 27th Louisiana was the first to arrive in Vicksburg but the last to see action. Other regiments have seen the elephant many times. We're green, and here, green is weak. After yesterday though, that green turned to red.

A Yank shakes his fist, and I yell, "We may be green, but you sure as hell couldn't tell it when we sent you runnin' like scared rabbits back down the hill."

I see the puff of smoke and hear the whistle. Corporal Willy Miller pulls me back down just before a minie ball hits the dirt in front of me. "Enough Private! Shoutin' won't send them to the devil. Save it for the next attack."

I wipe the dirt that kicked up from my eyes. "Yassuh, won't happen again."

He stomps his feet. "Shake it off, Lummy. We all lose our religion in times like this."

I don't know how to survive this. I want to come out being the same person I was in Winn Parish. I'll have to become somebody else to do that.

I ask the corporal, "You've been in fights like this before. How do you keep your soul?"

"Son, killing is the Devil's doin'. If you want to beat the Devil, then you got to be like him."

"But can you throw him out of your soul when it's over?"

He shrugs and walks on.

My mind is scattered, my heart aches, my body is exhausted, but my soul has never been more alive. Something about fighting makes a man come alive. Maybe we like it too much.

The field between blue and gray is silent, and so am I.

I find Jasper and James reloading their cannon in case of another attack. "Y'all okay?"

Jasper leans against a wheel. "Yeah, we done all right, I guess."

"Tell me about Greenwood. Did you run into any carpenters named Jake and Eli?"

Jasper rubs the back of his neck and looks at James. "Did you?"

James squints. "Yeah, one who talks God all the time and the other big and slow?"

I laugh. "That's them."

Jasper sits on a wheel hub. "Yep, they provided lumber and labor to help us build the earthworks near our gun emplacement. Good God-fearin' men them two."

"I worked with them on my way to Looseana. They doin' okay?"

Jasper nods. "Let me tell, we whooped the hell out of those Yanks at Fort Pemberton and...."

After hearing the entire story, twice, I return to my spot on the line and rest with my back in the hole I dug to get out of the sun and escape the shells.

It seems I'm always going somewhere never settling long enough to put down roots. I'm a Celt of the moving kind but also a Pict of the wildest kind. The savage fighting yesterday proved the latter. After this, I'll settle down. I don't want to fight anymore.

The smell of death drifts into the earthworks like fog crawling over hills. "Lord, give me better thoughts."

Nothing.

I want to go back to Winn Parish, but death waits for me there, too. I look into the sky. "Susannah, are you there?" I try to think about something else.

Granny Thankful's face pops into my head. Not five feet tall, but a formidable female. Not long before she died, we'd catch her singing and dancing around the house. We'd ask where she was going. She'd laugh. "On a journey don't you know? I'm gettin' my house in order to meet my Maker." Just before she passed at ninety-four, she'd say, "I'm goin' to a never-endin' homecomin' reunion dinner on the ground with the finest people and Jesus sittin' at the head of the table." She'd stare off into space like she could see it. In that moment, I believe she did.

Well, I ain't ninety-four, and I'm not quite ready for the end of my journey. Susannah would tell me that I've got too much life left to give it away to a cause everyone believes is so important. I've thought a lot about that. Getting shot at makes a man ponder his principles.

NOT MUCH HAPPENS for a few days, except we eat well, the wounded get doctored, and we're resupplied. We keep our heads down and duck at minie ball whistles and screams of the shells.

But those poor Yanks still in the field? Grant lets them stay where they lay, dead and wounded. I bet he's drinking every night leaving them in this field of blood and pain. I would.

Sarge returns from headquarters. "Boys, the general sends his compliments. The 27th Louisiana Volunteer Infantry distinguished itself one more time." He pulls a message from his pocket. "Let it be known to all troops on the field of battle that in the first assault made by the Yankee invader, the men of the 27th Louisiana captured the first enemy flag and prisoners in this conflict. They are to be honored by all troops and seen as the example to follow." He holds the paper high. "Signed by General Pemberton himself." We give a hearty cheer, and an extra ration of whiskey is afforded all.

Soon after our short celebration, Sarge orders us, "Can't rest on your victories, men. Drop your muskets and get these breastworks lookin' better. Put your hands to the plow, keep lookin' forward, and you might just get out of this thing alive. Don't worry about the kingdom of heaven. It's always waitin' on you. Get your asses up and go to work."

Hog Fart grumbles, "Gettin' preached at, and it ain't even Sunday."

Sarge belches out, "Hoe your row to the end, boys. Hoe your row."

CHAPTER 26

BLOODY SUN RISING

DAWN, MAY 22, 1863

Many thoughts traverse a man's mind when he realizes he might die.

THE SILENCE IS so loud I can hear it. It buzzes in my ears like bees swarming a queen in an old hollow tree—endless humming. Deafening. I'm straining to hear anything moving in the gully below. Not a cricket chirps—just J.A. snoring softly. He stands half asleep, half awake, musket in hand. Any small footstep of a night creature, and we're at the ready.

I elbow J.A. "How can you sleep with forty thousand Yankees out there? And standin' up?"

"Hell, I don't know. I just do it."

I shiver. It's always the coldest just before dawn, even in May. The sun battles darkness to chase away the lingering coolness hiding in the hollows and behind the ridges. My shiver ain't about temperature. A hollow cold hides in our souls this morning, gray and blue—a cold that chases my soul from my body, wanting to be anywhere but here.

"It'll be a hot one today, but we ain't budging."

Hog Fart whispers, "Damn straight, Lummy. But what's that smell?"

"Death."

Hog Fart whimpers. "The Yank wounded don't moan like they did."

"Either they're asleep or dead. Don't matter."

In the last assault, several Yanks crowded behind a small farmhouse to our left thinking they were safe. One dug a trench with his flag waving overhead. I guess everybody's looking for glory. He found it that day. Bullets rattled him like a baby's toy. Our men grabbed the colors but not his body—a very nice war trophy presented to our colonel. That choice makes me sad—a captured flag over a soldier's life. It makes no sense. War doesn't make any sense until you're in the middle of it. Then it doesn't have to. I tear up for the dead soldier. But only for a moment.

Without warning, a squirrel cuts loose chattering like an owl swooped down at him. It's not even light enough to shoot. It's been starry all night, but now the moon is darkened by drifting clouds and fog rising from the river. I can't see a thing in front of me. All is quiet, except for that dang squirrel barking. His call echoes across the field of death.

I've never heard a squirrel go on like this before daylight. Clearly, he's upset about something. City boys don't know the sound. We farm boys do. Something's coming. Something unfamiliar. Something wanting to remain unseen and unheard.

We've watched that big fox squirrel in the hickory still standing. "Big Red" we call him—bushy red tail with fur to match. White blazes his face and covers the tip of his tail. He even has white-socked feet. He's big as a small cat. He's escaped many a hawk and hunter to grow that big. Both sides want him. Big Red would be a meal fit for a king in these dusty trenches. He's not made a sound until this morning. Like Grandpa Temple used to say, "No need to talk unless you got somethin' to say."

Big Red has something to say this morning.

But still, my lips smack at the thought of him in the cookpot. Too many good memories of Ma's squirrel dumplings back home. I need to stop thinking about that. My guts have already retreated to my backbone and growl like a hungry bobcat.

I peek over the parapet. "Better'n the rats we'll be eatin' soon, huh boys?"

J.A. laughs. "Glad we saved that old hickory. At least we can dream about dumplin's."

Isham peeks at the tree. "How could Big Red survive everythin' that's hit that tree?"

One squirrel in one tree. Alive. Brave. His call breaks the stillness of the morning, but we can't see the red ghost. He doesn't want to be seen. Is it a warning? Is Big Red saying, "Hide!"

Will the Yanks attack this morning? We watch them and they us. They wave, and we wave back. We signal before we fire our cannons, and they do, too. They seem harmless. So much like us. Some Missouri boys have friends from their own state across the hollow dressed in blue. This war tears the best of people apart. I want it to stop but can't do a damn thing about it.

Waiting, silence, stillness—a strange solitude to find among hundreds of stinking, loud, and helpless men. I think of the saints at St. Paul's Catholic. The statues and paintings looked scary at first but became friends who helped me search my soul—just windows into heaven.

The shadowy ghoulish faces of my brother soldiers slowly become recognizable with the first touch of morning light. The saints in these trenches wish their angel would whisk them away to heaven. Not me. I want to live.

Pastor Dobbs at New Zion Baptist church never spoke about the quiet friendship we can have with God. He worried too much about appearances—dancing and cursing, paying tithes and being in church every time the doors open, drinking and fornicating. It's easy to condemn things you don't understand. I knew the difference then. It quelled the rage I learned growing up with Pa's anger and violence. Creator brought peace even to that storm back home in Choctaw County.

There won't be many saints amongst us soon. We'll all have to become demons today.

How can I do this? Fight? Wound? Kill? Survive? And still be sane? I nearly lost myself in the first attack. How can I do this again today? I have to be someone else to kill. I'm resisting. I'm weakening. I have to be the man who picked Kneehigh up over my head and slammed him on the street. I hate it. But I want to live. I give in.

I need mad dog, nail hard, teeth-gnashing rage. I don't want it anymore. I don't want to fight. I *have* to fight. I don't want blind uncontrollable rage anymore. There ain't no other way. Not here. Not this morning.

I ain't afraid. Pa pretty much beat the fear out of us when he beat the hell out of us. We Tullos boys never looked for a fight but never backed down if for the right cause. This Cause just ain't right though, as much as I love Missis-sippi. "Boy, don't you blame this on Missip. She wasn't like this 'til white folks pushed the Choctaws out." I look around to see who's hearing my sermon.

Who's right in all of this, anyway? When the day is done, who will be the winner? Whose side is the Good Lord on? Both sides claim God as their champion, but how we can both be right and call on him for help? I'm sure neither side is right. There's a fine line between those who fight the devil and those who fight for him. I'm sure I'm both. God must be worn slap out with all this holy self-righteous bullshit.

"Maybe he'll just kill us all and let that be the end of a nation that claims freedom for all but still chains people. He brought the flood for much less."

J.A. elbows me. "Stop your damn preachin'. Now ain't the time."

"When is? The South works slaves. The North uses them as an excuse to invade. The South grows cotton by slave labor. The North buys every bale of cotton they sell. Both get rich, and the Negro stays a slave."

Sarge barks, "Quiet on the line!"

I whisper, "The only reason a poor white farmer scratchin' out a livin' on a small chunk of land is so hard on a Negro is it keeps him from being the lowest rung on the ladder. It's wrong, and we're all covered in the shit of it all up to our necks. Nobody's clean." I stop. No, I don't.

"This war's just one big baptism to get everybody clean—not in pure spring water but in the blood of men that leaves a stank that can't be washed off. When this is over, we'll still stink."

Sarge points his finger at me. "Stop it!"

I want to scream, but I mumble, "We ain't gotta do this. We're all on the same side. We're all human bein's, and there's only one Massuh."

Isham elbows me. "Best keep your good eye on them woods down there. They're full of Yanks." He's only looking out for me. This day can't be called off.

Why don't Grant and Pemberton meet under Big Red's tree and settle this thing over a table of dominoes? Let the black dots on the white bone pieces be soldiers. That way, nobody goes under the dirt. There'll be plenty of bones lying around to make many sets of dominoes after this.

The boys in blue wait in a shadowy cane patch across the deep hollow. I don't hate them. I can't. Why should I? I could've been friends with these men under different circumstances. We could have played cards and drank coffee together around the fire. But no, we'll kill each other for beliefs we know little about but are expected to die for in this place soon to be forgotten.

A shot rings out, and we duck. A sharpshooter tries to fool us into believing that's all the Yanks will do today. I'm thinking too much. It makes me want to throw up. I do just that.

Hog Fart dances to miss getting puked on. "Dang, its bad enough smellin' dead Yanks, but last night's puked up hardtack and beans, too?"

I turn to watch the field. I'm better now.

Early on, I saw Negroes as human beings, especially after meeting Susannah. It always hurt me the way folks treated their slaves. Fear of the unknown causes the ignorant to hate a person they don't know. Until I knew different, I joined in the "niggah" jokes. If I didn't, I'd be suspect.

Growing up I had to hide my feelings about black people. They are meant for so much more. They have good minds just like white folks and talents wasted on picking cotton and slopping hogs. How could the sweet little old ladies at the New Zion Baptist church teach me that Negroes had no souls? I guess if you make Negroes less than human, then you can treat them like animals to be bred, beaten into submission, and sold for profit. If you make them animals, then beating them ain't so hard.

When I looked into Susannah's eyes, I saw a window back into my own soul. That can't happen if there's no soul there in the first place. Truth be told, I would have married her right there at home, but it'd been hell to pay. You just didn't do that. Not in Choctaw County, Mississippi. On the courthouse steps in Greensboro, Susannah was just property. In Mr. Gilmore's home back in Winn Parish, she became my wife.

Now she's gone.

The night before I left for Winn Parish, I slipped away to meet Susannah. But no Susannah. I went to town the next day, and Lester had the pleasure of telling me that Susannah was gone.

"Yeah, that slick gamblin' fella in his high dollar duds took her in a Bucksnort card game. Bet he's gettin' a bath from her right about now, and who knows what else."

Lester, the schoolyard bully who became town bully, was the sheriff's nephew. He made everyone laugh and afraid at the same time, always at the expense of some tortured soul. The tortured soul was me that day. It was like first year of school all over again. The girls asked a couple of us boys to swing the jump rope for them. Just as dust started to fly, Lester pushed down the girls, jumped in, and told me and Poole, "Keep that rope goin'." I winked at Poole.

We went a few rounds, but at the right moment, I yanked the rope taut. Lester's feet caught the rope as he went up, and his face hit the ground hard. He got up, shook the dust out of his hair, and spit the grit out of his mouth. His eyes burned red as the sun rising in front of me now. He didn't wade into me like I thought he would. He just hit me hard, once in the belly. I just took it.

Lester was stunned. He expected me to cry. I didn't. I just stood still. Lester stared me down and walked away. I went around the corner of the schoolhouse and puked. Mrs. Crow, our school marm, made me sit on the schoolhouse steps for the rest of play time.

She smiled, gave me a lemon drop, and winked. "I saw what you did. Thanks for taking up for the girls. Don't do it again, but if you do, just don't let me see it."

A stick snaps, and I point my musket at the faint gleam of bayonets in the fading darkness. My anger spikes. It's not enough. Not for what's coming up this hill. I need more. I go back to that moment when Lester told me Susannah was taken away.

"She's gone, niggah lover! Somebody else straddles her tonight." Belly laughs erupted all around. Lester bowed and turned to give me another challenge. I didn't want it. It just wasn't me. Never has been. I hated fighting. I hated the anger. I hated the way my Pa treated us boys, whipping us within an inch of our lives for little or no reason. Yet my blood boiled.

Lester's half-pint sized side kick cousin, Nehemiah nicknamed Kneehigh, cursed and kicked dust at me saying he'd try me on if I wasn't too scared. The thought about Susannah being with another man against her will as they continued their cat calls was too much.

Lester grabbed his crotch. "She's sweet as chocolate fudge. Think I'll go get me some. They can't be far."

I'd had enough. "You sorry son of a bitch."

Kneehigh ran quick as a swamp rabbit to head butt me in the stomach. He was fast, stout as a cypress stump, but like in first grade, I stood firm and took the blow. That's all I remember, except hearing a collective "uh oh" from the gathering crowd.

Poole yelled, "Don't do it, Lummy, don't do it." Ladies covered their mouths, men shook their heads, but some hid smiles for a job well done. Poole pulled my shoulders back as I came to my senses. My hands were full of Kneehigh's long red hair. He moaned, "Don't hit me, please, don't hit me." Poole told me later I picked Kneehigh up by the skin of his back and slammed him down on the hardpan street. Poole and I slipped away before Sheriff Platner arrived.

"You'll be throwed in jail this time for sure, boy. You best high-tail it on out of here. Go after Susannah. If you love her, she's worth it." I only saw Poole once before I left.

That night, Elihu heard Kneehigh said I started the fight. "He's pressin' charges. Lester's the sheriff's nephew. You best go, brother." There was nothing to keep me in Choctaw County that I couldn't find wherever Susannah had gone. This anger, this rage, would be the death of me or someone else. I needed to go somewhere and find the real me I knew lived deep inside. I had to leave then, and I don't want to be here now.

I didn't like the me I saw when I hurt Kneehigh. I don't like the me I saw three days ago when the Yanks attacked. Pastor Dobbs preached, "You can't conquer the world 'til you conquer home." He was right on that one. A man is created for a purpose in this world, but I won't know what that is until I meet the man on the inside. I have too many layers to find the true me inside.

As a kid, I mostly stayed to myself wandering alone in the woods sketching, writing poetry, and meditating. I've always found God easier on the outside than the inside of a church house. I've come to know Him better on the inside than the outside of me, too. I just want the outside to match what I feel on the inside. That's a tough one.

Once I sneaked out the back door at a revival in town when the mouthy preacher squawked, "You can't worship God under a tree. You better be at church every time the doors swing open, or when your time comes, the pearly gates'll swing closed with a loud clang." As I feigned stomach trouble to go to the outhouse, I thought, Preacher, I been worshippin' God under a tree for years, and I'm only twelve years old. Guess I'm a rebel in more ways than one.

Here I am going soft again, and those Yanks will be coming up the hill any minute. The Kneehigh thing was the worst of it, but it certainly didn't start there. Pa was a hard man, and though I have no regrets leaving because of the beatings and abuse he dished out, I still loved him as my father. He only did to us what was done to him, probably got it worse. All I wanted was to be with my Pa. I'm glad I made peace with him before he died. What am I doing? I need rage if I'm going to survive this thing.

The whippings that brought blood to the backside of our britches started when we boys were old enough to work with Pa. My problem was Ben got it rough from Pa, as did I. Then Ben took his anger out on me. I got a double dose. When I turned seventeen, I'd had enough of Ben.

Ben worked at a sawmill near Columbus and came home on a rain break with a friend of his. We'd just got home from the Sunday service at Mt. Pisgah Baptist Church, and I laid my Bible down to change clothes. Ma was frying chicken. It smelled good. Ben and his friend burst in laughing, smelling of moonshine. Ben slapped my head and punched my shoulder, knocking me off balance. "Told you, Colu-u-umbus ain't but a damn sissy who squats to piss." He'd hit my head with his boney elbows and then turn to his friend, laugh, and call me nasty names. I'd had enough. I tried to dodge the blows when I saw the hunting knife Pa had made me out of a broken crosscut saw blade. It'd shave the hair off your arm. As Ben threw another blow, I slashed his arm. He let out a yell. "You cut me, you bastard."

I was done with Ben. "Hit me ever again, and I'll kill you where you stand." Ben left me alone after that.

My anger boils thinking back on that. For me to fight and not hate the bluecoats, I have to go somewhere else in my mind. I just don't want it to take over my soul.

Not long after I cut him, Ben went back to the sawmill. He never forgot that day, saying often, "If I ever get in a scrape, I want Lummy on my side. He'll kill you."

My anger is nearly full-blown now. I'm fighting mad. Mad dog mean. Remembering one more story should do it. On the way home from church one Sunday, Pa was riding our asses about losing one of his tools or something. Whatever he was mad about, I didn't do it. My little brother Jasper did it, but I wouldn't tell on him because I knew what he'd get—another plow line beating that'd leave his back bleeding like a whipped slave. As I jumped out of the wagon, Pa breathed insults and accusations down the back of my neck.

I planted my feet solidly to speak my words as respectfully as I could. "You ain't gonna blame me anymore for things I didn't do."

Pa's eyes blazed red. He front handed and backhanded me seven times, slapping my face so hard my head snapped from side to side. He finally stopped. I just stood there.

I stared him straight in the eye without a blink. "How long you gonna do this? 'Cause I can go all day." A boy seventeen should never have to tell his daddy that. I knew then one day I'd leave. Susannah taken away and the Kneehigh incident just made it easy.

J.A. shakes me. "Boy, you best come back from wherever you been these last few minutes. Them bluecoats are comin' again."

Smoke from the cook fire brings the welcome scent of chicory in the acorn coffee. I reach to get a cup moving with the smoothness of a copperhead. I can barely see the morning slithering over the ridge. Light creeps bloody red over tall oaks on the far hill like a fire burning our way. We'll soon feel the hot blaze of a thousand Union muskets.

The sun eases over the ridge still curtained by trees but not enough to reveal the danger Big Red announces. Blue coats sneak through the switch cane. Quietly. Stealthily. Nervously. Big Red saved us. We fill the lunette. Silently. Muskets primed. Hats pulled low. Grenades nearby.

Hog Fart whimpers. "I'm afraid, Lummy. What we gonna do?"

I hold up my coffee tin. "Offer them a cup of coffee, what else?" I set the cup down. "We're gonna yell like devils crawlin' out the pits a hell and kill 'em all. Ain't nothin' else we can do, dammit. It's what we signed up for. Get your rifle up and make sure it's got a cap."

I grip my musket. I find a target less than a hundred yards away. The bluecoat bully "Lester" is in my sights. I try to push Ben and Pa's faces out. Don't matter now. The anger they gave me this morning will be my salvation. My heart pounds. I ready my musket as I steady my soul. A bloody sun rises this morning.

CHAPTER *27*

NO MORE
FRONTAL CHARGES

MAY 22-23, 1863

Demons don't come from the Hell below us.
They come from the Hell within us.

HOG FART CRIES out. "Why don't the damn Yanks charge and get it over with?"

I cover his mouth. "Sarge'll beat the hell out of you if you don't shut up, boy!"

Possums and other night scavengers still work the field. When the sun's first rays peek over the hill, they scamper away.

"Lummy, where you at, son? I need you for a minute."

"Yassuh, Sarge, what can I do?"

Sarge takes off his hat. "Talk to the Good Lord for us. We're all brave and fearless men, but we need His strength to make it through this one. This fight will be worse than the last. Anybody wantin' prayer, c'mon. J.A., keep watch. You get plenty of prayer hangin' around Lummy." The men half-heartedly laugh.

I don't know what to say, especially after talking about fighting like a demon when the Yanks come. It's hard to mix killing and my true nature of peace. But I know this—it'll only be by the grace of God any of us live.

J.A. stands close enough to hear but keeps his eyes to the front of the lunette. "Take your time, Lummy, the Lord's listenin'."

I pull the small Bible Mary gave me from my pocket. "I don't have the words, but here's a psalm. *The Lord is my light and my salvation so whom am I gonna fear? The Lord is the strength of my life, so who shall make me afraid? When my wicked foes came to eat my flesh, they stumbled and fell. Though a host should encamp against me my heart shall not fear, though war rises against me in this will I be confident. One thing have I desired of the Lord that I may dwell in the house of the Lord all the days of my life. For in the time of trouble He shall hide me in His house, and He shall set me up on a rock. And now shall mine head be lifted up above mine enemies round about me. Therefore I'll offer up sacrifices of joy. I will sing praises. Hear, O Lord, when I cry and have mercy and answer me. Lord today we hear You when You said, 'Seek my face.' My heart said, 'Thy face, Lord, will I seek.' And with my brothers here, I say, amen."*

Company F whispers, "Amen."

Sarge squeezes my shoulder, and J.A. gives me a nod. The men start back to their places on the line when a loud long grunting noise erupts like a cross between a lop-eared braying mule and an overgrown hog rooting in slop.

Sarge turns, "What'n the hell is that? Sounds like Satan risin' out the depths of Hades." We duck when the noise explodes again. "We gotta find out what that is. Sounds like it's comin' from the 7th Missip Infantry."

Isham squints looking in the direction the sound came from. "Sarge, them 7th Missip boys went somewhere else, and the 43rd Missip replaced them."

"Hell, them boys must have the screamers pretty bad to make that racket when they go to the shit ditch."

J.A. laughs. "Yeah, I want to make a sound like that when the smell follows you back from the ditch, Sarge."

"Shut the hell up and keep your eyes on them bushes down there."

We hustle to our positions with the love of God in our hearts but the wrath of God in our hands. We don't hear the strange grunting noise again. It couldn't have been our imagination.

At 11:00 a.m. sharp, Yankee cannons unleash hell.

J.A. yells above the roar. "They rainin' fire and brimstone like God did on Sodom and Gomorrah!"

I lean over to J.A. hiding in his bombproof. "Pastor Dobbs said the main reason God destroyed those wicked cities was because they didn't care for the the poor and needy."

He shakes his head.

I whisper, "It's us not treatin' Negroes in our land right. We might be gettin' what the Lord promised Abraham. Hellfire's rainin' down and there ain't a righteous man to be found."

J.A. cups his ears. "What? Can't hear you."

Since he can't hear me, I say out loud, "I'm on the wrong side of things. And it don't make the Yanks right any more than it makes us wrong. I just don't believe I'm doing the right thing."

I'm too torn up about all this. One thing I'm not torn up about though right now is staying alive. And those men in blue don't want me to.

At noon a thin line of skirmishers cautiously test the waters, but we wait. In a massive surge like a steam locomotive starting down the tracks, the thick blue lines shove forward to begin the assault. Behind the skirmishers come men carrying planks, ladders, pick-axes, and shovels. That's the plan. Those boys will be the easiest targets. That doesn't make me feel any better.

Their infantry trot down Graveyard Road in the calm of men resigned to die but with hope for a better ending than last time. They march in fine order turning this way and that in perfect precision. They march across Mint Springs Creek and up the slope within a rock's throw of our rifle pits, cheering like the victory is already won.

J.A. shakes. "Them boys is cool as cucumbers. Pretty marching can't stop bullets, though."

Sarge yells, "Get your muskets up and your heads down."

It's a grand sight. The Yanks must still believe we'll run at the first sign of a shiny bayonet. Wishful thinking for men who know their time is up. In a flash, they make their dash. They come at us like torrents of rain pounding on a tin roof so terrific a man can't hear himself think. The charge comes just after the last shell explodes over McNalley's Arkansas artillery boys, taking out half the gun crew. Our guns make good targets for Yank cannons. I fear for Jasper and James. My fear becomes anger, and I let loose with the fury of a swamp cat. I hate it. It hates me.

Quick as lightning, a thousand Confederate soldiers rise up as one man over the parapet to unleash hellfire without mercy. A great, gut-belching, high-pitched yell is thrown down at the charging Yanks having as much effect as our bullets. The great blue snake staggers. It writhes left, then right, men trying to escape deadly volleys pouring out like the wrath of God's angel armies. Many lie down where their comrades found shelter in the attack a couple days ago.

The Yanks scramble for cover, and more bodies litter the field. They fill the ditch in front of us, and their squirming stirs up the rotting bodies. The stench is unbearable. I'm thankful we're the defenders. I'm thankful I'm born of the Picts who deliver the surprise blow to send the Yankee legion scampering back to their camps. What did it sound like when thousands of blue-painted naked warriors attacked that Roman legion above the wall in Scotland so many centuries ago? I feel like I was there. We keep loading and firing our muskets.

It amazes me how well protected we are behind this parapet, and yet they come. Redans and lunettes—fancy names given to fortifications a man can hide behind where he has free license to murder men as easy as shooting pigs in a pen. If enough dead pile up in the pit, the boys charging up the hill will just climb over the bodies and walk right into our lunette. It ain't gonna happen. We're just filling graves because we're ordered to.

We build the same fortifications. We charge up the same hills. We fall into the same muddy ditches filled with blood, piss, and shit as them. And the generals still make us charge.

I load my rifle and scream, "We're all crazy!"

I shoot another Yankee down.

The weakened Yanks hide just a few yards away in the same pit I fell in three days ago. With the Yanks too close for effective cannon fire, Jasper and James run to where I duck down.

Jasper peeks up over the wall. "Watch this!" Jasper cuts a cannon ball fuse, James lights it. I scramble back expecting it to blow when Jasper hurls the grenade over the parapet just in time for it to explode in the middle of the Yankees. The screams of the enemy are unbearable, but I quickly go to cutting and lighting fuses. They hurl the shells as fast I light them.

Jasper laughs like a kid playing a game everytime he hurls. "Better'n playin' that stick and ball game the college boys taught us, huh?" He laughs to stay sane.

Blood splatters up in the air. The Yanks scream in agony. Men just like us. Nothing special about them except it's their day to meet the Lord face to face. That doesn't sound so bad. Just get it over with and be at peace from all this shit I had no part in starting in the first place.

I whisper, "Lord, forgive my cussin'."

Jasper slugs my shoulder. "Don't worry, I won't tell Ma."

"Get back to work, boy." He shrugs and lobs another grenade.

Yanks shout, curse, beg, moan, cry, pray, and die. Only a man himself knows what's in his heart in such times. We act brave, but the truth? None of us want to die. We all just want to go home. I won't be killin' hawgs after this. I puke, wipe my mouth, and light another fuse.

My face burns hot with anger. I need it now more than ever. It takes away the pain of killing. I think about Lester and rage seizes my soul. A Yank pokes his head up, and I split his skull with a pistol shot. A blue soldier raises his bayonet over Hog Fart, and J.A. slashes his throat with a short sword. We scream like demons. And all falls silent. For a moment.

What am I gonna do with all this anger when this is over? Will I be able to find my soul again? I can feel mine running away.

We gasp for air in a lull. I want to run to the woods where the Choctaws used to dance and deer don't run away. Alone, just to be with the Great Alone, and maybe find my soul again. I don't know if I'll make it through this to get there. If the Yanks would retreat, so would I. I can't take this anger through the thin veil to Granny Thankful, Pa, or Susannah. I must leave it here.

I pray. "Lord, will I enter the Pearly Gates if I die in this anger?" I shudder. Can't think on that now. I have to fight. I have to live. This can't be the end of me. Susannah wouldn't want it.

The smoke is so thick the Yanks can't see us nor we them. Take a peek, and they'll blow your head off. I wait for the next charge. It's quiet as a graveyard at midnight. I glance up at the old hickory. Big Red's white painted red nose peeks out of his knothole home—alive, surviving, dodging every shot. I wonder if Big Red prays for us or thinks it's all just stupid when there are good hickory nuts in the ground for the digging. A shot rings out, and Big Red disappears.

I try not to look at the Yanks' faces. It makes the killing easier. Look into their eyes, and I see myself. It's hard to shoot a man who looks like he could be your brother. Some men put muskets in their mouths, afraid to get bayonetted, sick of the mud and rain, weak from the screaming shits, and weary of the misery of the mosquitoes. They're tired of being part of the human race that's bent on ending itself.

Doc Simpson sneaks down the line, checking the wounded. His stare burns right through me, but I feel like I can see all the way to the depths of his soul, and nothing's there. Empty. Hollow.

"I'm done with all this pain. Say a prayer for me, Lummy." He stands so fast we can't pull him back down in time. A single shot rings out, and blood sprays in my face as the ball blasts out of the back of his head. He sits back with with a letter from his wife in hand.

I read the few words, sobbing.

J.A. asks, "What's it say?"

"I've found another. I won't be home when you get here. Goodbye. She didn't even sign her name."

Isham takes the letter from my hand. "She was all he talked about."

J.A. sniffs. "I guess Doc wanted to feel the pain that ends all pain."

I wipe my eyes. "At least he didn't feel nothin' when it hit him."

Sarge crawls over. "Sorry about the Doc, but the Yanks are about to try us again. Get ready."

I snatch a grenade in a rage and light the fuse. I'm happy when I hear the thud of the metal hitting a body. "Take that fire and brimstone you sons of bitches!" I'm losing control.

A bluecoat rushes over the parapet just as Jed—who caught the spy earlier—launches a grenade. The young private drops his rifle and catches it. He smiles as the blast shreds him from the waste up. The lower half stands quivering. His legs finally collapse, and we push what's left out of the way. I don't know how much more of this I can stand.

Jed's left side was blown away. I guess the spy returned the favor. A collective moan drifts up like ghosts rising in a graveyard from the anguish in our rifle pit. I moan, too, inside. I can't think about that. I have to keep fighting.

Not to win. Just to live.

I scream, "God, where are you?" Here I am calling on God, fighting like a demon. No answer. The Yanks want me dead. I have to fight. "Alright dammit! I'll call on the one who will answer!"

A dark rage rises like smoke from a cauldron. I slash with the knife Pa made me. I use my fists. I crush a man's head with my rifle butt, screaming like a beast out of hell. It takes a certain kind of evil to do this. I invite that evil in.

The Yanks back off for a second. I yell, "Damn Yanks! Don't you know killer demons don't come from the hell below us? They come from the hell within us!"

My demon within conjures up old memories and disappointments, the beatings and injustices, the bullies and foolishness of hatred and meanness. I have to if I want to survive.

"Lord, just don't make me like Cain."

J.A. pushes me back when a Yank charges with a short sword. He plunges his knife in the soldier's back. "You ain't Cain, and he ain't Abel, damn you!" He rushes back to the firing line and loads for another shot.

I whisper, "Cain and Abel. The first killing. And we're still killing each other to this day."

The muskets stop. The smoke clears. But the crying yet remains. The smell of burnt powder and rotting corpses rises like a fiery dragon to burn our lungs with a painful, awful stench. As the blood red sun retreats over the hill, so do the bloodied Yanks. We shake hands, glad to be alive.

Hog Fart sits in the bloody mud and cries. "Why can't it just be over?"

I give him a cup of water. "It is, for now."

It's deathly quiet except for a lone crow signaling the others that the feast is about to begin. The same loud grunting noise we heard this morning erupts.

Hog Fart yells, "What is that God awful noise?"

J.A. peeks over the parapet. "It ain't the Yanks comin' back."

Jasper stands up from organizing grenades and equipment. "Me and James know. You ain't gonna believe it. When the 43rd Missip moved up, they brought a danged camel with 'em."

Hog Fart scratches his ear. "A camel? Heck, ain't never seen no camel."

J.A. strains to see it. "Why'n the hell do they have a camel all the way from Africa?"

James, proud to have the answer, swells his chest. "His name is Douglas, their mascot. He carries band instruments and supplies but mostly does what he wants. They must love that damn thing. They said he broke loose in Iuka and hurt some boys. He tore up everythin' in sight, but they kept him. They say he don't like horses much."

J.A. laughs. "We need to see Douglas soon."

Sarge grins. "I say we turn him loose on the Yank's camp."

We relax as the big blue snake slithers over the ridge. I'm tired. Tired of the killing. Tired of men hating each other. Tired of the human race.

I need to release the feelings in my soul. I don't know what to write, but I want someone to read my soul's last thought if I'm killed. I pray as I write.

God's Friend
I say to the One I love, so full of grace,
Speak with me like Moses, face to face.
Walk with me now, then take me away,
In You, O Lord, I'll always stay.

When darkness becomes my dearest friend
Stay closer to me than a brother then.
Into Your Soul my soul as a dove descends,
I see the light of life's long journey end.

So I ask you Father for everything,
I take only the good to me You bring.
So down I lay my life in love,
Send Your angels to wing me far above.

J.A. whispers, "Read it again, Lummy. It's a prayer for all us boys expectin' to die." He wipes a tear, not from fear of death or pain, but of sorrow for the lives given in sacrifice.

DARKNESS LIES THICK on the field of death tonight. Sarge handpicks six men. "Sneak into the field in front of us and report back what you see. Pair off and watch each other's back."

I crawl along the ground, pistol in hand. J.A. follows with a knife in his teeth. Steps in the darkness stop me cold. I turn with my pistol cocked. A young Creole from G Company drops beside me. I relax the hammer on my pistol. "What'n the hell are you doin'? I almost shot you!"

"Askin' these boys for forgiveness. There ain't no priest to give absolution."

"What'd you do so bad you gotta do it this way?"

"Our men found out I'm a good shot. So they loaded their rifles and gave them to me. I killed at least fifty Yankees today. I aim for the head." He sobs. "Please, suh, I know you're a prayin' man. Ask God to ease my sorrow for what I did."

"JoJo?" He nods. "You worked provost with us last fall. You cooked our rations one time."

"Joseph Antoine is my Christian name. The boys just call me JoJo."

I waste no time, but the words don't come easy. "Lord, forgive JoJo tonight in this field of death and suffering. He only did what he had to. Ease the pain in his heart, Lord. Amen." He sheds tears without a sound, disappearing into the darkness.

In a half hour, we're back. Sarge asks, "What'd you see?"

We dump haversacks full of Yankee hats. Hog Fart and Isham count eighty altogether.

Sarge rubs his chin. "Damn, boys, every one of them has a bullet hole in it."

I pray for the souls of the men who wore them.

MIDMORNING SATURDAY, MAY 23rd, and it's a pretty day. We wake stiff and sore from fighting and repairing damaged earthworks through the night. A corporal runs through the lines yelling in a whispered voice. He jumps into our trench, slips, rolls over a couple of times, and hops right back on his feet like a circus performer.

We laugh, and J.A. yells, "So, circus man, what's the big news?"

The corporal shakes with excitement, breathing hard. He holds up his hand and swallows hard. "We heard the Yanks jabberin', and they're as happy as fleas on a dawg. Grant called us a gritty bunch and declared no more frontal charges. Ain't that a gift from the Lord?"

J.A. pats my arm. "Your prayer worked, my good friend." I shrug like it doesn't matter.

"No, dammit!" He yanks my jacket sleeve. "Keep sendin' them prayers up for us. Your jawin' with Him makes the difference." J.A. calms himself. "Say that prayer you wrote again." Men gather around. The corporal removes his hat.

When I finish, all say, "Amen."

I step away for a moment and stare into the cloudless sky, "With all the killin' I've done, Lord, am I still your friend?"

J.A. puts his arm around my shoulder. "If you ain't, nobody is."

I backhand his chest. "Jasper, James! Let's go see us a camel!"

CHAPTER 28

SIEGE

MAY 23, 1863

Profound truths are the most obvious but often overlooked. "Stay alert."

RAIN PATTERS LIGHTLY through the night, and dawn holds clouds to shield the burning sun. The guns lie silent this morning. Yank dead remain in the field. I'm tired and want to sleep. A shell explodes. The stillness is shattered. So is the possibility of sleep.

An educated soldier named Gunnard stops by at dark. We tell about our battle experiences, and he writes in a little book. I never thought about writing my story. Who'd read it? Then he shares his experiences.

Gunnard fought several battles with the 3rd Louisiana Infantry—Elk Horn Tavern, Corinth, places like that. We squat in a half-circle around him, listening for shells, dodging the ever straing minie ball. Gunnard is a master storyteller. He weaves in and out of his stories like a hawk through the trees after a squirrel.

"Boys, this is the roughest a-a-and toughest scrape I've been in yet. But take heart. Men defended Greece from an invader just like we're doin'. A wicked Persian king wanted the whole world for himself. We're like the brave three hundred Spartans who defended Thermopylae."

"Thermometer who?" Hog Fart asks.

Gunnard laughs. "Thermopylae, my fine illiterate friend. The world will remember the name Vicksburg throughout the ages, too. We're fighting for the same reason—freedom from an oppressor. Yep, they'll write plays and sing songs about our bravery one day."

Being remembered through the ages comes at a high price when all God wanted us to be was good children in the Garden. "Ain't none of us good children now, not after what we've done to each other here."

J.A. pats me on the back. "It's all right, Lummy."

Hog Fart whispers, "Did he call me a bastard usin' that fancy word illegitasamy? Do I need to kick his ass, so he'll know how to socialize properly with folks from Looseana?"

"He meant no harm. He just said you can't read. And he's from Looseana, just like you. He just don't sound like it."

Hog Fart rubs the back of his neck. "Well, damn, if that's all he spit out, then that's all right by me. Hell, I can't read nary a lick no how."

I say in perfect English, "They call that accent a gentleman's education, my fine young fellow."

Gunnard turns. "Damn, friend, where'd you go to school?"

From the corner of my eye a bluecoat creeps like a cat on an unsuspecting mouse. A scrawny little Yank points a pistol at my chest. I don't know if he's trying to get a look at our defenses or got drawn into Gunnard's story. Maybe he wants to be a hero. I don't know. He never got the chance to tell us. He cocks his pistol.

Quick as a rattler strike, Gunnard pulls his pistol and shoots the Yank between the eyes. I can't believe his quickness and accuracy. The Yank stays still, his eyes roll up into his head and his pistol still aimed at my chest. Hog Fart gently relieves the dead man of his sidearm. I'll see that in my dreams tonight.

"That's how we boys in the 3rd Louisiana do it." Gunnard holsters his pistol, living up to his stories right before our eyes. Then he grimaces for a minute, rubbing his shoulder where a small spot of blood leaks through. I thank him for saving my life.

"Think nothing of it. Lummy, is it? You'd done the same for me."

"In a heartbeat."

Gunnard reloads the round in his Navy Colt. "Stay alert, and you'll stay alive. The Yanks didn't come for a picnic. It'll all be over when Fightin' Joe Johnston kicks their asses. Gotta go now. I'll catch you butternuts later."

I like Gunnard. He brings cheer to a dark place.

Hog Fart yells, "We ain't no damned butternuts."

I push him back against the earthworks. "Shut up, he's a corporal."

Hog Fart pops his head back up. "We ain't no damned butternuts, *suh*."

Gunnard salutes as he walks away. Hog Fart laughs but drops facedown, and then we hear the whistle and a thud in the dirt behind us.

"Heard it comin'. Almost got me, boys."

The body of the Yank Gunnard shot finally goes limp and piles up at my feet like a sack of potatoes. I'm sorry for him, but he knew better. We all know better. We may talk between the lines when it gets dark and be friendly if a truce gets called, but the rest is killing time.

Stay alert. It's a simple truth. Gunnard forgot that once and got wounded as a result. It only takes one time.

The guns are silent, and the afternoon is peaceful. We clear the dead from the rifle pits, gently laying bodies in a row, blue and gray. Uniforms don't matter when you're dead. Respect does.

After cleaning my musket, I eat and rest in my bombproof for the night. Like the other boys, I dug mine deep to escape shells and bullets but also to get a little shade from the sun in the hottest part of the day. Quiet comes, and I can still see the blank stare of the Yank Gunnard shot.

I sleep until I smell acorn coffee boiling. Isham brings me a cup as we trade places. He stood guard last night and settles in for a snooze. The morning heat dries the dew-covered hillsides.

"What'n the hell is that?" Hog Fart wrinkles up his nose, then he gags and pukes.

J.A. sniffs. "Yank bodies swellin' up and bustin' open in the field. It's an awful smell, but a worse sight."

I cover my mouth and nose with a rag. "And the buzzards that soar highest now fly low." Their graceful flight can't make up for their ghoulish mission. A loud shriek comes from just over the parapet. We grab our muskets. A Yank screams "bloody murder," as Ma used to say. A buzzard must've thought him dead and pecked a wound.

The guns are silent, yet there is no peace. And Grant lays siege to our city set upon a hill.

CHAPTER 29

WHEN THE SMOKE FINALLY CLEARS

MAY 24, 1863

Trials a man survives make him more alive.

A WARM BREEZE brings the scent of the muddy Mississippi River into the earthworks. It smells like fresh-plowed ground. Honeysuckle helps mask the awful odor of human waste and swollen corpses—if the wind blows the right way. A welcome reprieve from the rags we tie over our noses and mouths. The smell still creeps in as the heat rises. And cottonwood seeds snow like Christmas time.

The Yanks must be having it hard today. They took a lot of losses. For a second, I sob for them. But only for a moment, after all, they invaded Mississippi like a locust plague destroying everything in their path. They came to steal Vicksburg. They crossed the deadly space between us. They charged with no other intention than to make us bait for buzzards and possums. They killed boys in my company. They did only what they were ordered to do. Just like me.

A sharpshooter's musket brings death early. A boy gets his head taken completely off by a random cannon ball. I'm glad I didn't see it. I've seen more than I want. We expect another attack today, and if they come, we'll kill them all. I hate these thoughts. It's not who I am. It can't be the true nature of the Yanks either.

J.A. wipes sweat from his arms. "You'd think the men runnin' the two governments, claimin' to watch over us, protectin' us, and lookin out for the common man, could find a better way to solve their fusses."

Sarge stomps his way towards me. "Shut the hell up, all of you. Nobody wants to hear all that shit. Stay ready. Them Yanks hope we don't lob a grenade at 'em. Keep it up, and you'll catch one in your lap. And Lummy, I swear, that talkin' out loud will get you killed."

A whitish, foul-smelling, thick liquid splatters next to me. We jump back holding our noses and checking our pants for splatters.

J.A. looks up into the sky. "Buzzards. They did that to me once when I walked a creek goin' to my fishin' hole. I saw their shadows pass by as I sloshed along. One made a loud screechin' sound, and a shit bucket full of puke fell from the sky. I ran under a willow tree quick." I hope Sarge is distracted by the buzzard puke. He isn't. I didn't know I was talking out loud. Sarge only says such things to keep us alive. I quietly move a few yards down the line.

"Pssst, hey, Reb." It's coming from the ditch in front of us. "I agree with you. Sure wish you butternuts would quit so we can go home. What do you say, butternut? Will you give it up? Grant'll take good care of you boys. No prison camp or nothin' like that. Just go home."

"You lie like a damn dawg. We ain't no damned butternuts, you ignert ass. We're gray-suited Looseanans ready to pour it on your sorry asses again if you ain't had enough."

Sarge looks surprised. It's quiet for a moment.

"Don't mean no harm, Reb."

I don't want this conversation, so I try to end it.

"You think we should surrender? Tell me, where's Grant? Drunk? Where's Sherman? With his head up his ass?"

The Yank whimpers, "They said nobody's goin' home 'til you men lay down your muskets."

That same small, pitiful voice resides in me. That's a voice that gets a man killed.

"So, Yank, lay down your muskets and crawl over here. We won't shoot nary a one of you."

The Yank says nothing after that. I lean back, tired of war, tired of talk, tired of bad food and little sleep, and very tired of our prison behind these dirt mounds. We can't get out, and the Yanks can't get in. I hate it for the Yanks lying in the mud and filth a few feet away. Then again, I don't. After all, they came looking for it. It reminds me of Thermopylae, the Trojan Horse, and George Washington's battles, but Grandpa Temple's stories were best.

The Tulloses are Scots, but we had another name before that—Picts, the people painted blue. Grandpa Temple said the word means "the ancestors." We didn't come from somewhere else. We were always there. We lived peaceful lives until threatened. We were one with the land. Our people just wanted to be left alone in the hills above the two walls, enjoying the world as we understood it. We believe there's a thin line between the land of the livin' and the place of the dead. We included them in all we did. Granny Thankful spoke often of those things.

The Romans built two walls to keep us out. End of the civilized world the Romans claimed. There wasn't anything civilized about men who raped, plundered, killed, and burned. They built walls to protect themselves from free men attacking the invaders. Walls never control people who see them as nothing more than manmade hills to climb over. "Never kept us from raidin' the bastards, though," he'd say.

The Romans tried to end our ancestors' way of life. The massacre of the 9th Legion changed that. They came to take what wasn't theirs, and they disappeared into the wilds of Pict land without a trace. Romans. Nothing but bullies. Now a Roman legion dressed in blue sits across the gully. They ring our defenses with cannons, not catapults. They're armed with muskets, not bows and arrows. They've built their own Hadrian's Wall, not to keep us out, but to keep us in.

Isham wakes from a bad dream and yells into the night. "No more frontal assaults, you say? Why, Grant? Lost too many men? Where's Sherman's army? Lost your pride?"

A Yank laughs. "Bet Ole Shermy is fit to be tied with what happened here."

There's nothing funny about that. Many a good boy died in front of the 27th Louisiana Lunette. It's just crazy. A hundred years from now, no one will remember this place or why we fought and died here. They won't re-member how we hid behind these earthen walls in our own filth, nursing our wounds, living with death, starving. Nobody will remember that most of our men fight for home and family, and most never owned a slave or ever wanted one.

I elbow J.A. "You awake?"

"Am now."

"Ain't it strange some men brought Negroes to cook and wash for them?"

"They treat them fairly well, from what I've seen."

"Some are restless, hoping they be freed soon. Some already ran off."

"Hell, I would."

I check the cap on my musket. "Most of these boys fight for their lives, home, and family."

"That'd be me. Now go to sleep."

John Hall of Company G brought an old slave along to tend to his needs. Jasper threatened to whip him the other day for treating him too roughly. Hall walks through the rifle pit this morning complaining about Jasper chastizing him.

I tossed a clod at his boot. "If all you got is complain about a man you keep chained, Hall, take it on down the road. I don't want to hear it."

"May I sit?"

"Yeah, if you shut up about your slave."

Hall rubs his eyes. "My first wife, Tranquillam died in childbirth. I married her sister before I enlisted. She writes nasty letters sayin' how I left her with all my bad children."

I try not to be too hard on him. "Ain't a reason to treat that old man so bad, is it?"

"No, it ain't. Guess I could sell him like Isaac in E Company did. Said his wife and kids were starvin'. My family could use the money, too."

"Why not set him free and trust the Lord will bless you."

"What do you mean, set him free? By God, I'm fightin' for my family, our Negroes, and our country. What's that old man gonna do if I don't take care of him?"

Hall doesn't understand. Slavery is too ingrained in his thinking to separate it out.

The world will keep turning no matter what happens here. This war will end one day, and little will change if John's thinking prevails. Pushing that aside, I just have to hold on. And live.

It's madness. What becomes madness breeds madness. This won't be the last battle of the last war. Makes me wonder how civilized we are with dead and rotting bodies a few feet away, wounded screaming into the dark night, and Grant doesn't have the mercy or the decency to bury the dead and tend to the suffering. Heathen anyway.

My Creator taught me better. "Hell, I'd get shot tryin' to help those men."

Jasper plops down beside me. "Shoot you deader'n dirt."

"I just wish… I need to stop all this cussin'."

"Get your mind off it and write Ma a letter." Douglas the camel bellows out one of his regular grunts of dissatisfaction for being tethered. "Think I'll get James and go see Douglas again."

I'll write Ma, but don't expect she'll ever get it. I borrow an envelope from a boy in the next company over and set pen to paper.

Vicksburg,
May 24th, 1863

Ma, I hope you're safe from the Yanks. We heard Grierson made a ride down through Missip. I pray to God he don't come your way. We saw pretty hot action few days go, but we held the bluecoats off. We don't hear much now from outside, and rumors can't be trusted. We hope General Johnston will attack Grant soon so we can squeeze the Yanks flat like a corn fritter between our two armies.

I put in a bit of dirt from our defenses. Should I die on this sacred hill of honor, I want you to have a piece of God's troubled earth where I stand to defend our home. I know you worry, but me, Jasper, and James made it through the fightin fine. They're good soldiers. You'd be proud. You heard from George? I wish I'd said more to him and Elihu before I left home.

We don't get paid no more, so I can't send money. I would if I had it. Tell my sweet cousins Mary and Emaline hello and that I read the Bible Mary gave me. It gives great comfort.

Make sure you tell them about Douglas the camel the boys of the 43rd

Missip have as a mascot. He's a one hump camel that gripes and grunts because he don't like horses or bein tied up. If he gets loose, he kicks up a fuss somethin terrible. I wish you could see him.

Don't worry, Ma. We'll make it through this. Trials a man survives make him a man more alive. I don't understand it all, and it seems such a waste of good men, but I'm committed to this thing bein over, one way or another. I just hope I'm not a lesser man for it.

Though what I see everday is gruesome, my soul has hope. You taught me that no matter how bad life gets, the Lord makes it come out right somehow. I never wanted to admit it as a young man, but I am my momma's son. I'm proud to say it now. Tell all to stay strong and trust the Creater who gives life. Pray this will be over soon.

Your affectionate son,
Lummy

CHAPTER 30

YOU AIN'T GOTTA HAVE FOUR LEGS AND BRAY TO BE AN ASS

MAY 25, 1863

The dead rest just as good under the sun as they do under the dirt.

SARGE SHAKES HIS fist. "Grant's madder'n hell, boys." We cheer quietly not to draw unnecessary cannon fire. "We beat back that cigar-smokin', whiskey-guzzlin' bastard and that looney redheaded Sherman who sees gray ghosts behind every bush. Thought you'd just walk right in and take our guns out of our hands."

Hog Fart finds his bravery. "Can't snatch a bone out of this dawg's mouth!"

Sarge sits on an ammunition box. "Now them chickenshits gonna lay in a siege. Keep your muskets up and top knots down 'cause they're lookin' to take your head off at the neck. Short of makin' him your wife, protect the man beside you with all you got. He'll do the same for you."

The stench is unbearable. Bloated bodies ooze green and don't look human anymore. Jacket buttons pop off, and the scavengers roam freely. If this is Grant's way of punishing us for not letting him walk into Vicksburg, he's just making us meaner. I'd understand if it was our boys lying out there. The wounded, the dying, the dead are dressed in blue lying under a red hot skillet sun. Some have been there since the first attack on May 19th. It ain't right.

Their suffering is nearly insufferable. We pass a little water and hardtack to those in the ditch under the parapet. We warn them not to come over unless they make it clear they want to surrender. They stay put. I would.

Sarge inspects our muskets. "General Pemberton offered Grant that if he won't take care of his dead and wounded, we'll do it for him."

J.A. shakes his head. "It's the right thing to do. Grant. What a bastard."

A whimpering Yank begs, "Spare some water?"

Hog Fart hands it over on a willow stick.

I lean close to the berm and ask him, "Don't Grant care nothin' about y'all livin' like haints in a graveyard?"

The Yank cries out, "Grant won't gather the wounded if we don't take your positions. So here we sit." It ain't this man's fault he can't retreat.

"Makes no sense." He doesn't say anything. "Guess you don't have to have four legs and hee-haw to be a jackass."

The Yank chuckles. "That's for damn sure. I might shoot Grant myself if I make it back." We throw more hardtack biscuits over to ease their hunger— and to ease our consciences.

Grant grudgingly agrees to a ceasefire. At 6:00 p.m., white flags go up. Gray and blue rise out of their hiding places. Conversations are had, coffee and tobacco are traded, brothers embrace. I ask Sarge to let me visit my brothers across Glass Bayou.

"Get on back here soon as the truce is done. I need every good man on the line."

"Yassuh." I wander down the line to find Jasper and James still blackened with burnt powder from the last assault. They look as ghoulish as the dead in the field.

Jasper fingers his ear like he's trying to get a bug out. "I'm tryin' to open it up so I can hear."

James elbows me, grinning. "Helluva fight, huh, Lummy? They attacked three times May 19th and twice on the 22nd. Couple of our men were killed, a few got wounded, but we held. Our Lieutenant Eubanks got hurt pretty bad. How about y'all?"

I look down. "We lost a few."

Jasper interrupts to change the subject. "Sure could do with some of Ma's squirrel dumplin's."

James licks his lips. "And some cat-head biscuits and cane syrup Pa used to get in Bankston."

I squeeze his shoulder. "I'm just glad we're alive and together."

Jasper stands to stretch. "Let's go meet Yanks we missed with our cannons and grenades."

We walk to the field where hundreds of blue covered bodies litter the field. I've never seen anything like it. I don't want to ever again. We tie rags over our mouths and noses to brave the stench. James pukes twice when an arm of a body he drags breaks loose. He just stares at it. I take the arm and lay it on the chest of the corpse. Our men work as hard as the Yanks to bury the fallen. Gray men working side by side with men in blue—what a novel idea.

Jasper stops dragging a corpse for a minute to rest. "Bet ole Grant and Sherman are cussin' up a storm that we get along so good together. Regular men ain't got no issues. We're just common men with a common problem—generals."

I can't disagree. "Ain't no two-legged braying asses in this field. Just good men shakin' hands, makin' friends, and respectin' each other."

I scan the field. We desecrated and violated this land with hate and anger, death and murder. Only the blood of good men can wash away the stench of the wrong done in this place. Good men always have to die for the wrongs of evil men.

Two officers talk, one blue and one gray, enjoying each other's hospitality. The Yank officer bids farewell. "Good day, Captain, I trust we shall meet soon again in the Union of old."

The Reb captain pleasantly replies, "Forgive me, but I cannot return your sentiment, suh, for the only union you and I may enjoy, I hope, will be in the kingdom of God to come. Good-bye, suh." Well said in such a terrible place. Bugles blare, and we're ordered back to our trenches.

I shake a few Yank's hands. "Keep your heads down, you hear?" They wave.

As I pray on the way back to the lunette, two brothers embrace. The Reb wipes a tear. "We can't get any mail out now. Tell Ma and Pa I'm alive and doin' alright."

His blue-coated brother says, "I'll write them a letter right now." They go their separate ways.

Jasper and James catch up, and I pull them close. "Thank you, Lord."

CHAPTER 31

A LONG WAIT

JUNE 1, 1863

Like the brave 300, we'll hold the pass. Funny thing, they all got killed.

THE SHOW STARTS early this morning. We take a potshot here and there. It works if a man finds a target without taking one in the head himself. It's easier shooting a man whose face you can't see and name you'll never know. It ain't the same shooting a man you've become friends with.

The attacks are over. Joy is short-lived when Sarge says, "It's official. We're in a siege."

Hog Fart elbows me. "What's a siege?"

"Don't know, never been in one before." Nobody here has. We don't know what to expect.

Shortages are worse now that the Yanks have completely ringed our defenses. Our rations have been cut, and we're also running out of percussion caps. No food and no way to fight, and we don't know when we'll get either. Uncertainty to misery. The misery is that nothing happens.

Our captain stops by. "Boys, the Yanks raised a flag of truce demandin' our surrender. If we don't, they'll bomb the town."

Sarge snickers at this. "What in the hell do they think they've been doin' up 'til now?"

We laugh.

Our captain stiffens. "Men, we must strengthen the breastworks. I know it's extra duty, but we gotta make a good go of this. The Greeks besieged

Troy for ten years and still couldn't take the city. I know you can do this." He moves down the line to the next company.

Hog Fart cries. "We could be here ten years?"

J.A. whispers, "He didn't mention the Trojan Horse."

I rub my face. "I wouldn't tell that part, either. We're in for a long ugly wait, I'm afraid."

Cap comes back. "When General Johnston gets here, he'll send Grant and Sherman packing. Keep your heads down and the Yanks out."

He looks around. "These hills are stronger than the Trojan walls, and those Greek archers ain't got nothing on us crack shot Looseana boys. It won't be easy, men. There'll be disease, lack of water, and food will be hard to come by." He looks at the ground realizing his despair has gone too far. The silence takes its toll. "That war started over a beautiful woman named Helen whose face launched a thousand ships. Our lady is Mississippi, the Confederacy, and our sweethearts and wives, sisters and daughters.

"Good news, a courier sneaked past the Yanks last night with eighteen thousand percussion caps." We cheer as his assistant doles them out sparingly.

"Treat them like gold. Make every one count." He trots down the line to the next company.

"I came here for a beautiful woman, too—soft hair, dark eyes, velvety skin, and a face that'd launch ten thousand ships." Damn, I'll never hold her again. "I need to quit cussin'."

J.A. laughs and pats me on the back. "Yeah, you do."

Shots ring out, and a furious barrage sends us scampering to our bomb-proofs. It's over as quickly as it started.

Cap returns, hat in hand. "Colonel Marks is wounded. Is there a praying man among you?"

The men all look at me.

"Bow your heads...." I beg for mercy.

ALL KINDS OF reports come but none we can take for gospel. Lee whipped

Hooker. Bragg beat Rosecrans. Johnston is in Canton with 30,000 men and Loring not far behind with 10,000. Good news, if true. But who knows. Rumors come frequent as the scavengers.

The only thing I can compare a siege to is the time Jasper and I shot a tricky boar raccoon we called Ole Grayback because his dark hair turned silver over the years. He ran inside the hollow of an old oak. We beat on the tree, tried to smoke him out, but nothing worked. Talk about an angry raccoon. He'd growl at our every move. He'd outsmarted Uncle George's prized dogs every time. Talk about an angry coonhunter. He was once offered five hundred dollars for his best dog. Uncle George refused. That's more than most folks make in a year. Still, they couldn't catch Ole Grayback. We stood there scratching our heads. I cut a switchcane to poke him out.

"Jasper, get ready. He'll come out quick as lightnin'."

I jabbed it up the hollow of that oak hard as I could. That old boar coon let out an awful scream and bailed out looking for blood. I fell back, and the coon came right at me.

I yelled, "This ain't good!"

He was mad as a nest of stirred up hornets with teeth sharp as needles and claws like straight razors. I was up on my feet just as the coon bit my boot. I screamed when his teeth sank into my big toe and didn't turn loose. I danced like a holy rollin' revival preacher aiming to save souls at a camp meeting trying to get him off my boot.

Jasper yelled, "Hold still!"

He shot, but missed.

"You dang near shot my foot off, you dern fool." I fired at him straight down as I jumped straight up, but I missed. I cursed but was relieved I didn't shoot my own foot off. Finally, the raccoon shook loose. I yelled, "Get him!"

Ole Grayback lunged at me. I fell on the ground backing up. Jasper shot him, but he still came after me. I pulled my gun up just as Ole Gray Back leaped. I shot between my feet, and he landed on my knees. I lay on my back for a minute. Jasper's eyes were big as saucers. We started laughing and could hardly stop. That night we gorged on roasted coon and sweet potatoes. We spit enough shot out of Old Grayback to make a couple shotgun loads. That meal would go good in these trenches tonight. My stomach growls—sounds like that old coon again.

Like that old coon, we're holed up in these hills poked by cannons and muskets. It'll take a lot of jabbing to make us come out. We'll wind up on the Yankee supper table if we do.

Just before midnight, a Yank takes a jab. "Heard you got a new commanding officer."

Hog Fart yells back, "Now who'd that be, Billy Yank?"

"That'd be General Starvation, my good man." They belly laugh.

"Keep laughin', Yank, we're still here, ain't we?" I try to sleep.

NOT A CLOUD in the sky this morning but very warm. A mockingbird in his gray coat with a grasshopper in his beak lights on one of the Arkansas cannons. He knows nothing of the instrument of death upon which he sits. I'd eat that grasshopper right now. If John the Baptist ate locusts, so can I if there's a little honey to go with.

It's going to be a long wait.

There's not much to do between dodging cannon shells and minie balls except take a potshot every once in a while. The Yankees throw up their flags just to draw our fire. They shoot holes in ours, and we shoot at theirs. Better than at each other. Sarge orders us to save our bullets.

Night falls but brings little rest. A dirtclod lands at my feet.

"Hey, Reb, you asleep?"

Isham yells back, "Poke your head up and find out."

He whispers, "Get your heads down, the cannons are about to open up."

Shrapnel tears up a few tents in the rear and wounds three men. Mortar shells fly high in the night like shooting stars racing across the dark sky. A pretty sight until they land.

I stare up at the heavens. "Susannah, do you see me? Can you hear me when I talk to you? I know you're just on the other side of the thin veil. Can I touch you? Can you come to me? Should I stand up and let a Yank bullet send me to your arms? I want to come to you, my darlin'. I don't know how long I can hold on."

J.A. whispers, "It's all right, Lummy. It's all right."

The Yank's don't let up until morning. My spirit is low.

WE'VE BEEN IN these trenches three weeks, and it's been about that long since we've had acorn coffee. We receive a fair amount of rice and beans, but the stores of cornmeal are depleted. There's no meat except for a little mule.

Gnawing the last bit of meat from a rat leg, Hog Fart holds up the bone. "Nothin' but a squirrel with his tail shaved."

"Wonder what disease we'll catch eatin' these things?" I try not to think about it too hard as I take another bite. It gets so bad, men in the 26th Louisiana pick corn out of cow piles in the woods behind us. I breathe deeply and swear I can smell Ma's good cooking. Familiar scents waft over from the bluecoat side. "Dang it if that ain't salt pork and biscuits with a wisp of real coffee."

J.A. spits. "They do it on purpose." He throws a dirt clod over into the Yank's trench.

We hear a clank and a man curse. "Hey, that was our morning coffee, you Rebel bastard!"

J.A. laughs. "Sorry to disturb your breakfast, shithead."

I laugh to cover the sound of my guts growling like Old Grayback. Our meager rations can't feed a rat. Some make theirs last. Men who don't expect to live out the day wolf theirs down in a couple of bites. When cut to quarter rations, men desert. Hunger is a powerful enemy, but being locked up in Yankee prison camp doesn't sound good either.

Everybody cheers when Cap stops by to pass out tobacco. "Great news, men. Our river batteries sunk the *Cincinnati,* one of the Yankee's finest ironclads. Hundreds of town folk came out of hiding and cheered. We needed that victory."

Cap licks his finger to check the wind direction. "Just right." He loads his pipe. "Do me a favor. Everybody light up. I want the Yanks to smell this fine southern tobacco." The calming aroma reminds me of sitting on Grandpa Temple's knee listening to his stories. I rarely smoke, but I join in to let the Yanks know we ain't done yet.

I draw in slowly, savoring the taste. "Do I hear cannons rumbling?"

J.A. elbows me. "Nope, that's thunder in your belly."

I look at my smoke. "As good as this tobacco is, I can't eat it." It crosses my mind, though.

TODAY, A GOOD friend to the lunette finally gives up the ghost. An old poplar tree slams into our lunette. It took at least a hundred cannon shells and who knows how many minie balls to bring her down. It stood proudly though wounded terribly. Today it falls.

I check on Big Red in the hickory tree just down the hill. We haven't seen his bushy red tail lately. Maybe he went over to the Yanks. They surely have better food and more of it.

We're cooking rations against the fallen poplar tree when a shell buried in the woods explodes. I'm hurled back with a half-cooked ration of meat on a stick. Two men's whiskers are singed off, while another splashes water on his smoking long hair. The boys knocked to the ground slowly stir and regain their senses. One man is severely wounded and taken to the hospital.

J.A. picks up tin plates and cups scattered when the blast went off. "I'll be a suck egg mule if that ain't a sight." He pulls out his liquor ration and holds it high. "To our good luck and the Good Lord for watching over us."

Liquor and the Good Lord. Not a common combination, except in these trenches. I'm sure God turns a blind eye in times like this. I lean against the old poplar tree wondering if I'll be cut down by a cannonball.

Isham bumps my cup with his. "If anybody survives, it'll be you, Lummy."

"Dang my talkin' out loud." I sip a little whiskey and shrug it off.

J.A. pulls me up. "Let's work on the earthworks. It'll get your mind off of it."

We work alongside Negroes pressed into service. They sing and joke as they work.

J.A. rests on his shovel. "How can they be happy workin' like mules and livin' off of bits of cornbread and salt pork?"

"Sure makes me think twice about complainin'."

JUNE 10TH, AND it gets hotter every day. The Yanks don't come at us anymore. They have to be as tired of this as we are. It's impossible to get our minds off hunger and disease living in a hill bank expecting death anytime. I hunker down in my bombproof and dream about Susannah—coal-black eyes, slender hips, girlish grin, laughing at my silly jokes. What will I do now with Susannah gone? My heart aches worse than my belly. I try to sleep.

I wake to heavy rainfall for my turn at watch. The rain and mud make life worse in the trenches but bring a cool and pleasant evening. I occasionally take a peek through a sniper's hole. I can't talk in standing guard duty, so I can only listen as the men tell jokes to keep up their spirits. It's not long before their stories go nasty about women. Hearing them talk is like taking a big slug of clabbered milk. You just want to spit it out.

One time, Pa, my brothers, and I came in worn out and hungry from a hot and windless day working on Uncle Rube's farm. We all liked that old bachelor. He made us laugh and let us sip a little moonshine when Pa wasn't looking. Ma had a big pan of biscuits and fried rabbit on the table. I ate so fast, I nearly choked. I took a big gulp of cold sweet milk. Or so I thought. When it filled my mouth, I spewed it out like a Yankee cannon. I just knew Pa would slap me sideways, but he'd taken a drink at the same time.

Wet, hungry, and exhausted in this dirt hole having to smell Yankee coffee and salt pork cooking? I'd be happy to drink that clabbered milk right now.

CHAPTER 32

NO CANNONS? GRENADES WILL DO

JUNE 14, 1863

A shell, flyin' or rollin' downhill, will blow you to high heaven just the same.

W E'RE LOSING TOO much weight. They give us a new concoction called "cush-cush," a mixture of ground peas and meal we're supposed to bake into bread. It ain't fit to eat. Nobody complains. At least not out loud.

Overzealous, misguided men rail on like revival preachers. "If a man complains, he's a coward. If he talks about goin' home, put 'em in jail."

I just wish they'd shut up.

General Shoup orders them, "If you can't say somethin' to inspire us to fight, then sit down. Encourage them to stay strong, or I'll sit you down." They sit down.

Hard rain showers make the rifle pits into mudholes. A man can break a leg just walking picket. One man slipped in the dark, cut his leg, and bled to death.

J.A. gripes, "Damn, gettin' killed on your way to gettin' killed."

Sometime during the night, the Yanks hit a prime target in town with a shell. Smoke trails in the sky this morning. They said they'd bomb the city. I hope the town folk made it to their caves. We dig our bombproofs a little deeper into the parapet wall, just in case. We stretch blankets over the entrances and enjoy being out of the blazing sun.

The Yankees digging trenches up to the 27th Louisiana Lunette are almost close enough we could cook meals together. Don't think that'll happen.

News reaches us about lost battles in Virginia and Port Hudson near Baton Rouge expected to fall any time is nothing short of discouaraging.

One of the 31st Louisiana boys comes by the lunette today with his chest poked out. "The Yanks charged us and eighty got in, but we killed forty and took the other forty prisoner." I needed to hear that. Not about men being killed, but that we're holding. It's good news, I reckon.

Yank sharpshooters spend more ammunition in a day than we have on hand. Fortunately, another courier brings 20,000 more percussion caps for our muskets. But like our rations, cannon ordinance is all but gone. That *ain't* good.

Jasper feels like he's of no use. "Lummy, it's awful. Anytime we fire a shot, the Yanks bear down on us with fifty guns. They take out our cannon, and the others got no ammunition. If the Yanks come again, we're done for."

General Shoup gathers up the artillerists. "Got an idea, men." I sit by Jasper's and James's disabled cannon to listen. "You've done a fine job with your cannons, but that time is passed. You understand explosives better'n anybody. You will now retrain to become a grenade and thunderbarrel unit."

James responds, "Say *what?*"

"Listen to me now. A shell's a shell, flying through the air, lobbed over a parapet, or rolling down a hill. It blows you to high heaven either way. Some of you did that at the 27th Louisiana Lunette, didn't you?"

Jasper yells, "Ain't nothin' to it, Gen'ral. Light the fuse and lob them over like apples."

General Shoup points his finger at Jasper. "That's the spirit." He salutes and says to a captain from the 3rd Louisiana standing at a small table with various types of explosive rounds. "See to it." I move closer. A man can always use a little extra training.

He demonstrates hand grenades, larger rampart grenades, and thunder barrels—hogshead kegs filled with rocks, metal, or anything that can do serious damage to flesh.

I lean over to Jasper. "Hell's coming for the Yanks." I head back to the lunette after a few minutes. When Jasper and James finish training, they get permission to visit me. I'm cleaning my rifle when they jump into the pit.

James punches my bad shoulder. "How you doin', Lummy?"

I rub my arm and grin. "Worse now you're here." I polish my rifle barrel. "Y'all learn how to lob grenades better and roll thunder barrels down a hill? You could show 'em how you chunked dirt clods at each other back home. I got hit more'n once." Tightness seizes my chest. "Jasper, James, be careful with them grenades. Keep your eyes on the fuse. They can get away from you in a heartbeat, and then yours will stop beatin'. I saw a Yank get the top half of his body blowed off in the first attack. Terrible sight."

Jasper heaves, but nothing comes up. We sit quiet for a minute.

"Brothers, I ain't tryin' to scare you. Just get rid of anythin' with a fuse burnin' quick as you can, that's all."

THE 27TH GETS a leave for a few days rest in town. With my brothers close by I decide to rest in the shade trees behind the lunette.

Sarge doesn't argue. "See you soon, Lummy. Let Bowen's 2nd Missourah boys do the snipin' and night watch. You earned a rest, son."

I thank him. "Hey, Sarge, bring me any newspapers you find and something sweet, if you don't mind."

While the 27th is in town, our rations get cut again. A third pound of peas, two-thirds of five-sixths of a pound of meal—a measurement I don't understand—a half-pound of mule beef including bones and gristle, a little sugar, some lard, soup, and salt in like amounts that can't keep a man on his feet, much less ready to fight. We starve, and nothing can be done about it.

Yankee diggers are only ten paces from the lunette. It won't be long before they come for us. A shell explodes overhead, and Jasper and James rush to the rifle pit with grenades. Other men carry thunder barrels. I race to the line, ready to help. As they launch the deadly bombs, I fire and load, shooting one Yank after another. James lights the grenades and Jasper lobs them high in the air so they explode a few feet above the ground. Yanks scream and yell, cry and curse.

James grabs a thunder barrel. "This 'uns full of small shells."

Jasper lights it and pitches it over the parapet. The first big explosion goes off, then the shells burst, scattering shrapnel in every direction. Blood splashes high and falls like rain. They go back to lobbing grenades. One comes back as fast as Jasper throws it over landing where James lights the next grenade.

I yell, "James!"

He hands the lit one to Jasper, grabs the returned bomb and launches just in time for it to burst about fifteen feet above their heads. He grins like a demon and keeps lighting grenades and handing them to Jasper. Jasper's arm gets tired, so James takes his turn throwing.

I shake my head. "Is this battle ever gonna end?"

Just as Jasper starts to throw his last grenade, a terrible force knocks him down. I grab the grenade Jasper dropped and throw it just in time. A cannonball had found its way into our rifle pit, blowing Jasper's hat off. James throws a bucket of water at the cannonball buried into the soft dirt. Thankfully, it didn't go off.

Finally, the Yanks retreat, and I check on my brothers. Jasper's dazed but gets up, dusting off his pants. He puts on his hat, but it falls apart. "Well, what do you think about that?"

I take a hat from a dead soldier and hand it to him. "This will do."

The two boys sit down on the hard dirt. I bring water. They nearly choke drinking so fast.

I check Jasper's head. "How's it feel?"

"All right, I reckon."

James laughs. *"Lucky* is the word."

I'm glad he doesn't have a crease on his head like Mr. Wiley got in the Mexican War.

James laughs. "How about that little skirmish, big brother? You didn't worry too much?"

Jasper cleans his nails with his pocketknife. "Why didn't you take leave in town and go see all the pretty girls?"

"You know why, little brother."

James kicks Jasper's shoe. "So when I write Ma and tell how you had your eyes on all the pretty girls in Vicksburg, what's your sweet wife Isabella Ray gonna say?"

Jasper raises his hands in surrender. "You're right. I'm done. I'm out. No more talk like that. I'd appreciate it if you keep that last remark to yourself."

James pokes his chest. "You're safe with me."

Then it hits me hard in the heart.

Jasper lays his arm on my shoulder. "Susannah?"

I nod, and a tear drops. "I wish I could joke like that about a wife I get to go home to one day." We sit in silence.

James looks to the western sky. "Looks like a rain comin'."

I stand up. "I'm fine. Boys, just love who the Lord gives you and be true as best you can. They deserve it."

I ease up to the line to listen for diggers and to be alone. It crosses my mind to stick my head up and take a bullet. I can't do that. I still believe the Good Lord has something for me. Susannah wouldn't want that either.

Jasper takes me by the shoulders and gently shakes me. "I'm glad you're here, big brother. We do better with you around. You watch over our souls."

I clear my throat. "Y'all know this ain't lookin' too good. We can't last long if that damn Johnston don't show soon. Them boys y'all just blowed up? They've got more to replace them. They're diggin' a mine underneath this lunette to blow us to high heaven. Pay attention Jasper, and watch after James, you hear?" I walk on.

A shot rings out. A man down the line peeking into a sniper hole gets his eye shot out. Did he make a mistake or a choice?

I can't make it that easy.

CHAPTER 33

SIFTED LIKE WHEAT

JUNE 15, 1863

*Don't stay mad too long at the man next to you. He may just save
your life in the next scrap. And there* will *be a next one.*

JUNE 15TH, AND it's hot. There's hardly a blade of grass or a bush in
sight. The trees we felled before the Yanks came lay flat from the shelling. The dirt is as powdery as the loads we pour into muskets—like Ma's
flour after she sifts it for baking. *Sifted.* Pastor Dobbs preached that Satan
would sift Peter like wheat. That couldn't have been a pleasurable experience. It ain't here, either.

Hog Fart returns from town early and hands me yesterday's Vicksburg
newspaper printed on wallpaper.

That ain't a good sign.

"Got no money, and them boys just gonna get in trouble, anyway. I come
on back to be with you, Lummy, that all right?"

I nod, but really, I've enjoyed not talking to anyone.

The little news rag has nothing of value except to laugh at the Yankee
lies about our enormous casualties and how they run the river blockade with
ease. True or not, doesn't matter. We're sifted down to bags of skin and bone
with little food except the rats we catch. The Yanks could take us if they
make one mad rush from all directions. If they do—oh, well.

James complains when they dole out rations. "Might as well eat it all in
one bite. I might die today." I eat a bit at a time to make it last. Either way,
hunger pangs don't go away.

Hog Fart begs, "Lummy, can you spare a bit of hardtack? I'm so hungry I could eat the slop out of a dead hog's rear end." I heave, but there's nothing in my stomach to puke up. Hog Fart laughs. "Gotcha, didn't I?"

"Shut the hell up or go somewhere else." I hurt his feelings. "Sorry, I just ain't in the mood to hear about eatin' out of a dead hawg's hind end."

"I shouldn't have said it, I guess. But don't you forget how I got my nick-name, you bastard."

I like that boy. You can't stay mad too long at the man next to you. He may just save your life in the next fight. And there *will* be a next one.

I've heard about people going crazy with hunger to the point of eating each other. I'd rather shoot myself. The Lord surely would understand. Both happened in the Bible—people eating each other and people killing themselves.

Thunder booms in the west. I spy a strange ship in the air across the river. "What is that?"

Hog Fart squints. "I don't know, but there's a long rope tied to a big basket hooked to a big round ball floating in the sky."

Heavy thunder then booms east of us. I glance back at the strange ship. "Hog Fart, dark clouds comin', so you best find cover or you'll get soaked."

Douglas the camel bellows back at the thunder, almost like he's trying to tell us something.

Hog Fart cups his ears. "Lummy, that ain't storm clouds comin'. Them's Yankee cannon."

A whistle becomes a scream. My skin crawls. *"Get down!* It's goin' over, but not by far."

The shell slams into the embankment behind our rifle pit and blows dirt all over us. Hog Fart rolls on the ground screaming. I jerk him up and peek through a sniper's pipe. The Yanks are marching directly at us. The blue storm lets go of its thunder when they charge.

A sergeant yells, "They're comin', boys! Put them bayonets on, quick!"

Hog Fart's knees shake as he puts a cap on his rifle. "Ain't they had enough? Ain't none of us gonna live to see our mommas ever again."

They come in a fury to take the 27th Louisiana Lunette. But we're mean-er. They scramble up the hills in four columns attacking the breastworks like they're just going to walk right in.

Wrong again.

What's wrong is another senseless bloodletting that'll end with dead bodies and no change. But the damn generals will give account to someone someday, even if it's only to God.

I guess Grant wasn't serious when he ordered no more frontal assaults. Maybe it's just a trick to make us slack off. There won't be any tricks coming from this side today. We have the high ground, and our boys are shooters. The Yanks slip and slide in the powdery dirt. I'm reloading when a blast of hot wind knocks me back. A lone cannon on our right pours fire into the side of the Yank's advance.

The Missouri men yell, "Hurrah for the 3rd Looseana." It's only one gun, but the canister fire blows holes in their lines big enough to drive a wagon through. It's awful—the screams, body parts scattering everywhere, blood covering the ground like snow in the wintertime.

Now I understand why they call it "sacred ground." It's ground washed in blood.

A colonel waves his hat. "Give them the hot lead, boys. Make your brothers down the line proud they joined in. Enfiladin' fire, damn, that's the ticket. Hurrah for the 3rd Looseana!"

We fire faster and fight harder, cutting men down like making hay.

The colonel yells again, "No way in Heaven, Hell, or on Earth are you taking this hill! Not today, by God!"

Jasper and James steadily chunk grenades, tuning out the screams and groans of the wounded and dying. The Yanks make a mad rush only to run into a gray brick wall. Finally, they back away, dragging their wounded and dead with them. When they stop shooting, so do we.

We watch for a second charge that never comes.

I elbow Hog Fart. "Wonder what the talk in Grant's headquarters will sound like tonight?"

He grins. "Probably more drinkin' than talkin'."

The Yanks cannonade us all through the night while we repair our defenses—defenses they failed to take yet again.

Will this ever end?

MORNING DAWNS PLEASANT with cottony white clouds floating by, as if all is well with the world everywhere. And it is, at least for the morning. We receive rations hardly enough to stave off starvation. Anything is good when you have nothing. The Yanks know we're having a hard time food wise. Our nightly talks are had in good spirits. But there's always at least one wise ass.

A Yank tosses over a hardtack biscuit into our little group huddled against the wall. Starvation is written on it. We immediately chunk it back over, politely inscribed, *Forty days rations and no thanks to you.*

"Don't mean no harm, Johnnies. We just want to know how much longer we gonna be out here in the sun and skeeters."

Hog Fart finds his bravery. "Best settle in, Billy Yank. There's no place we'd rather be than right here. That fine beef steak and sweet taters I had for supper surely will help me sleep well."

"Yeah, but when's the circus show?"

"What circus show?"

"You got an elephant to go with that camel? Pemberton's the best damn ringmaster ever." They laugh.

"Poke your damn head up, and we'll show you the elephant."

"No need to get testy, Reb. We figure if you don't put on a circus show, we could put that critter on the spit. Bet camel tastes better'n mule and rat."

"You're right about rat, but give mule a try. You might just like it better'n beef cow."

"Give 'em hell, Johnny Reb."

"Give 'em hell, Billy Yank."

We laugh, but keep our heads down.

CHAPTER 34

SOLDIERS WITH FEW EQUALS

JUNE 18, 1863

Water runs downhill. So does a man's spirit in a siege.

LIGHTNING FLASHES ALL around. It's tough to know when God throws thunderbolts or Grant spits artillery shells. Either way, I keep my head down. And my spirit sinks lower. The corn meal gave out yesterday. We only have a few days' rations left. A man gets edgy when his stomach clutches his backbone.

I don't know how much longer I can hold out.

The Yanks are close enough to throw notes over. A Yank dangles a hardtack biscuit tied to green switch cane. It bends just low enough Hog Fart can untie it without getting shot. They laugh, and so do we. We both need a breather. The Yankees sing hymns like they're at a funeral. We're all attending our own funerals on this dark evening.

Hog Fart whispers, "How can them boys come down here, kill our friends, and have God's sacred tunes on their lips? Don't make no sense."

My only answer is to join in quietly with the Yanks. Hog Fart shrugs and whistles the tune.

THE 27TH LOUISIANA returns from town at daylight in a thick fog. J.A. walks to his spot on the line, scratching his head. "Damn, fog's so thick the birds are walkin'."

Sarge tosses me copies of the *Vicksburg Daily Citizen, The Daily Whig,* and Yank newspapers out of Indianapolis and Chicago. I look up expectantly.

"Here you go, boy." He pitches me a chunk of hard molasses candy, too.

"Appreciate it, Sarge."

"Heard you boys were in a scrap. You all right?"

I nod and change the subject. No sense rehashing death I've already put behind me. "Where'd you get the newspapers, Sarge?"

"I commandeered them just for you from the good citizens. Enjoy the rock candy, but I want the papers back for purposes other than readin', if you get my drift."

"Hell, I get your drift every time you head to the screamer ditch."

"Ain't you the funny man? You heard what I said."

"Sarge, what was that up in the sky back towards town the other day?"

"That, my young friend, is what they call an observation balloon. We saw it from Sky Parlor Hill. I guess the Yanks want to see what in the hell they're blowin' up."

"Well, ain't that somethin'. Man hoverin' in the clouds like buzzards."

Sarge grins. "Take the rest of the day, son. You've earned it."

I settle down into my bombproof, suck on the smooth candy, and read newspapers. A quiet respite, even if only for a few hours. For a moment the world around me fades away.

The papers say over a hundred women and children have been killed or wounded here from the shelling. A Yankee colonel named Daniels lost six hundred Negro soldiers in a charge against Port Hudson. A Chicago paper says General Robert E. Lee is invading Pennsylvania. Another tells of other happenings around Vicksburg.

I throw the papers down. "Dang fool war ain't never gonna end. We ain't givin' up, either."

A shell explodes overhead, and I draw back into my bombproof. My heart sinks low. I enjoy the last taste of candy as it fades away with my hopes.

JUNE 19TH, AND the diggers are so close we hear every whisper. Just before sunup, a drunk Yank yells, "You best leave now. We're gonna blow you to high hell soon." His friends yank him back down, cursing. Soused or not, though, there's some truth in his drunken words.

I find Jasper and James. "The Yanks are minin' underneath us and will blow this lunette. When you ain't on duty, stay away from the parapet." I look into my brothers' eyes, their faces gaunt from lack of food, their souls weary of the killing and constant threat of danger. They're wasting away. "You boys hold on. We're gonna make it out of here alive somehow. Like Pa used to say, 'You gotta bow your necks, boys.'"

James wraps his arms around me and Jasper around him. "It's all right." But it's not.

Gunnard comes down the line walking slowly, stepping over men and trash. I motion him over. "Jasper, James, this here's Gunnard, best storyteller in the whole damn army."

Gunnard takes off his hat. "Don't mean any harm, Lummy, but I bring only a story of heartbreak today. Weren't you friends with that young boy who never got his papers signed to go home?" Gunnard hands me a small Catholic medallion on a chain with the inscription *"Mary conceived without sin, pray for us."*

I recognize it and my heart sinks.

Gunnard kicks the dirt. "There's no easy way to say this. Poor young Granville was standing in the pits yesterday at six o'clock, doin' his faithful duty, when two minie balls shot clean through his head just above the right eye. He said nothing when he fell. They took him to the hospital, but he died soon after. I knew you'd want to know."

Tears fill my eyes. "He never took this little medal off and was the most faithful of us all goin' to church. His momma'll want this." I wail for a moment, and Gunnard pats me on the back. Nobody says anything. Sarge stands to block the scene, but no one looks our way.

Finally, my tears run out.

Gunnard stands slowly. "Lummy, you were a good big brother to him. His ma and sister need to know. Would you consider writing them with your kind, God fearin' hand? I found paper, and my captain said he'd get it out somehow. What do you say?"

"Be glad to."

Sarge steps up. "I'll make sure he gets time to do it."

Gunnard places his hand over his heart and quotes Shakespeare. "Hell is empty, and all the devils are here"—pointing at the Yankees, he places his other hand on my head—"but God's angels are here, too, though some are with you now, Lord." Gunnard hands me the paper and slowly walks away, holding his hat in his hand.

Sarge crouches down to look in my eyes. "You all right?"

I nod, and he moves back to the line. I choose not to go see Granville's body, though. Some things are best remembered as they were.

Sarge brings me an envelope with President Davis's picture like the one I sent Ma last Christmas. "You done?" I nod. "Men, gather around. I want you to hear Lummy's words to Granville's folks back home."

Jasper and James stand beside me. "I had some help writin' this letter. Our good friend Gunnard made sure I got the right spellin's. Thank him too."

Vicksburg, Miss,
June 19, 1863

Dearest and Most Respectfully Mrs. Amelia Alspaugh and Your Daughter Gertrude,

I write this letter with great sadness that your young and brave son, Granville, has been killed by the Yankees. It is a loss to all who knew him, and we thank God for his presence with us here in Vicksburg. We know that our pain in no way could ever match that of a loving mother who watched him grow and a faithful sister as a loving companion. He spoke of you often and lovingly. There was nothing more on his mind than return-ing to you as soon as possible. We cherished our time with Granville as he was faithful and cheerful in the worst of trials here. Granville was a hard worker, never shirking his duty, even in the lowest of moments. He did fi-nally send a Yankee to meet the Good Lord and saved many of us at crucial times when the Yankees attacked. He enjoyed playing games and made me a chess set out of bullets for Christmas. He was always doing something for another. Now Granville loved all the pretty girls. He made us laugh with his hopes and dreams of marrying every one he met. I know that some poor, sweet young lady will not have the husband of her dreams because Granville gave his short and promising life for his friends. The Master once said, "Greater love hath no man than this that a man lay down his life for his friends." Granville did just that, a soldier with few equals. He loved you, Sister, very much, and looked forward to being with you, Bobbie, and Wright again after the war. Granville asked me to serve as a big brother to him. I had the privilege of getting to know your son and brother as a soldier and a friend. When this war ends, and the Lord allowing me grace and mercy, I will come visit you to tell you more about your son. Enclosed is Granville's medallion. He wore it always.

Affectionately, on behalf of all soldiers in this place,
Private Columbus "Lummy" Nathan Tullos

"Sarge, all right if I pray?" He nods. "Lord, there ain't a righteous man amongst us except by Your grace and mercy. But why him? Why a young boy so bright-eyed and bushy-tailed ready to live a good life? Where's Jesus now when we need Lazurus raised? I know Granville would say, 'Don't cry for me.' Give him rest, Lord, and protect us, Amen."

Gunnard gently takes the letter from my hand. "Straight from the Psalms, my good friend, and as God heard David crying out, he hears you now. I'll make sure this gets through the lines. Before I do, I'll read it to the men in his company."

I nod and walk away. It's very quiet in the rifle pits tonight.

The Yanks hurl a rock over. A note is tied on with a string that reads. *Sorry about your friend. He must've been a good kid. God bless you boys.*

CHAPTER 35

FREEDOM COMES IN STRANGE WAYS

JUNE 20, 1863

Hell from below can bring freedom from above.

THE SUN BURNS bright early this morning, and the Yanks shell us like we've never seen. The Yank gunboats come close to town with flags at half-staff but back away. No one knows why.

J.A. elbows me. "It was for Granville, the best damn soldier this army ever had. Better'n the blue devils on them gunboats wavin' their flags." I thank him.

By midmorning, we hear digging underneath the lunette. They're close. The Yanks pitch a funny-looking grenade over. Fortunately, it doesn't go off. We've not seen one quite like this. It's egg-shaped, about four inches long and two inches wide with a percussion cap on one end and a wooden arrow about six inches long out of the other to make it fly straight. James runs it down to the 1st Mississippi Light Artillery to show Company C's captain.

With the new grenades and extra shelling, we expect the Yanks will attack today. They're killing our nerves more than anything. Anticipating an explosion is almost worse than assaults.

This war is strange. The Yanks don't want to be here anymore than we do. They're friendly, trading boxes of sardines, coffee, and paper for our tobacco. We enjoy lively conversation filled with news and bad jokes. There's kindness and respect even among men killing each other. It's never easy to shoot those boys. But when it comes time, we go at it.

Constant shelling and sharpshooting wears on us like rain washing away a mud bank. "Lord, I'm ready to be washed away."

Jasper jumps into the rifle pit. "Wash nothin'. Teach me how to play chess." I look at every piece Granville so carefully carved by his hand. It's hard to get my mind on the game, but it's a good diversion. The good feeling doesn't last very long.

Sarge's report doesn't make things any better. "Lieutenant Colonel McLaurin was wounded in his side by a minie ball yesterday. Major Norwood was shot in the leg this afternoon."

I dump the chess pieces on the ground. "I can't play no more." Jasper picks up the pieces. Sarge just walks on. I walk away. The anger that kept me alive is gone. I don't have the strength, and I don't want the Devil in me any longer. I haven't felt this bad since the day I found out Susannah died. I hunker down in my bombproof and sit alone.

THE YANKS ASSAULT the 31st Louisiana line, but they counter to capture the enemy's pits and some prisoners, including a lieutenant. The Yanks try to retake the ground on the morning of the 23rd but are repulsed with heavy loss. We perk up hearing about the 31st Louisiana's fight. Though we still have fight in us, we're sun-blistered, half-starved, and shaking with fevers and dysenteric sickness. Fortunately, town ladies turn out to care for the sick and dying men.

A runner hands Sarge a message. "It seems some of the good citizens in town have been hoardin' whiskey. Company F is ordered to search every household in town." We find sixty-nine bottles of whiskey in a merchantile at the corner of Clay and Levee Streets.

Sarge screams at the proprietor. "You had this all along, and men are sick and dying for *you,* fool!" We grab Sarge before he slaps the overstuffed man and empties his store of everything.

On the way back, Sarge points to a case of whiskey. "That one's for y'all. Make sure the rest gets to the doc." No two ways about it. We got drunk. It was the best night's sleep I've had in weeks. A light rain cools the air and keeps the mosquitoes away.

I wake feeling much better this morning, June 25th.

Sarge waits for us at the cookfire. "Lieutenant Colonel McLaurin died last night. He will be missed. Y'all rest up. Nothin's gonna happen today with the rain last night. Besides, it's gonna be a scorcher."

Suddenly, a rumbling like the Devil clawing and scratching his way out of Hell belches below us. An eruption of dirt, fire, timbers, and men rises into the air at the 3rd Louisiana Redan.

Sarge yells, "Get your rifles, the Yanks blew their mine."

As soon as the dirt comes back down, a wave of bluecoats rush in like Satan's demons. My heart tries to leap out of my chest—Jasper and James are there with their artillery company.

Sarge says, "Lummy, go. The rest of you stay here."

Isham pitches me my musket and Hog Fart my ammunition pouch. I run like a demon let loose from Hell crossing Glass Bayou and sprinting up the hill where 1st Mississippi Light Artillery Company C is positioned. A great cloud of dust settles over the intense fighting in the 3rd Louisiana Redan. I catch up with the 6th Missouri Regiment pushing forward to join the fray. I arrive as fierce hand to hand combat is at its worst.

A colonel jumps up on top of the rifle pits yelling, "C'mon, my brave boys, don't let the Third Regiment get ahead of you."

I yell in the ear of the Missouri man beside me. "Who is that?"

"Colonel Erwin Clay, grandson of Henry Clay!" No sooner does the colonel get the words out of his mouth than a sharpshooter takes him down. The Missourians are appalled and surge forward to push the Yankees back down the hill. Our men on top of the crater mercilessly pour fire into the writhing blue mass that can go neither forward nor backward. The battle rages for two hours. The Yanks throw up a makeshift parapet across the crater, but our boys rolling live shells into the crater soon end the attack. Nothing is gained but a loss of life on both sides.

When it's safe, I find Jasper and James huddled together like rabbits hiding in a thicket. Jasper glares at me like a dog defending his last bite of food, and James stares wide-eyed into space. My heart leaps for joy that they're still alive but aches for the damage done to their souls.

James cries, "They came at us like demons out of hellfire, Lummy. We just kept chunkin' grenades and rollin' thunder barrels at them." Jasper says nothing. I don't know if it's from exhaustion or shock—probably both. Victories aren't always sweet for men doing the killing.

Jasper looks up into the sky. "Six Missip boys were buried alive today. Wonder where the rest of Company C is?" He stares at me with bloodshot eyes. "Lummy, I saw a Negro cook get throwed higher'n that old hickory at your place. He landed near the Yankee line. Damnedest thing I ever saw. He jumped up and ran like a rabbit to the Yank trenches."

"I reckon that's one way to get your freedom."

CHAPTER 36

OUR MINE BEFORE YOUR MINE

JUNE 27, 1863

I was taught to let others go first, but not today.

I WANDER OVER to find my brothers making grenades. Jasper laughs. "That explosion hardly rattled the 3rd Louisiana boys. They're just itchin' for the Yanks to come back."

I grin. "I just ain't that eager to get my head shot off."

James sets down a grenade. "Me, neither. Hey Sarge, need to stretch my legs. Okay if we go over to Lummy's lunette to eat?" He waves his hand giving permission.

Jasper pulls on my shirt and points. "Lummy, look here. This is one of the wooden shields we use to protect ourselves from sharpshooters while we're firin' cannons."

I count the splintered dents. "Thirty-eight musket bullet marks?"

"Yeah, and that was my shield."

"Get your stuff, and let's go." They grab their rations, and we rough house on the way. We laugh, talk, and tell old family stories, trying not to think about the horrors we've witnessed.

There's a buzz of excitement in the lunette as we come up the hill from Glass Bayou. Captain Wiggs has gathered the sergeants and corporals for a quiet discussion.

Sarge pulls us aside. "Boys, keep talkin' like nothin's different, but back up from the parapet. We got a little surprise for them Yanks diggin' under our lunette."

Our diggers scramble out of the countermine like rats with dirt so thick on their faces we can only see their eyes and smiling teeth. "We heard 'em talkin' last night. They're about to blow their mine. But we beat 'em to it. Cover your ears and hold onto your asses. It's fixin' to blow."

A robin flies down on the last patch of weeds near the 27th Louisiana Lunette. He cocks his head sideways listening for a worm. The mine engineer is doing the same, except he's not listening for a lifegiving worm. He's listening for death. The ground beneath us rumbles and shakes. The earth swells for a moment and settles back down. It's over.

A digger sighs, "That's it, boys. Them Yank diggers will be down there forever now."

Captain Wiggs announces, "Well done, men. My ma said I should always let others go first. Just couldn't do that today."

Men from other regiments come running. Gunnard grabs me. "You hurt, Lummy? I was so scared I went to shakin' like a dawg trying to shit a peach pit."

James looks up, gnawing on hardtack. "My mine before your mine, huh, Mistuh Gunnard?"

A soldier from the 43rd Mississippi races over. "Come help us. Douglas got loose in all your confusion. The Yanks'll surely shoot him."

I grab my rifle, and several of our boys along with Jasper and James take off running. We get to the rifle pit just as a Yank blows a hole through Douglas's rib cage. A collective groan rises from both sides, gray and blue. Douglas tries to walk but struggles to stay up. His legs collapse. A long slow grunt belches from the animal we all have grown to love. Douglas the camel dies.

Colonel Moore yells, "Dammit, Douglas survived Iuka and Corinth. How in the hell did he get loose?" He shakes his fist in the air. "You dirty rotten son of a bitch. You'll get yours."

A sergeant pulls him down. "Now, Colonel, you know Douglas escapes every chance he gets but never wanders off too far. The countermine goin' off at the 27th Lunette made him go crazy."

Colonel Moore is beside himself. "I knew this was bound to happen, but they didn't have to shoot him. You men the best on the line?" I'm not one of the sharpshooters, but I nod with the other five. "Then shoot his camel killin' ass."

The Yank sharpshooter ducks, but three shots make their mark. We think he's dead. It's dark when a medic drags him back to the Union lines. I think the Yanks wish that boy dead. They loved Douglas as much as we did.

I take the evening watch. "Hey, Reb, sorry about Douglas. We all liked watchin' him stomp and grunt. Sorry, but our boy's carved him up for supper. I couldn't. Too much like eatin' a pet yard dawg."

"Apology accepted. But we got the dumbass who shot him, didn't we?"

"You got him in both legs and once in the shoulder. He lost a leg, though."

"Could've been worse. He could be dead."

"I dunno, Reb. I bet he wonders now if it was a good trade, a stump leg for a camel. I believe he got the worst of it. But that ain't the worst. Now they're carving his bones for souvenirs. Anyway, you boys of the 27th got the best of us this mornin'. You beat us to it."

"Beat you to what?"

"You blowed five of our miners to kingdom come." He sniffles. "My cousin was one of 'em."

"I'm real sorry about that. Y'all close?"

"Grew up huntin' and fishin' and goin' to church together. Gonna miss that boy."

"What's his name?"

"You mean, what *was* his name?"

"Naw, what *is* his name?"

"George. Why you ask what his name is?"

"George ain't off in the clouds somewhere. He's right here with us. We just can't see him. There's just a thin veil betwixt us and him. My Granny taught me that. It's true if she said it."

The Yank is quiet for a long minute. "Thanks, Reb, you give hope to this hurtin' heart."

"I'll say this, and then we best be done. With your cousin here with you, what's the worst that can happen now? You go to God and back to fishin' with George in Heaven. Think about it."

He sighs. "Amen, brother."

Brother.

I sigh, too. Brothers caught in a mess neither of us started but might be the end of us both.

SUNDAY MORNING, JUNE 28th, St. Paul's bells ring, calling folks to worship. I wish I could attend, but I pull double duty today. I enjoy quiet moments in the cathedral of open air, trees, clouds floating by, and birds singing. And with the saints right here, too.

A soldier from G Company trots into camp. "You ain't gonna believe it. Soon as the priest opened the church doors after service, them damn Yanks sent a shell right in amongst us. Lucky only a few got hurt. The Good Lord's gonna make them pay for that." He runs off cursing.

J.A. laughs. "Maybe it's too dangerous to be a Catholic."

Sarge reads a Mobile paper to us. "Port Hudson has been attacked twenty-five times but still holds. They're puttin' up a heck of a fight. I wish we had the strength and ammunition to make a charge. Grant and Sherman wouldn't expect that."

A man can't do much more than stay alive on our meager rations, no matter how spirited he is. We get paid, but Confederate money is only good for the shit ditch.

Sarge gets up from his hogshead. "We got us a new major. Some feller named Jesse Cooper. Don't know where he's from, but I know where he's headed if a Yank sniper gets sight of him." We half-heartedly laugh. None of us are immune to Yank snipers.

J.A. whispers, "Major of what? Hell, we ain't got the strength to even have roll call."

And the Yank diggers get closer every night.

GUNNARD COMES BY this morning, June 29th, to compliment us again on counter striking the Yank miners. "A job well done, my good friends.

My fine meal today consisted of hardtack, a little molasses, and the finest fried rat in these hills. Never tasted squirrels any better'n their cousins who'd rather crawl than climb." He snickers. "Speaking of rats, I believe we have more blue rats burrowing underneath our redan again. I've come to inquire of your Captain Wiggs about the fine art of blowing bluebellies to hell before they reach us first." We point to where the Captain sits calculating numbers.

A Yank yells, "I know you like rats, but how's that mule meat workin' out for you?"

Gunnard, not to be outdone, says, "Why, the 27th has a rather large one roasting as we speak, and we cordially invite you to share the most tempting of fine cuisines. Shall we have a table reserved for you fine gentlemen dressed in blue?"

"Smartass Reb."

Gunnard salutes. "My day is complete."

It's not all bad. We boil our suger ration down to make hard candy. Mule meat is coarser than beef, but it tastes just as good. Someone finds a pond full of crawfish, and the Creoles go to cooking. We each get a steaming cup of fine gumbo. That runs out fast. So it's back to mule meat, poke salad, and rice soup, but who's complaining?

HOG FART WAKES with his hair stuck out in every direction. "What day is it?"

I have to think hard. "I think the 30th of June but...."

The silence is shattered by a second mine exploding underneath Gunnard and the 3rd Louisiana. I run as fast as I can, thankfully to find my brothers pulling bodies from the dirt.

Jasper yells, "More'n a hundred men got killed or wounded. They didn't attack the crater this time. They just bombed the hell out of us."

Just another unnecessary waste of life.

They demoralize us, holding up bread loaves on poles so we can see. We're so hungry. Many are sick from disease and sun exposure. We need relief. We need to get out of this place. I wish I could fly away to a peaceful sandbar in the Mississippi River and escape the madness.

J.A. asks, "When the Good Lord comes for me, would you say words over me?"

"If I do, it'll be after a long and prosperous life."

He slumps. "I hope so."

We're tired. We want to go home.

TOMORROW IS INDEPENDENCE Day, and rumors fly that Pemberton is asking terms for peace. We're ordered not to fire at all today.

A Yank whispers, "Grant'll treat you better if you surrender on the 4th of July." Some say Pemberton was a traitor from the start and planned to give up Vicksburg when he took command. I don't believe that at all.

It's not Pemberton who writes a letter threatening mutiny if decent food isn't had soon. It's not Pemberton's name signed at the bottom, but "Many Soldiers."

I would have signed it.

THIS AFTERNOON I find Jasper and James dozing against a rifle pit wall. "Boys, looks like Pemberton's gonna surrender tomorrow."

James wipes dust from his eyes. "I ought to get my musket and go after that damned Pem—"

"No time for that, little brother. We got bigger hawgs to skin right now."

Jasper thumps James's head. "Shut up, James, and listen."

James nods, though aggravated.

I pull them close. "This storm is about over, and there'll be bright sunshine somewhere on the other side. We're gonna do what the Yanks say and stay alive."

Jasper blinks in disbelief. "I can't believe we made it."

"We will get separated again. Jasper, James, keep your mouths shut, don't cause a ruckus even if men around you start somethin'. It's over, you hear me? It's time to survive."

James sniffles. "We ain't goin' together, Lummy?"

"Probably not. They'll keep us in our regiments. Stay alive. I'll do the same." I pray, hug them both hard, and leave for Company F at the 27th Louisiana Lunette.

I can't do this anymore—be strong for my brothers, Hog Fart, and others. I've never felt so low, weak, so ready to die. I'm just a sack of bones, and my skin is dark as acorn coffee. I've had enough of this. J.A. hands me a scrap of paper he saved for a letter to his wife.

I shake my head.

He pushes it back. "You need to write your wife more'n I need to write mine, Lummy."

J.A. knows Susannah is dead. I start a letter too difficult to write. I date it July 3rd, 1863.

I think, *Either I die, or the world changes today....*

CHAPTER 37

SURRENDER

JULY 4, 1863

Never judge a defeat you've yet to experience.

PEACE BLANKETS THIS broken land like fog thick on the river. No one stirs. No one talks. But the birds sing. It's been a while since they've serenaded us. A breeze brings some relief. We need it. I sense a glimmer of something I'd nearly forgotten. Through the anger, pain, killing, madness, and betrayal, somehow I feel hope for the first time in weeks. It's a strange sensation.

At 8:00 a.m. July 4th, a flag of truce is carried from our lines to the enemy. Men shake their heads and shout, "Say it ain't so, we ain't gonna surrender. Hell no!" Sarge quiets them down. He's glad it's happening. At least his men will live and maybe go home.

The 3rd Louisiana men take it badly. They curse, break their muskets against trees, and scatter their ammunition. I expect they'll start ripping their jackets to pieces any second. Instead, they rip up their flags giving each man a small square as a souvenir. They refuse the Yanks the satisfaction of capturing their banners as war trophies. Let them waste themselves on anger.

"I might just make it out of here alive yet." Things quiet down, and I sit to rest my eyelids.

J.A. punches my shoulder. "You made it, you bucket-headed out-loud-talkin' fool. We must be livin' right to see this day."

"Ain't no holy souls in this damn army except on the bottom of your boots." I grumble at being rousted from a daydream about Susannah.

Dreaming is the only way I get to be with her now. I roll over to get it back, but it's not to be had.

J.A. punches me again. "Get up. It's ten o'clock. They're callin' us to stack our muskets. Maybe the Yanks'll give us food. I swear my guts are stuck to my backbone."

J.A. is the best friend a man could have in siege. Next to Poole back home, he's the best I've ever had. Proverbs says there's a friend who sticks closer than a brother. Poole is that. J. A., too.

We straighten our ragged uniforms and leave the rifle pit to see rows of blue lines patiently waiting. I'm ready—ready to get this over and for the Lord to point me in the next right direction. I hope it ain't to a prison camp.

The 27th Louisiana Volunteer Infantry Regiment files out of the trenches in good order. We stack our rifles and march to the city. I sneak my pistol to a lieutenant when I hear officers can keep their side arms after the surrender.

Some men wish we'd fought to the last man. Some men are dejected, some cry, some curse, and some break into fights. Some men blame Pemberton. "Damn Yank sympathizer planned this from the beginnin'." I don't believe that for a minute. Some blame Richmond for not sending supplies. But all blame Johnston for not coming to our rescue. There are as many reasons as we can dream up.

Folks hang their heads when we march into town. To our surprise, the Yanks are respectful, even encouraging to our beaten army. There's no laughing or belittling, no poking or goading, no degrading sarcasm from the Yanks—only words from seasoned men who know what we suffered these past forty-seven days and why. One regiment sends up a resounding cheer for the brave lads who defended the Gibraltar of the South.

All along the way into town Yanks smile, salute, and yell. "You gave us hell, Johnny Reb."

"Wasn't for lack of guts you men surrendered. Heck, no. It was for lack of beans. That's all."

"Now there goes a fightin' man's army right there."

J.A. whispers, munching a piece of fresh-baked bread. "Just knowed they'd be itching to kill us all."

They lost many friends and brothers. But they know we lost ours too. Inward pain is as horrible as the smell and sights outside our trenches after the attacks. We're just human beings who survived a great storm together. That's how they welcome us out of the trenches—as human beings. Gray or blue, it doesn't matter anymore. We have to take care of each other.

Union General Logan leads the band playing "Yankee Doodle," that old song from the first revolution. Soldiers step out of line to share bread and cooked beef from their haversacks. Cups of cool water are given every man. Some of our men collapse from fatigue, hunger, and despair. It's a sorrowful time, but we're glad it's over.

I whisper a Psalm, "I will extol thee O Lord for thou hast lifted me up and hast not made my foes rejoice over me. Say that to thank God for not only keepin' you alive but puttin' you in the hands of these honorable men."

J.A. and Isham repeat the words.

Hog Fart asks, "What does extol mean?"

I just pat him on the shoulder. He winces a bit.

A reverend preaches, "For his anger endureth but a moment, and in his favor is life. Weeping may endure for a night, but joy cometh in the morning." I've been looking for this morning a very long time.

We reach town at 2:00 p.m., many in better spirits. I'm not sure how I'll feel when I see the U.S. flag above the courthouse. I stretch to see it waving proudly, flapping majestically in the breeze that rises from the great river. Love for my state brings truth to my soul. I'm glad it's there. It was the first flag over that courthouse, and I pray it will be the last. My heart fills with hopeful pride at the sight. It brings a bit of peace to my soul.

We march with our tails dragging, as they say, but perk up when a loud commotion erupts where merchants keep shop. J.A. yells, "Are them blue bastards pillagin' civilian property?"

We bristle, and the Yank guards draw closer. A captain rides up. "You men now can know the reason you had to surrender. Understand what's happening. General Grant gave strict orders—no civilians or their property is to be harmed. We follow that order to the letter, but some of your merchants, shopkeepers, and speculators squirreled away enough food and supplies to carry you men another month. They were getting rich on the black market. I'm sorry, men. You gave us hell. But cheer up. When my boys clean those buzzards out, you'll have a helluva party tonight."

Men and women fat and well-dressed are thrown out of their houses and shops in front of the very men who protected their evil doings. They won't look at us. They're too ashamed. They should be. Men died because of lack of food almost within sight of their shops and homes.

I feel for the knife Pa made me. "Damn them. I could kill them all."

J.A. grabs my arm. "They'll get theirs soon enough."

"Already are."

The Yanks pile everything on wagons and follow us down the street. We stop to rest across from the Rock House where General Pemberton is headquartered. The Yanks driving the wagons distribute foods ready to eat. It stings my soul that our own people thought so little of us.

It's not simple wrongs that make a man detest his own people. It's human greed that causes my anger toward those who'd rather make a dollar watching men starve.

I look up at the Yankee flag again. It wasn't that long ago I honored it. Susannah, Old Bart, and all their people have been treated like animals for too long. I see how the Yanks treat us now and what this war has come to mean.

I count from the top to the twentieth star on the flag. "It's still there, right where I left it."

I look at my ragged clothes, my thin body, and my friends who sit with me. The world suddenly looks different. I won't ever be the same again because today the rebel flag loses any meaning it ever had for me.

"I've been fooled. The state's rights cause was nothin' more than a cover up for keepin' slaves chained and the rich gettin' richer. Damn 'em, makin' out like the Yankees are devils sent down here to deprive us of life, liberty, and the pursuit of happiness when slaveowners been doin' that to Negroes for years. Just because a white man makes a Negro lower than a dog to keep himself from bein' the lowest rung on the ladder don't mean I buy that horseshit." I want to stand up and shout. I start to get up. "I'm never gonna be the same, and I'm sure as hell done with this army."

J.A. punches me. "Shut up and stay down, Lummy. Here they come, and you'll damn well go wherever the hell they tell you."

He doesn't understand that's exactly what I mean. "I may have been a fool, J.A., but I ain't no fool's fool."

J.A. puts his hand over my mouth and points to the road. A group of Yankee officers stop at the Rock House. "That'd be Grant." They're all gussied up except a bearded one in a plain blue coat with a half-smoked cigar in his mouth.

I elbow him. "He's shorter than I imagined."

Grant leads the way up the steps first to extend his hand of friendship to General Pemberton. Mr. Wiley told me about Grant and Pemberton fighting in the Mexican War together. If they were friends back then, you can't tell it by the way General Pemberton receives him. Our general and his staff appear to be in a bad mood. I guess I would be, too. Pemberton barely speaks to Grant and doesn't even offer the man a seat. When Grant asks for a glass of water, he's told where he can find it himself.

"Suck egg mule, look at that," J.A. whispers.

I shield my eyes. "I don't care that we did get whooped. Ain't no call for Pemberton to be a horse's ass about it."

J.A. swats his hand at Pemberton. "Don't speak well of southern hospitality, now does it? My momma sure taught me better'n that. Guess ole Pemberton missed that lesson."

Grant salutes Pemberton and walks down the steps shaking his head. He starts for his horse, but turns abruptly and beelines toward us under a shade tree. We're a beaten mob, ragged, downcast, grieving, and looking the part. We're eating food his soldiers gave us.

Grant removes his hat and wipes the sweat from his forehead. "You men doing better, gettin' fed? My men best be treatin' you good, or I'll give them a worse ass whuppin' than you gave them. You men put up a helluva fight, and you have no reason to be ashamed. It's time you get on with your lives, 'cause you got lots of good days left to live." He studies us for a minute.

"Sure wish I'd had you boys in my army. We'd taken Vicksburg in the first assault." Grant turns for his horse but stops. "But don't tell anybody I said that."

We laugh. J.A. stares at the general who defeated our army until he mounts his horse and rides away. "Maybe we should've been marchin' for him instead of Pemberton waitin' on that coward Johnston, yellow as a crook neck squash and just as soft when cooked."

Hog Fart chimes in. "I hope President Davis cooks Johnston's ass up real nice when he reports to Richmond. That bastard could've saved us from prison camp if he'd done his duty."

I nod in agreement. But what does it matter now?

Lying back against a hitching post, I just can't get these Yanks out of my mind. Why are they so kind? Do they truly believe the Union is worth dying for? Do they believe Negroes like my Susannah should be free? They seem sincere. They act like they believe what they say. There was always something not quite right about our cause. I can't give much thought to that now. I'm more concerned about where the Yanks will send us. Grant rides to the river landing to congratulate Admiral Porter.

Isham leans up. "Damn, there's sixty steamers docked in front of the Prentiss House Hotel."

Hog Fart sobs. "They gonna take us to a prison camp, ain't they?"

I put my arm around him. "I don't know. We'll just take what we get. Don't worry, we'll stick together." We've all heard horror stories about those camps, on both sides.

What to do? Where to go? What's the right choice? Will I have a choice? Will they parole us or imprison us? What's the best path if we're set free? Too many questions with no answers.

I could go live and work with Ben and Mr. Gilmore, or I could go home to help Ma in Choctaw County. I need to settle my soul down. I'm all jittery inside. This war brings too many uncertainties. I calm myself like the Catholic priest taught me.

Sarge comes by. "Good news, boys. Grant's gonna parole all men willin' to take the oath not to take up arms against the Union. At least, not 'til we get exchanged."

Nobody cheers.

It's hard to know what to do when I get set free. I know what we're expected to do. Go to Enterprise, Mississippi, wait to be exchanged, and be ready when the 27th Louisiana is reassembled to go back to war. I ain't going down that road. Right now, I just want to run off in all directions at once. I need to think about what I'm going to do—and why.

At the end of the day, General Grant lets us go back into our camps to rest before we get our parole papers. Once back in camp, we're fed again, doctored, and given tents to sleep in. They want us healthy enough to march in a couple of days. Formal paroling of prisoners starts July 7th. The march to Enterprise begins on the 11th.

It's hard to believe that we can mill around with the Yanks, playing cards and dominoes. We play the stick and ball game again. It's good to have some fun.

One Yank guard tries to joke, "A long ways from eating mule meat, huh, men?"

Hog Fart blurts out, "Better'n this beefsteak." We throw clods at him as he laughs with his mouth full of good Yankee beef.

The Yank shakes his head. "Guess a hungry man can get used to anything."

Two Wisconsin men bring by their eagle mascot, Old Abe, and congratulate our bravery.

J.A. rubs the massive bird's back feathers. "Meanin' no harm, but we thought this bird was a buzzard. We seen enough of them bone pickers for a lifetime."

The Yanks laugh, and we rub the bird's back feathers.

A Yank corporal hangs his head. "Sorry about ole Douglas. He was a sight to behold, a magnificent beast. I thought so much of him I got a souvenir bone, so I'll never forget his bellowing at night." The Yank holds up the piece of bone. "I do believe this piece probably came from a mule. There's been enough of these souvenir bones sold to make up a herd of camels."

The Yanks issue five days' rations, and we gorge on bacon, hominy, peas, bread, salt, and real coffee with sugar. They give us candles for light and soap to wash off the unbearable stink of the siege. I scrub thirty minutes trying to clean off what can't be purified by soap and water. I scrub until my skin turns red. The more it stings, the harder I rub.

A middle-aged Yank guard says in a fatherly way, "Son, no amount of rubbin' will peel off that pain. Just give it to the Lord. He'll take it away. Let Him clean your heart so you can be the man you used to be. I can't imagine the things you men saw and had to do, but the Lord forgives. And know this, the Lord forgets." Good words that bring a tear.

Early evening, we fall exhausted into our tents with full bellies and better spirits. I can't sleep though. My soul is yet unsettled. Stars stare at me like eyes in the darkness—Granny Thankful and Pa, Amariah and Amanda, Lucille and Mr. Wiley, Granville, and Susannah—waiting for my decision, my choice, my next step. I don't know what to do. My life never has run in a straight line. Why must I always walk upstream against the current? My choices are made for me. And I know the One who makes them.

Today I found my independence. I know what to do. Today, we laid our muskets to rest from a battle we didn't lose. Today, I surrendered more than my musket. I surrendered to set captives free. I surrendered the old way that refuses others the right to be who God created them to be. I surrendered all that holds my soul back from living the convictions God put in my heart. But tonight, I surrender me.

I'll soon take the oath to never take up arms against the Union again. Some will pledge truthfully. Some will lie. I can't do that. I'll keep my word. They'll call me a turncoat, traitor, worse than a Yankee. But there are things in this universe that need to be set aright. And what I've given myself to this since I left Winn Parish ain't it. I heard it said, "Fool me once, shame on you. Fool me twice, shame on me."

I look up at the stars. "I won't be fooled again. Now I know what to do."

It's dark and quiet this 4th of July night. No cannon blasts, no whistle of minie balls, no sound of good men struck down. I never knew silence could sound so good. I close my eyes.

Peace is good, if only for a little while.

Lightning Source UK Ltd.
Milton Keynes UK
UKHW010011180522
403157UK00008B/134/J